Just Between You and Me

A Novel About Losing Fear and Finding God

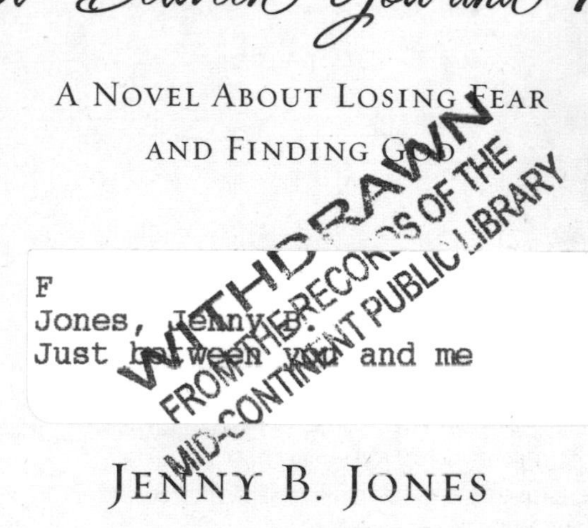

Jenny B. Jones

Thomas Nelson
Since 1798

NASHVILLE DALLAS MEXICO CITY RIO DE JANEIRO BEIJING

Published in Nashville, Tennessee, by Thomas Nelson. Thomas Nelson is a trademark of Thomas Nelson, Inc.

Thomas Nelson, Inc., titles may be purchased in bulk for educational, business, fund-raising, or sales promotional use. For information, please e-mail SpecialMarkets@ThomasNelson.com.

Publisher's note: This novel is a work of fiction. Names, characters, places, and incidents are either products of the author's imagination or used fictitiously. All characters are fictional, and any similarity to people living or dead is purely coincidental.

Library of Congress Cataloging-in-Publication Data

Jones, Jenny B., 1975–
Just between you and me : a novel about losing fear and finding God / by Jenny B. Jones.
p. cm.
ISBN 978-1-59554-851-1 (pbk.)
I. Title.
PS3610.O6257J87 2009
813'.6—dc22

2009024969

Printed in the United States of America

09 10 11 12 13 RRD 6 5 4 3 2 1

To my sweet, sassy niece, Katie Beth.
May you walk boldly and fearlessly for Christ
all your days. Your giggly, squealy joy for life
makes me smile. I love you, curly girl.
Always remember . . . I'm your favorite aunt.

Though the mountains move and the hills shake,
my love will not be removed from you.

—Isaiah 54: 10

Prologue

To some women, fear is a man walking out the front door and never coming back. To others, it's looking at that black dress in the back of your closet and knowing—without a divine miracle or the return of the corset—you'll never be a size six again.

For me, in this moment right now, it's a Parisian river calm enough to lull a baby to sleep. And yet my palms are so slick with sweat, I can hardly maintain my grip on the boat rail. My heart beats violently in my chest and I haven't heard a word that's been said in the last hour.

"Here we go. Step off nice and easy." Pierre, our guide, assists the captain by leaping onto the dock and tying the small vessel in place.

The crew of *Passport to the World* climbs out one by one. I go last, waiting for the black spots to subside as I stand and fight with gravity's pull on my wobbly knees.

"You did great, Maggie." Carley, my friend and producer, pats me on the back as I focus on everything but the water. Unlike the rest of my coworkers, she's the only one who doesn't ignore the fact that I turn into a psychotic mess anytime I have to shoot a location involving water. Sometimes I can get an intern or another cinematographer to cover for me, but I have to pick those battles. And the lazy Seine is not worth calling in a sub.

"You need therapy," Carley says.

"I need a chocolate éclair."

She shields her eyes from the noonday sun and hands me a Dasani from her bag. "Let's get some more footage at that café by the Champs-Élysées. I'm considering of coming to Paris for my honeymoon. What do you think?"

My job as cinematographer for the travel show can be as glamorous as the Eiffel Tower at sunset or as unattractive as a night in a leaky hut in Cambodia. Last year we became the number one show on Travel TV, picked up a few awards, and got moved to a killer time slot. I should be on top of the world—thrilled with life. But somehow lately I'm not.

My pocket buzzes, and I reach in and pull out my phone. My dad. Calling again. And two messages from John, my boyfriend. Are men born with a guidebook on how to be a nuisance? I could travel to the ends of the earth and some man would find me and expect some big sacrifice from me. Like a text. Or a date. Or a returned call. But I'm a busy person! I have things to do. Cities of the world to film. A week-old *People* magazine to read. And a candy bar in my bag that has been calling my name for the past two hours.

Getting out of the rented sedan, I stretch my arms, then reach for my camera.

"I want to talk to the café owner," Carley says. "Will you translate again?"

"Sure." We walk across the busy street and into the quaint restaurant. "Where's the owner?" I ask a waiter in French, reminding him who we are and why we're here.

He jerks his head toward the back. "He's taking a cigarette break." The slim man stares at his full tables, his brows furrowing as someone shouts out a drink order.

"If it's okay, I'll get him." I shoo the waiter away. "Don't worry about us."

I weave through the diners and back into the bustling kitchen, throwing up a hand in greeting to the staff. "*Bonjour*!" My eyes land on a partially opened back door, and I slip through it, blinking at the sun.

Beside me a Dumpster rumbles, and I gasp as I see two little legs sticking out, wiggling with the effort of digging.

"Hey," I say automatically, then call out a greeting in French. "*Salut*!" I walk up to the Dumpster and tug on a dirty shoe.

A head pops up, and I'm face-to-face with a small boy, face smudged with grime, fear making his eyes as round as dessert plates. He flings from the trash like a little gymnast, his feet landing on the ground.

I hold out my hand. "*Attends!*" Wait!

Without a backward glance, he takes off in a sprint, running as fast as his little legs will carry him, dropping food behind like crumbs on a trail.

I sling my camera over my shoulder and race to the edge of the building, my lens trained on the slender blur. "Wait, please!" I shout to him in two different languages, but he just keeps moving.

"Beggars."

I whirl around and find the restaurant owner behind me. "Did you know him?"

He gestures toward the direction the boy ran. "What is there to know of one such as him? He is a thief and a public nuisance."

My heart twists in my chest. "But he's so young. So thin." I step back toward the restaurant. "Obviously he was hungry."

The owner laughs, his belly making his shirt dance. "I have a business to run. I cannot feed every stray dog that shows up here."

My breath catches with the insult, but I bite my tongue,

knowing Carley would throw me out like a stale croissant if I made him mad and ruined her interview. "Does he live nearby?"

"Who cares?" He slams the lid down on his Dumpster and flings open the café door. He steps back inside, leaving an odor of cigarettes.

Who cares? Sometimes I ask myself that very same question. Could I have helped that little boy if he hadn't run away?

For a moment I stand there, the yellow sun beating down on my red head. Who am I to help anyone anyway? I'm a girl with a camera and a suitcase. Nothing much more to give.

Because I've seen the world.

But sometimes I wonder . . . has it ever seen me?

Chapter One

I sit at my dining room table and swirl linguini noodles around my fork. Unease has me on high alert as John relights a reluctant candle.

"When are you going to fix this place up?" He sets the lighter down and smiles with the confidence of a man who knows he makes a pretty picture. "We should've gone to my apartment."

"But I haven't been home in weeks." I glance about the dining and living room area. Okay, so I meant to buy some prints to hang here and there. But one day you're looking at art, and the next thing you know a few years have gone by, and your walls are just as bare as the wood floor. "It's not like I'm here much anyway," I say around a bite of bread. "But thanks for cooking me dinner." I blot my mouth with my napkin and wonder at the strange gleam in John's eye.

"Maggie, do you know what tonight is?" He grabs my hand, and I watch his large fingers cover mine, making them disappear.

I untie the scarf at my neck, a treasure I carried with me from my last trip to Ecuador, purchased from a street peddler who couldn't have been older than eight or nine. I reach for my goblet of ice water and tip it back.

"Tonight is our five-month anniversary." John keeps talking. Actually, I don't know that *boyfriend* would be the right label for him. More like frequent date when I'm in town.

John's hand strokes across mine, and my stomach does a little flip. Not the good kind that makes you want to break out in a show tune. More like the sort of quivering that happens when you've swallowed one too many bites of questionable sushi.

I tune back into the romantic scene unfolding before me and plaster on a smile. The candlelight illuminates the dark center of John's eyes. "I want you to know how special you've become to me," he says.

There's a feeling in the air, and I don't like it. A feeling that says, *Things are about to get messy and out of control.* Messy I can handle. The contents of my purse are a testimonial to that. But this relationship business? Let's just say I'm a better cinematographer than I am a girlfriend.

I clear my throat and interrupt him just as he appears to be on the verge of a sonnet. "John, I, um, was wondering how your day went."

He blinks. "Did you hear a word I said?"

I bat my heavy eyelids. "I'm really tired. We filmed way into the morning, and then I was on a plane for twelve hours."

Oh, there goes that compassionate look. The one that promises to care for me in my every moment of jet lag, sleep deprivation, and PMS. You'd think I'd be grateful to have found that. I know I should be.

"I think we should talk about our relationship, Maggie. What our next step is."

"I have an interview with the National Geographic channel."

His face freezes. "What?"

"Even Carley doesn't know. It's very hush-hush." I nod and study the ice cubes in my glass. "It's in a couple of weeks. They just called today."

"Would this job involve more travel?"

Lately John has been hinting that I try to stick closer to home more. Every time he brings it up, I get these little itchy hives on my neck. "It's the chance of a lifetime. I'd be the producer of one of their TV shows." I see his eyes light up at that. So why don't *I* feel more excited? I should be oozing with enthusiasm. It's like when I got saved last year, a lot of things changed for me. Including my attitude about my career. And I have no idea what to do with this feeling of ennui I now wake up with every morning. "And it would get me that much closer to the people who could make my documentary a reality."

He leans back and rests his elbows on the chair arms. "You've had five rejections on your documentary proposals. Let it go."

"Maybe." And—just like the value of ESPN and foreign sports cars—here is yet another area in which we will never agree. I've approached a few companies about backing this idea I have for a series of documentaries. Everyone has said no. Even John thinks it's silly.

"People have done plenty of films about underprivileged children." John reaches for my hand again. "You know I think you're gifted at what you do, but budgets are tight out there for projects, and they're not going to fund something that's been done a hundred times."

I don't want him to be right. But he probably is.

His smile is warm, filled with care. "You need to learn the difference between work and a hobby."

I grip the stem of my water glass. "You're doing it again."

"What?"

"Talking to me like I'm a child."

"I just want the best for you."

John works as an attorney for our network. Sometimes I think he finds my career behind the camera a little beneath me. Or him.

"Maggie, tonight is a very special night."

Uh-oh. Here come the dreamy eyes again.

"I care so much about you. And recently I've realized those feelings have grown into something more. I'm crazy about your laugh, your smile, your sense of adventure. I want to tell you that I—"

"Boy, am I tired." I like how John and I are a casual couple—we go out when I'm off the road. We talk; we text; we e-mail. We do pad thai and a movie. We do *not* do the L-word. "Maybe we should skip dessert and call it a night."

He leans forward, his face too close to mine at this small table. He runs the back of his fingers across my cheek and down my jaw line. "Maggie, I love—"

Ring! Ring!

"Oh, sorry." *Yes!* "Gotta take this." John's face crumbles into a mask of frustration as I answer my phone without even checking the display. Whoever it is, I owe them a *big* one. "Hello?"

"Maggie?"

My heart plunges like a runaway elevator. "Dad?"

"I've been calling you for weeks. Didn't you get any of my messages?"

"I've been out of the country." I wince at my own tone, but it's Dad, after all. The man who only contacts me twice a year, and usually it's just to tell me some distant old relative has gone to the great beyond. Heaven forbid he get crazy and call because he wants to see how I am. Or acknowledge a birthday.

"What is it?" John whispers, and I hold up a finger to wait.

"Maggie, I don't know how to ask you this, so I'm just going to come right out and say it. I . . . I need you to come home."

I snort into the phone. "Right." Maybe when the planet starts rotating the other direction. "I was just there a few Christmases ago."

"That was five years ago."

"Oh." Seems like only yesterday to me.

"Your sister showed up last month . . . and we need help."

"I'm sorry. I can't come see you guys right now. The show is wrapping up for the season, and I have to catch a plane in four days."

"Look, you know I wouldn't ask you if I had anywhere else to turn. Last week I had to go back to the plant to work."

"Why would you go back?" Dad retired five years ago after giving his life to the local tire factory. It got more of him than his family ever did.

"I don't have time to get into that now."

"Where's Allison? Is she in trouble?" My quirks are more socially acceptable, but my younger sister's? Not so much. There's no telling what she's done this time.

"Gone. She's just gone, okay? The point is I . . . Can't you just visit for a few days?" His tone snaps like a rubber band.

It occurs to me that this is the longest conversation I've had with my father my entire life. I mean, he's using real sentences and everything. "Dad, if you or Allison need money, I'll gladly send some. I can have it wired tomorrow. But I can't just up and leave. I have to fly out to Taiwan next week to tape, so I can't simply abandon work."

"I don't need your money!" he growls. "I need . . . help." Silence crackles on the phone. "I need help, Maggie. Please."

I close my eyes at the plaintive tone. Never have I heard my dad like this. It scares me almost as much as the idea of going back home to Ivy, Texas. Though I don't owe this man anything, I feel the familiar twinges of guilt.

I think of my sister, three years younger than me, and at the age of twenty-seven, she has yet to grow up. When I left home after graduation, I pretty much never looked back. And if I have any regrets, it's that I left Allison to be raised by a heartless grump who was only home long enough to criticize. At least I had Mom until I was sixteen. By the time Allison was thirteen, she only had me and Dad . . . and then I left. I took off with a suitcase in one hand and guilt for leaving my little sister in the other.

"It's just not doable, Dad. I have too much going on right now. I'm sorry."

"This is for Allison."

My sister—my Achilles' heel.

"Think what you want about me, Maggie, but she's never needed you more. In fact . . . I think you're the only one who can save her this time. Do it for your sister."

I close my eyes against the inevitable. "I'll be on the first flight out tomorrow."

An hour later, with the excuse of fatigue and a need to pack, I escort John to the door.

"How long are you going to be gone?" His face radiates such care, I find myself drawn into his hug.

"Three days. Then I'll fly out to the show location."

"I'll miss you."

I smile at his predictable statement. Of course he will.

He pulls back and cups my face in his hands. "I wanted tonight to be perfect. I needed to tell you that I—"

"John . . . I think we should use this time apart to really think about our relationship."

"I think about it all the time."

And here's another one of our problems: I don't. "I believe you and I are at two different places here. Two different speeds."

He takes my hand, kisses it. "You're tired. I'll let you pack."

"No, I'm serious."

"Call me if you need me." He presses his lips to my forehead. "Talk to you soon."

I shut myself in and take comfort in the click of the locks . . . and slide to the floor.

Me, scared?

I've counted snakes in the rice fields of Cambodia. Eaten things that crawled down my throat in Botswana. In the Amazon, I dodged mosquitos as large as birds.

But I, Maggie Montgomery, world traveler, have never been anywhere quite as frightening as home.

Chapter Two

"And if you just sign here, here, and here, I'll get you the keys to your rental."

I scribble my name on the Hertz agreement and wait as the woman types in a few more things on her computer. I think she's gotten every detail about me but my bra size.

"Sure you don't want the weekly special? We've got a good deal running."

Lady, you could pay me, *and the deal wouldn't be good enough to keep me in Ivy a week.* "Three days is all I will need the car, but thanks." I take the Focus key from her chipped-polish fingers.

Turning down an offer of help from a gentleman in the parking lot, I heave my suitcase into the Ford, only banging my knee twice. I decided I'd just catch my connecting flight to Taiwan from Dallas, so I packed for three weeks.

Pulling out onto the Dallas highway, I crank on some country music and let Carrie Underwood sing to me about her cheatin' man. Ivy didn't leave much of a stamp on me, but I've never outgrown my love for good country music.

God, I know we haven't talked much lately. I've been really busy the last few weeks. But obviously you have something up your holy sleeve, or I wouldn't be eastbound and trucking, headed straight for my own version of hell. Why am I doing this? Why is it Dad only has to mention

Allison and I'm doing his bidding, no matter how awful it is for me? Maybe this will wipe the slate clean once and for all. I'll swing by, do whatever needs to be done, and leave my old Ivy ghosts forever.

Two long, tedious hours later, I stop the car at the Jiffy Qwik gas station and fill up. The gauge reads half a tank, but I might as well get some. What if there was a wreck between here and the five streets to Dad's, and I had to wait forever and ran out of gas?

On this last day of March, the sun warms my skin as I stand outside my car, and I toss my light jacket in the backseat. The pump clicks, and I head for the door to pay, as the miraculous invention of pay-at-the-pump has yet to make it to Ivy. Nothing about this place could be easy.

A bell tinkles overhead as I step inside, and I immediately inhale the scent of popcorn and convenience store hotdogs. Instinct kicks in, and I go directly to the aisle with candy. It's like I have the gift of sugar prophecy. The Lord just tells me where the goods are. Wrapping my hand around a Snickers and some SweeTarts, I decide to suck up some more time and peruse the wall of drinks. When I'm not in close proximity to my father or clingy boyfriends, I can stay away from the stuff. This is not a time for self-control, though.

Meandering to the front, grabbing things as I go, I throw my purchases on the counter. Two candy items, plus four Little Debbies, five packs of chocolate minidonuts, a box of Oreos, peanut butter crackers, and some strawberry Jolly Ranchers so I can say I got in some fruit servings.

"Someone have a sweet tooth or a life crisis?" The clerk lifts one penciled eyebrow in judgment.

I smile and dig out my debit card. "I got gas at pump three."

The register beeps with each item as "Marge" scans my loot. I feel better just looking at all that comfort food. There *are* some things in life you can depend on.

"You look familiar."

A blush moves up my neck. "I'm just passing through town." I avert my gaze and stare at the Oreos.

"You Constance Montgomery's daughter?"

And here we go. "Um, yes."

"Crazy Connie." Marge laughs as she whips out a plastic sack. "I haven't thought about her in years, but I couldn't miss that wavy red hair. You look a lot like her."

"Uh-huh. Thanks." My hand shakes as I sign the debit slip. *Let's go, Marge. Throw the stuff in the bag and let me leave.*

"I remember you. You and some friends went streaking through my tulips one spring."

I close my eyes and swallow back a groan. "That was a long time ago. I'm sure my daddy made me apologize."

"No." Marge smacks her Juicy Fruit. "I didn't get no apology."

"Oh. Well. I'm sorry then." *Aw*kward! "If it's any consolation, I've given up my streaking ways and keep my clothes on these days. I leave the skin flashing to young Hollywood." Not to mention the morning I turned twenty-eight was the day I woke up to a new relationship with Miss Clairol and some dimples on my thighs.

"You were just like her," the woman says, not letting this go. "Always in trouble, always doing something crazy." A reluctant smile grows on Marge's chapped lips. "Your momma was a fun lady, though. She'd come in here and get a bunch of junk just like this." She hands over my bag. "Usually had a song on her lips and a twinkle of mischief in her eye."

I blink back a tear at the unexpected description of my mother. She died when I was in the eleventh grade, and my sister and I lost our champion. Our joy. Like a bad sunburn, the memory of that dark time still remains tender to the touch.

I gather my purse and bag without another glance at Marge.

"Have a nice day." As I turn to the door to make my escape, another woman walks through.

"Maggie?" Her eyes round as she squeals. "Maggie, it's me!"

I blink at the short, chubby black woman who's approaching with arms stretched wide.

"Beth?"

Her arms swallow me in a fierce hug. "You look amazing." She eyes my figure, my clothes. "I was a size six once." Beth laughs. "Before I had four babies in nine years. How long are you in town?"

"Just a few days." I stare at the woman who was once my best friend. I practically lived at her house after my mom died. I couldn't stand to be home. Not with my dad. And not with the memories. "I'm here to see Allison, then head back out."

Her mouth forms an *O*. "Yeah, I heard about your sister."

"What do you mean?"

"Nothing. Nothing at all. I'm sure your daddy will catch you up."

"That would require him turning off the TV and talking. Maybe you could fill me in."

Beth reaches out and pats my shoulder. "Not my business."

This from the girl who used to write people's business on the gym bathroom wall.

"Well, I better get back home. Mark has the kids, and they've probably got him tied up and stuffed in a closet by now." Her expression darkens. "He just lost his job at the tire factory."

"Oh, I'm sorry. But Dad said he just went back to work there." Things are starting to get weird.

"Yeah, there's talk of the plant closing, so some of the managers got jobs elsewhere. They were lucky to get your dad to pinch hit. Last month Reliant Tires laid off one hundred and fifty employees. My Mark got the cut, as did all the third shift." She shrugs. "I actually popped in here to get an application. Time for mama to go to work."

"I'm really sorry." Could I get any more lame? Sometimes when I'm in the real world, I long for the safety of my camera to hide behind. Like now.

"Stop by the house and see the kids. Let's hang out before you leave."

"I'll try, but I'm not even here long enough to unpack my suitcase." Lies are okay if they're super polite, right? "It was good to see you."

"Hey, we're having a multiclass reunion the first weekend of May. You should come back for that."

So people can remind me of all the lunatic, half-illegal things I did in my youth? Um, no. "I'll see you later, Beth."

"I'll friend you on Facebook!"

I all but run to the car, holding my bag like a security blanket. I don't even get my seat belt on before I'm popping SweeTarts like Rolaids.

Okay, I can do this. Three days. That's all I have to give my dad, my sister, and this town. Three days.

Putting the car in gear, I head back onto the road and drive toward my old house. The home where Crazy Connie taught me to dance on the edge. Where I left a sister behind. And where I buried memories that must never be exhumed.

Chapter Three

Why rush a good homecoming? I decide to take a little detour and cruise through the town. Very little has changed. The high school's bigger, the water tower is whiter, and the Ivy Lions now have a new football stadium. But other than that, same old place.

Before I know it, I'm on the outskirts of town at the Ivy Gardens Cemetery. My mother's final resting place.

I step out of the car and let the warm breeze ruffle my long hair. The gravel crunches beneath my flats as I walk down the path, past the oldest graves, and stop in front of the stone of Constance Marie Montgomery. Thirty-seven years old.

Beloved Daughter, Wife, and Mother.
Fearlessly She Lived. Joyfully She Loved.

I trace my finger over the letters and numbers on the grave. "Oh, I miss you." The strain returns to my eyes, and the tears begin to swim. I swipe them away. I haven't cried since the funeral, and I'm sure not going to start now.

Lowering myself down to the grass, I sit Indian-style. "So . . . um, I came back home." Is it just me, or is this awkward? "Work is going okay, I guess. Our show won an Emmy last year. Well, for cable, but still. I'll be interviewing for a new job soon."

I pull at a blade of grass and twirl it around my fingers. "It would mean traveling even more, but I wouldn't mind. I've got your gypsy blood, you know." Sniffing, I blink the moisture back as the memories flow. "I know it sounds like I have it all together, Mom, but I don't. And I wish you were here to talk to. Especially since talking to your headstone feels very Lifetimey at the moment." It does. It really does. "But I'm a mess with men. And my job . . . I don't know. I want to make my mark on this world, you know? I want to be . . . somebody." Having no other choice, I rub my dripping nose across the sleeve of my jacket. "Why did things have to go so wrong? Why does *everything* in my life go wrong?" I don't want to be here. In this cemetery. In this town.

"Watch out!"

I turn my head at the distant voice just in time to see a blur of brown fur charge my way. I jump to my knees, but the force of a defensive tackle throws me to the ground.

"Oomph!" My breath lodges in my throat, and I use all my strength to push the beast away. "Get off me!" Licks to the face. Ew! "Stupid dog, get off!"

"Gandalf, down! Heel! Stop!"

I dodge the slobbering dog tongue and find two human legs beside me. "A little help, if you please."

I see the light of day again as the dog is physically removed. The owner snaps the leash on the collar as I dust off my clothes.

"Are you okay?" The man holds out his hand, and I finally look up.

Oh my. This one is beautiful. As in he could be Patrick Dempsey's fraternal twin. The cuter one. I swipe at my cheeks and bring back dirt. Great.

"Let me help you up."

"I'm fine." Nothing a fresh change of clothes and some new makeup wouldn't cure.

"You don't look fine," he says as I stand to my feet. Before I can back up, his hand is on my face, his fingers brushing lightly at my cheeks. The eyes behind his sunglasses find mine. "Better. You just had some dirt smudges."

"I wasn't crying." Omigosh. Did I really just say that? "I mean, I—"

He wraps his other hand around the leash once and smiles. "You don't have to explain anything to me. But, um, yeah, you were."

"A gentleman would not point this out."

He shrugs. "Maybe I'm not a gentleman."

"Your dog doesn't seem to be either. You might want to think about some obedience classes."

"Not my dog. I'm training him for a friend." The wind filters through the man's dark, wavy hair. He reaches down and pats the chocolate Lab.

"How nice." I brush more grass off my jeans. "And I'm quite all right."

Mystery man's mouth quirks. "Oh, I can tell." He pushes his sunglasses onto his head, and I get the full impact of his blue eyes. Eyes that probably made many a girl forget a curfew back in the day.

"You know, sometimes it helps to talk things through with a stranger." His expression holds a dare, a gleam of mischief, and something else that has danger signals blaring in my head.

Clearing my throat, I look away. "I haven't talked to my mother in a while. I was just updating her on my life." I kick a small piece of gravel with my toe. "I was telling her about my life . . . as a Britney Spears impersonator. I really think I'm gonna make it this time, and she would be so proud. And then there's the fact that I just got out of prison, and I haven't robbed a bank in three whole months." My eyes glaze with longing. "Unless you count that Victoria's Secret store. But I was newly released, and a girl has to have her frillies."

He rubs a hand over his stubbly jaw. "Is this your way of telling me to butt out?" He glances at my mother's grave. Then does a double take. "Maggie Montgomery." Suddenly the affable charm is gone.

"And you are?"

"Connor." He studies my face. "Connor Blake."

The name does not ring a bell. And neither does his cool yet handsome face. "Nice to meet you, but I should be going."

"Just in the neighborhood or are you staying in Ivy awhile?"

His tone is anything but casual, and I find myself bristling. "I'm just here for a few days."

His mouth tightens. "You haven't changed a bit, have you?"

"Excuse me?"

Connor slowly walks toward me until there is barely a foot between us. "I said you haven't changed at all. You don't even know who I am, do you?"

I give him my most withering glare. "Should I?" Is he an old boyfriend? Did we go out? Blind date?

I watch the column of his throat move as he laughs. "Have a nice day, Maggie Montgomery. You have a nice *quick* visit." And he walks away, pulling his errant dog behind him. Leaving me rooted to the spot. My hands fisted in anger.

And I don't have the first clue why.

I wish Ivy, Texas, had a Holiday Inn, but the town is so small it only has one traffic light, so hoping for other accommodations besides my dad's house is wasted energy.

I shift the little red car into park and take a deep breath. Then ten more. *God, help me.*

My pulse quickens as the front door opens and Dad steps onto the old porch. Like the chipped clapboard on the Victorian house, Dad has aged since my overnight visit five years ago. Face cleanly shaven, hair now completely gray, he stands before me a thinner man. Not the beer-gut fellow he was when I saw him last.

He steps down and walks toward me.

I climb out of the car and put up my hand. "Hi." I stick my head in the back seat like an ostrich in the sand, then focus all my attention on wrestling with my suitcase.

"Let me get that." Dad stands behind me.

"Nah. I'm good. Almost got it." I bump into him, then hit my head on the car. "Ow."

"I said let me get it."

"I got it." I glance back his way and soften my words with a small smile.

He shakes his head. "Some things never change." Dad takes me by the shoulders and pulls me out of the Focus. "Go on inside. I'll bring this in and up to your room."

I stand there for one clumsy moment. "Fine. I'll, uh . . . just let you get that then."

The screen door creaks as I pull it open, and I walk into the small entryway. Memories of a misspent youth flitter through my head as the scent of home fills my heart. There's the staircase that Mom and I rode the mattress down like a sled. And there's the living room wall I crashed into when she gave me my first skateboarding lesson. Walking into the kitchen, I see the black ring on the Formica counter where I learned how to create fire using corn oil, two sparklers, and one shiny black FryDaddy.

I pour myself a glass of tea and listen as Dad mounts the steps to my room. Last time I was here, it was just like I had left it. Same purple comforter from the nineties. The bulletin board with movie and concert tickets hung on a wall. Still had the list of old boyfriends written on the inside of the closet door, with the dates of the birth and death of each short relationship.

Dad enters the kitchen and points at my glass. "You want some sugar in that?"

"No." He never could remember that I don't like sweet tea. It makes me a rare breed in these parts. "So what's going on?" Let's just get right to it.

He opens the fridge, and for the first time I notice it's not the harvest gold number we had growing up. The side-by-side stainless looks foreign in the kitchen.

"The old fridge went out last year. Had to get a new one. Zeke at the hardware store sold me this floor model."

"Nice." I move in beside him and get some ice from the door.

"I had planned on replacing the stove too, but things just happened, and I decided to put it off."

"Things like Allison moving in with you?" I watch him nod. "How long has she been here?"

Dad eases into a chair and wraps his hands around a can of Coke. "She started having trouble about two years ago. Things got . . . weird."

"You think everything's weird." How he ever ended up with someone like my mom is beyond me. They were night and day. Classic rock and elevator music.

His mouth thins. "Okay, things got crazy. Literally."

I walk to a nearby counter and lean my hip against it. "Like her senior year of high school?" Allison tried to kill herself just three months shy of graduation. Dad got her some help and some meds, but she never returned to school. Never got that diploma or even her GED.

"Similar . . . but different," he says, taking a deep pull from the can. "She's relapsed again. I don't know if she's on her medication, but if I had to guess, I'd say she is not."

I know enough of Allison's history to fill in the rest. "But you think she's on *something*."

He silently nods.

"And what do you want me to do about it? I can call some treatment facilities in Chicago, but they won't take her against her will."

"Allison's gone."

I set my tea glass down on the counter with a *thunk*. "Dad, if she's run off, then there's nothing you can do. She'll have to hit bottom and realize she needs help all by herself."

He lifts tired eyes to mine. "I know that."

"Then what's the problem?"

The front door slams, and Dad checks his watch. "Right on time."

Feet stomp through the living room and head straight for us. "I'm never going back there again!" A little girl bursts into the room, her red hair spiraling all over her head like a natural disaster. "Who are you?"

I close my eyes as the pieces click into place. "I'm Maggie."

She crosses her freckled arms and snarls. "Maggie who?"

I take in the bedraggled kid and long for the SweeTarts in the car. "Maggie—your aunt."

Chapter Four

"So you couldn't have told me Allison dumped Riley on you?" I pace the small kitchen as my niece sits upstairs watching TV. "Would it have really been *that* hard to give me a few more details? Cliff-hangers are only cool on television, Dad."

"I was afraid you wouldn't come." He pops the top off his Coke can. "You haven't seen Riley since she was three, so I didn't figure she would be much incentive to come back."

If guilt was a beer in my dad's fridge, I'd be drunk on it. "I haven't been a good sister or aunt, but I don't really think I have to explain myself to you." My sister got pregnant in high school, and I wasn't around for that either.

"Nobody asked you to," Dad snaps. "I need help, Maggie." He winces at his own words, and I know he'd rather snort nails than ask for anything from me. "I've had Riley for a month. In that time she's run off five different babysitters. Mrs. Bittle from across the street will help out in an emergency, but I've used up about all of her generosity."

"What's wrong with Riley?" I swallow back dread. "Is she like Allison?" My sister has a host of mental problems. And she's just mean.

"No, nothing wrong with that kid's head. She's smart as a whip, but she's been allowed to run wild." He steeples his calloused fingers.

"I'm just going to lay it out for you. Allison hasn't been any sort of mother, always on the move, and Riley's been in and out of school."

We Montgomery girls are nomads. It's in the blood. That's the one thing my sister and I have in common. I travel with work, and Allison travels with whatever spirit moves her. I can't count the number of cities she's been in, but it's almost as impressive as my own list. "Dad, you got me for three days. If you think I'm going to be able to work any miracles in that time, you're sadly mistaken. This is Allison's problem. Can't you find her?"

"I've been looking. Don't you think I've been looking for my own daughter?"

Our gazes clash, and I know he can read my mind like a script. *No, I don't think you've looked.* But Allison was the baby, his favorite, so I guess it's possible.

"I've called everyone I know. I've got Arlo down at the Ivy police department making quiet inquiries."

"Why quiet? Don't you want to find her? Riley needs her mom."

Dad studies his hands. "Because the state's stopped by a few times—social services. Your sister already has a ten-foot-tall file with them. And now that Riley's with me, they're checking up on her. They stopped by last week and she was throwing cookie batter in the ceiling fan while the babysitter sat in the La-Z-Boy and cried."

I can't help but laugh, though it's not funny . . . but it kinda is. My stoic father in charge of a ten-year-old demon.

"And a week and a half ago, she ran away from school."

"A lot of kids do that."

"It was the tenth time in four weeks."

"Oh."

"I have to work, Maggie. I just need some time. If you could watch her, I could do my job at the plant *and* find Allison."

Bitterness seeps through my blood like poison. "So you called me here to help *you* out. And *that's* why you didn't tell me the complete truth." *Because I don't owe you anything.* "I'm not sticking around. I'll do what I can in these next few days, but come Friday morning, I'm hopping on that plane."

Dad slowly stands and pushes in his chair. "I realize I haven't been any kind of father to you, and I'm asking for the moon here. But are you so cut off from us that you could let that child go into foster care? Do you want to see your niece bounced from home to home every time your sister screws up? I'm nobody to be asking you favors, but I thought maybe, just maybe, you might have it in your Christian heart to have mercy on a child."

The refrigerator's hum fills my ears. Upstairs, a TV blares.

Dad shakes his head and steps toward the back door. "Never mind. Forget I asked." Reaching for his cap hanging on a peg, he stuffs it on his head. "I've got to check in at work for a few hours. Do you think you can manage being her aunt for that long?"

"Yes." My tone makes me feel sixteen again. "I think I can manage it."

He jangles the keys in his pocket and opens the door. "Don't lose her."

I roll my eyes. "I've scaled the jagged mountains of Patagonia. I think I can handle a ten-year-old."

I've lost her.

Forty-five minutes into this babysitting gig, and I've misplaced the child. The little actress came down the stairs with her sweet words and cherubic face and asked me to play hide-and-seek. Of course I said yes. I didn't know she would go AWOL on me by the time I got to the count of forty-seven. But the pink bike that was slanted against the big oak is gone. And so is Riley.

This is why I have a pet rock.

I walk down the neighborhood street and call her name. After ten minutes and no sign of her, I hop in the car and cruise through town. An hour later, I'm still childless and feeling more than a little panicked. What if she hitched a ride with a stranger? What if someone kidnapped her? What if my dad thinks I'm the biggest loser ever?

I return to the house and rip through the front door, yelling her name. "Riley! Riley!"

No response from the quiet house. I run upstairs, a prayer on my lips.

When the phone in the kitchen rings, I fly down the steps like a woman after the last Coach bag on clearance at Macy's. "Hello?"

"Maggie?"

"Yes?" I rest my hand on my heaving chest.

"It's Beth."

"Oh, hey, Beth. Uh, now is not really a good time to catch up." I've lost a kid, and the woman is probably calling to see if we can do pedicures and pull out the yearbook.

"No, I'm sure it's not. Do you know where your niece is?"

Oh no. "You know Riley?"

"Girl, the whole town knows Riley. And right now she's standing in the middle of Ivy Square, pouring dish soap in the founding fathers' fountain."

"Fabulous."

"You want to get her before the mayor sees it. No need to leave any evidence—like a bubble-covered child."

"I'll be right there."

I pull out of Dad's subdivision like I'm in the Daytona 500. This is not how I intended to spend my evening.

Driving down Central Avenue, I zoom past Martin's Drugstore, Bailey's Hardware, and the Ivy League Diner—places that haven't changed since I was shaking my pom-poms for the fighting Lions.

Finding a shady Bradford pear tree, I pull my car into an open spot on the square. I look toward the fountain of Buford Chapel and Delroy Jackson, the two men who supposedly won a considerable amount of property in a poker game with some wealthy cattle farmers. They played for the best two out of three, and Buford and Delroy, two wandering trappers with questionable card decks, walked away with what would later become Ivy. The two men couldn't decide what to call their township, so they named it after a saloon girl they both fancied.

And now my niece is kicking up water in the memorial fountain, dancing like a sprite, with water shooting out of Buford and Delroy's concrete muzzle loaders.

"Riley!" I shout. "Get out of there now!"

She ignores me and continues to wade in the shoulder-deep water, bubbles spilling over the sides like the fountain is vomiting froth.

I finally reach the child and make a grab for her arm. Slippery little thing. "Get out."

Oh my gosh. Bubbles. Everywhere. They're mutating. They're multiplying. One day when she's a little less amateur, she'll know to bring food coloring too.

"Go away." The minx has the nerve to flip over and do the backstroke, lazy as she pleases.

I run around the side and try to latch on to her leg. "It's not quite spring yet, Riley. I know that water has to be freezing."

"I don't care." And to prove it she dives under.

"Hey. Where are you?" My heartbeat kicks it up a notch. "Riley? This isn't funny." I can't see her. Too many bubbles. I can't see her! "Help me!" Where's a nosy townsperson when you need one? "Riley, can you hear me?"

I hear the thud of running feet behind me, but I can't take my eyes off the water.

"Maggie? What in the world is wrong?"

Walking round and round the fountain, I fish my hand in the water and come away with nothing. No child.

"Maggie?" Beth grabs my shoulders.

I point toward the rising mound of bubbles. "Buford and Delroy have my niece."

"Just step in there and get her. And hurry up. The mayor can't stand for anyone to mess with his fountain."

I wave my arms around in there again. "I can't find her. Please, Beth. Please help me." I can just see dinnertime tonight. *Dad, Riley drowned in a sea of bubbles . . .*

A small giggle reaches my ears, and I begin to breathe again. "I hear you, Riley. Get out."

"Come and get me."

I bite back a blistering response.

Beth turns and stares me square in the face. "Maggie, you're not still afraid of water, are you?"

My chin inches up a notch. "Of course not. I just don't like it. And that is distinctly different than being afraid of it. Plus, who wants to get all sudsy?"

Her bemused expression grates on me as much as Riley's dramatic doggy paddle. "It's a fountain."

"Look how deep that is. She's *swimming* in it. I need help with a kid here, okay?"

"What you *need* is to get her out of my fountain."

Beth and I both spin around.

"Hello, Mayor Karstetter." Beth smiles at the town leader, her body shielding my niece's kicking legs.

"Do you know how much it costs to get soap out of that thing?

Do you have any idea how strapped the city budget is? I had to lay off Maudine Richardson just yesterday and—"

"I'll take care of it, James."

I turn and find the man from the cemetery standing behind me, hands on hips.

"You," I hiss.

Connor Blake angles his head. "We meet again." His blue eyes light on Riley. "And this time *you* brought the unruly beast."

"I'll have her out in a minute." As soon as I dig out a twenty from my wallet to flash in front of her freckled face.

"It's going to be expensive to clean that up . . ."

I try to smile at the mayor. "Send me a bill."

Beside me Connor laughs. "It's just that simple, is it? Tell me, has everything always been that easy for you to brush off?"

I look to Beth for help, but she's by the fountain dangling a piece of gum. "What is it exactly that I've done that's ticked you off so much?" I move a step closer, forcing myself to look him in the eye. "Why don't you just tell me who you are, so I can add you to the long list of people I need to apologize to for my wild and reckless past."

"Hey, Connor," Beth calls. "You could lend a hand instead of staring down my friend."

He crosses his arms against a chest a pro athlete would be proud of. "I'm the guy who's going to have to fix this mess. Again." He points toward Riley, who's now singing a song from *The Little Mermaid*. "This is the third time in three weeks."

"She's going through a rough patch right now."

"Then maybe her aunt should take care of her."

My mouth opens in a gasp. Who does he think he is? "Look, *Connor*, I'm sorry you've had to fix the fountain. I'll pay for any damages."

"You just handle getting the kid out."

I turn back to the frothy fountain. "Um, yeah. About that . . ."

Connor stares at me like I'm totally boring him. "You have thirty seconds to hop in that fountain and procure your niece before the mayor scares her with the handcuff talk again."

I steal a look over my shoulder. "Well . . ."

His nostrils flare. "Does everyone indulge you this much?"

And before I can hurl a one-liner, he's stepping into the water, the bubbles rushing to cover his khakis. Riley squeals as he makes his way to her. Connor scoops her up in his arms, the soap sluicing off his biceps. As quickly as he got in, he climbs back out.

"Get your hands off me! I'm calling the cops!"

Connor thrusts the sopping child into my arms, instantly soaking me. "This time she's going to work it off."

"Okay." *Good luck getting her to cooperate.* I have a feeling it will be like trying to negotiate with the business end of a rattlesnake.

Connor turns to the fuming mayor. "I'll have it cleaned out this evening." He shoots me a withering glare. "Again."

"Thank you." The mayor crosses his arms over his chest. "I'm glad some people still have some pride in their town." He storms off, stopping only to pick up some trash on the sidewalk.

"Have her at my clinic after school tomorrow," Connor says, swiping at his shirt. "She can clean some kennel cages to work off her *three* offenses."

"One," Riley snaps. "You can't pin the other two on me. You got witnesses? You got proof? I watch *Judge Judy*."

Connor Blake turns his steely eyes back to me. "Bring her to Ivy Lake Animal Clinic. If she's not there by three forty-five, I call your father and let him know how successful your outing with your niece was." He walks away, dripping in bubbles.

"Wha—who . . . how?"

Beth stands beside me. "Connor knows everything. Everyone.

Pretty typical when you're the town vet." She sweeps her hand across my forehead. "You had a big bubble on your face the entire time you were talking to him."

Great.

"You remember him, don't you?"

Unable to hold Riley any longer, I drop her to the ground and manacle her arm with my two hands. "Don't even think about running. No, Beth, I have no idea who he is. I'm sure if I went to school with someone who looks like *that* I would've remembered." Or acts like that.

Beth smiles. "You know—Connor Blake. He looked a lot different back then. President of the math club, science club, and robotics. I think he also held some sort of office in the Future Farmers of America."

"Not ringing any bells. Not that we hung out with the math, science, and techno-geek crowd." I strengthen my grip on a wiggling Riley and laser her with a death stare. "Don't even think about moving."

"He went away to college. And when he came back, he and your sister struck up a friendship. I guess anything he knows about you came from her."

"And you smell," Riley says.

I glance down at her. "And you have suds coming out your nose." She rolls her eyes and looks away.

"We weren't exactly nice to the nerds back in the day." Beth digs in her purse for her car keys.

"He's obviously forgiven you."

Beth shrugs. "I asked him to."

Chapter Five

"I asked you to keep an eye on her for two hours." Dad plunks down three dinner plates on the small kitchen table. "You said you had it under control."

"Yeah, well, I didn't know I was babysitting a little terrorist. Beth and a few other townspeople filled me in on some of Riley's most current escapades." Letting Mr. Miller's donkey out, reorganizing the shelves at the public library, and licking the pastries at the downtown bakery. Ridiculous! Okay, actually the pastry licking I can kind of understand.

Dad focuses on the table as he sets down a platter of grilled burgers. "Do you see why I need help?"

"What you need is the National Guard."

"This is your sister's only child." Dad grabs on to the back of a worn brown chair and eyes me. "Can you really just stand there and tell me you're going to walk away from this? Because, Maggie, if you do, she's going to a state home."

"Why do you care?" The words fly off my tongue, and I suck in my lips as if to bring them back.

He stalks to the fridge. "Never mind."

"I'm sorry." My voice is quiet, reluctant. We didn't talk like this in the house of Benjamin Montgomery, where his word was law. And if anyone but him had the final say, it was followed by just enough yelling and insults to make you wish he was a man who used his fists instead. Bruises, I could've reported. But mean words? Nobody ever cared.

Dad pours a small glass of milk and sets it beside one plate. "No, you're not sorry. You been waiting your whole life to talk to me like that. And maybe I deserve it—or maybe I don't." He looks into my face. "But we're not going to upset Riley any more than she already is, so you just keep your smart mouth to yourself around her."

He's weirding me out. It's like he's genuinely concerned for Riley. I guess it would be hard for him to hold his head up at Bixby's Coffee Shop if he lost his own granddaughter. "Do you have any leads on Allison?"

"I think she might be in the Houston area. One of her old boyfriends lives there. I know he was calling her a lot in the month leading up to her taking off. Or she could be down the street. She's still got a motley crew of friends here. Who knows?"

"How did you get this information?"

"Phone records." Dad throws down some silverware. "I had gotten Allison a cell phone. So I checked the bill."

Wow, I didn't know he knew how cell phones worked. Heaven knows he never calls me.

"Are we eating in this millennium or what?" comes a sassy voice. My father gives me a warning look as Riley stomps into the room. "I'm starving."

I ruffle the curls on her red head. "I guess you worked up an appetite with all that swimming." And law breaking.

"Whatever." She grabs a handful of fries and dumps them on her plate. Sliding into her seat, she grabs three Ore-Idas at once and takes a bite. Charming.

God, help me love this child. "So, um, I noticed Dad moved you into my old room. I thought tomorrow after school—and your work release program—we could go shopping."

"I don't like to shop."

I sit down and fluff my napkin into my lap. "Everyone likes to shop."

"It's stupid." She goes out of her way to avoid touching me as she stretches across the table for the ketchup. I pick the bottle up just before she grabs it and hand it to her with a smile.

"So then what do you like to do, Riley? Do you play sports? Play with dolls?" At this she snorts. "What about video games?"

"Nah."

Dad finally takes his seat, and I begin eating. Just an old habit. Until Dad is seated, no one touches their food. But looking at Riley, ketchup smeared all over her smart mouth, I guess that rule doesn't hold. I consider blessing our meal, but we were never a praying family. Dad didn't do church period. Dad didn't do a lot of things.

I take a peek at my sister's child, this little stranger. Allison always made sure I knew her P.O. box for the sake of gifts and monetary contributions, but visits were never allowed. She came up with a million excuses. And the sad thing is, I let her.

"Do you have friends at school?" I ask.

Riley takes a big bite of hamburger and talks as she chews. "Tons and tons. Everyone wants to be my friend. They line up at recess to play with me." Her monotone is as dry as an Arizona desert.

"Why don't you tell us what you learned at school," Dad suggests.

"Nothing." Riley shrugs. " I know it all."

"That's convenient." I take a sip of tea to keep my mouth busy.

"I used to know someone else who thought she knew everything." Dad looks at Riley and jerks his head my way. She spares me a small glance, then rolls her eyes.

"Do you have a favorite subject?" I ask.

"Lunch." Riley dips a fry in ketchup. "I hate school. And I'm not going back tomorrow."

"Yes, you are," Dad says.

"I'll run away."

"And I'll find you and send you back. Like last week. And the week before."

I stare at my niece's tornadic hair and too-short pants. What kind of life did my sister give her? "What don't you like about Ivy Elementary?"

She props her cheek on her hand and sighs. "The cafeteria gives me gas."

Three hours later, I throw myself on Allison's old bed. It's exhausting to watch TV when your mind is racing with all the things you can't say. Dad just sat there silently in his recliner while Riley complained about everything on the show. If I hear the word *stupid* one more time, I will not be responsible for my actions. And I don't even want to think about my phone call with John. The man is so nice. *God, why don't I just fall madly in love with him? He's the very opposite of my father.*

I tuck myself in bed with a travel magazine and read until the lines blur. As I turn the page on "How to Not Lose Your Shirt in Airline Fees," my ears perk at a noise in the hall. Riley's door. I stay still as a mouse and continue listening. Maybe she's just going to the bathroom.

But when the back door opens, I slide into my flip-flops and leap down the stairs.

"Riley!" I hiss when I reach the backyard. The cool night air swirls around me, and I cross my arms over my chest. "Riley!" A flash of light has me turning, and I follow the glow and look up. My old tree house.

I walk to the giant oak and set my foot on the first wobbly plank nailed into the tree. This ladder couldn't have improved with age. I mutter a silent prayer to not fall on my butt in the dark of night, because I know this kid will leave me for dead.

"I know you're up here." I gingerly reach the top, only to find the door above my head locked.

"Go away."

"I want to talk to you."

"Make an appointment with my secretary."

Mentally I do the math and calculate back to the year Allison gave birth. How is this kid only ten? "Let me in, Riley."

"I'd rather eat cow brains."

I give the door three taps in the center and one giant push. It gives instantly.

"Hey!" She blinds me with the flashlight.

I throw the door back and pull my body onto the floor of the tree house. "This was mine. You think I wouldn't know how to jimmy the lock?"

"Leave me alone."

I wrap my feet under me and look at the old walls as best I can in the sparse light. "I spent a lot of time out here."

She picks at the fuzz on a bunny slipper. "Yeah, and you locked my mom out."

I inhale at her harsh tone. "Yes, I did." Though it certainly worked both ways. "That's what big sisters do."

"You locked her out of everything."

I pick up a leaf from the floor. "Is that what she told you?"

"She said you were the worst sister ever."

Blade in heart. Twisting. "Well . . . I probably wasn't the best. Your mom and I were, um, *are* very different." How do I tell a ten-year-old that her mother came out of the womb hating me? I expected my mom to bring home this rosy baby that I could love—who would love me back. Follow me and adore me. That's what my friends' little brothers and sisters did. But she didn't. She just never did.

"Riley, I know you're scared. And I understand you're hurting and—"

"You don't know squat, lady." She sets the flashlight in her lap, and it casts warped shadows on her face.

"Your mother didn't leave because she doesn't love you. I hope you know that. She left because she's sick. She needs her medicine to do things our brains do for us naturally. And I don't think she's been—"

"Spare me. I've heard it a hundred times."

I'm really stinking it up here. "She does love you, Riley. And you must miss her a bunch."

"Miss her?" Riley chokes on a laugh. "I don't *ever* want to see my mom again."

Chapter Six

Everything in me wants to go back to Chicago. I've slept in more intolerable, body-cramping places than I can count, but nowhere as uncomfortable as the bed under my father's roof last night. I spent most the night just staring at the ceiling, my mind wide awake with a million thoughts—especially my conversation with Riley in the tree.

In between long stretches of tormenting thoughts were small spasms of fitful sleep. Minutes at best. And I dreamed of my mother. Even now when I close my eyes I can see her walking on a pool of water, holding out her hand.

"Come to me," she said. "Take my hand."

But I couldn't. I stood on the pier. Alone. Unable to step out. I wanted to, but I knew I would sink as soon as my toes moved from the ground.

I woke up with that remnant of regret. The taste of it in my mouth.

And this morning at breakfast, my dad hit me up to stay for an additional week. But how can I? I have a lot on the line at work right now.

"I'll pay you," Dad had said. "How much do you want?"

"I'm not taking your money. That's not the point."

"The school talked to Department of Human Services yesterday.

Riley's principal called me. You know they won't let me keep her if I'm working and don't have someone to take care of her."

"So you want me to say I'm living here?"

"Just say you're staying indefinitely."

"I'm on a plane to Taiwan Friday morning. That's not indefinitely."

"You're as selfish as your mother."

That did it. I walked out. I grabbed my iPod and my sunglasses and took a long run in the neighborhood, taking my frustrations out on the asphalt. When I got back, he was gone. But my bad mood was not.

I spend the rest of the day with my laptop, reviewing video footage I'd downloaded before I left. Not film for *Passport to the World*, but my own stuff I've been collecting. Hours and hours of children in the countries I've been in the last year. It's like God opened my eyes to other things that were going on around us as we made our travel show. It seems everywhere I go, I keep finding these children in unlivable circumstances—from poverty to prostitution. And yet I'm powerless to do a thing. Except pick up my camera and capture seconds of their lives. Flashing, fleeting images of life in motion.

Initially I had no idea why I was filming these children, let alone keeping the footage. But it soon became this conviction in me. Like here were stories that had to be told. And where were their voices? Sometimes I lie awake and night and wonder if *I'm* their voice. And that scares me to death. Who am I?

With instructions to get Riley at three o'clock, I leave the house and pull the Ford into the car-rider line at Ivy Elementary. And I wait for half an eternity. Whoever said patience is a virtue obviously never had to pick up a kid at school.

I feel some relief when I see her standing in a group with other students.

"Hey." I move my purse out of the seat so she can sit down. "Good day?"

She gives me the crazy-woman look again. "The best. In fact, I did so well, they want to move me up to junior high."

More like move you to a padded cell. "Dad showed me a few of your grades last night. I think fourth grade is a big enough challenge for you."

"I'm not stupid."

"I didn't say you were." I put the car in drive and slowly pull away, waving at the harried crossing guard in the orange vest. "You're a very intelligent kid, Riley. I knew that within ten minutes of talking to you. I just get the impression you don't try very hard."

"You don't know jack."

"About some things, that's very true. But I'm right about this."

"Just take me home." She stares out the window as we cruise through town. "I want some cookies."

"We have to stop at the veterinarian's clinic so you can work off your debt to society, not to mention Buford and Delroy."

"They're clean now, aren't they?"

"Delroy said to tell you he got a rash from all the soap."

I see her mouth quirk. Just a hint of movement, but I saw it.

"A good aunt would know I need food after school. What kind of adult are you?"

My tongue pauses at the roof of my mouth. She's right. Most people would know this. Why are kids so *not* user-friendly to me? I'm a kid-idiot.

"Here we are." I pull into a spot at the Ivy Lake Animal Clinic. Beside us a woman stands by her car and has a conversation with her wienie dog.

I open my door and get out. "Let's go, Riley."

"Now, Mr. Pickles," the woman says. "You get in that car right now. We're not staying here. You've had all the biscuits you're going to get out of me. I don't care if there's a lovely schnauzer in there, we're going home. In the car!"

I rest my hand on Riley's shoulder. "If Mr. Pickles likes this place, it can't be too bad."

She jerks her shoulder, dislodging my hand.

"Hi, I'm Maggie Montgomery," I tell the woman at the front desk. "Dr. Blake invited my niece Riley here to do some special work for him."

Her face wrinkles in confusion. "Which Dr. Blake?"

"How many are there?" I can only handle one.

"Dr. William Blake is still here part-time. His son, Connor, is our main vet."

"Connor."

"And what is the purpose of your visit?"

"Scoop poop," Riley snaps. "You know, slave labor. Break some child labor laws. That sort of thing."

"Sandy, I'll take care of this."

I do a slow turn and find Dr. Hotness standing right behind me. "Hello," I say, trying to model polite behavior for the child.

His eyes glitter with unspoken sarcasm as they briefly travel over my face before turning to my niece. "I'm glad you came today, Riley."

She shoots a few daggers in my general direction. "Like I had a choice."

Connor's voice is firm, but kind. "It's the right thing to do, and you're also going to be helping the animals out today."

"By scooping—"

"By cleaning cages *and* playing with some stray cats and dogs that we have here right now."

"Nobody wants them?" It's the first thing of interest I've heard from my niece.

Connor shakes his dark head. "We usually have a few animals here that people bring us. We try to place them in good homes. You'd be doing them a huge favor by spending a little time with them."

Some of the hostility melts off of Riley's face, and I openly stare at the man. How can he be such a jerk to me and yet so kind to Riley? Like he knows just what she needs to hear.

He reaches into his pocket and pulls out a granola bar. "Thought you might want an after-school snack."

With a smirk to her clueless aunt, Riley accepts the treat and follows the doctor to the office door.

"Pick her up in an hour," Connor says, without even bothering to turn around. "Don't be late."

I grumble all the way back to my car. Mr. Pickles is still being his obstinate self as I drive away. Must be some good dog treats in there. Because I can't imagine anyone wanting to hang out in *that* vet's office.

Fifty-five minutes later, I stand in the same parking lot. Spying the vet in the nearby horse barn, I walk that way.

He runs his big hand down the flanks of a chestnut mare. "Joe, get Daisy here her X-rays, and let's see if it's colic." Connor leans closer to the horse and speaks soft words to her as he rubs her head.

"Dr. Blake?"

His eyes shift to steel as he gives his assistant another order, then walks three steps toward me. "You're on time."

I frown. "You don't even know me. Isn't it kind of weird to make assumptions about my punctuality?"

"I know you, Maggie Montgomery."

"We went to school together, but much like you, I'm a very different person these days."

Connor's open stare has goose bumps dancing on my skin.

I readjust my purse strap. "Is Riley around?"

"No."

"What? Did she run off?" My heart stutters in my chest. "I *knew* this would happen. I don't suppose you microchipped her before she got away, did you?"

His face is a neutral mask. "She's in the clinic helping Sandy with a new kitten we're bottle-feeding."

"Oh." I pick a piece of lint off my shirt. Then another. "Can we just forget that microchip comment?"

"You have no idea what to do with Riley, do you?"

I take a deep breath and inhale the scent of warm hay and animals. "It's complicated."

He cocks his head. "Does it have to be?"

"Yes." *Now butt out.*

"Riley needs stability." His brow furrows. "She needs someone to love her."

"I'm her aunt, Connor. Not her guardian."

"You've had nothing to do with her."

I take a step back. "What is this? You have no idea what goes on with me and my family. So don't stand there and give me parenting advice, *Veterinarian* Blake. I don't know what I ever did so long ago to tick you off, but it's past time you got over it." I move closer again, sticking my finger in his chest. "I'm going to be honest with you, Connor. I was a reckless, holy terror of a kid. And I hurt a lot of people who didn't walk and talk like me. So if you were one of them, I'm really sorry. But a person can only carry around so many pieces of guilt in one lifetime, and your name isn't on a single one."

He removes my pointing finger, his thumb brushing over my hand. "Well, on behalf of anyone ever wronged by wild Maggie Montgomery, I'll be sure and spread the blanket apology. I'm certain it will warm hearts all over town."

My breath rises and falls like I've run a marathon. We stare each other down as the seconds tick by. "Look, I just really need to get my niece."

He slowly nods twice. "I'd say her life depends on it."

Chapter Seven

When I hear Dad leave the house the next morning, I make my way downstairs. I could seriously go for a bowl of Fruity Pebbles right now, but there's none in the house. Even though I've had it under control for years, my stress eating is back with a vengeance. I've eaten more junk in the last few days than all last year. My pants are not happy.

I pad to the fridge, my running socks sliding across the beige tiled floor. Opening the door, I stand there until I find the juice.

The phone on the wall rings, and I stay in my spot holding my Minute Maid. Do I answer it? On the seventh persistent ring, I pick it up. "Hello?"

"It's me."

"Yes?"

"Your dad."

"I know." I do a Riley eye roll.

"You have to go get your niece at school."

I glance at the clock. "She's only been there thirty minutes. How much trouble could she have possibly have gotten into?"

"I can't leave work. We have union reps coming today to discuss the company shutting down."

"So Reliant Tires is definitely closing. Why didn't you tell me?"

A buzzer sounds in the background. "I gotta go. Please get her."

"But wait, I—"

The line goes dead. I down two coffee mugs of juice and pray that Jesus and the vitamin C will get me through the day.

Twenty minutes later, I walk into the Ivy Elementary office.

"I'm here for Riley Montgomery." My sister had known from the beginning Riley's father wouldn't be in the picture, so Riley carries on our name. Crazy like the rest of us.

The secretary's lips thin. "Just a moment." She picks up the phone and talks for a moment. "Mrs. Chapel will see you now." She points to the hall behind her.

"Mrs. Chapel?"

"The principal."

"Oh." Boy, does that bring back memories. I follow the direction of her finger and find an open door. I knock twice.

A thin woman stands at her desk. "Come in." She shakes my hand with a weak grip.

"I'm Maggie Mont—" I clamp my mouth shut, recognizing a look I'm coming to know. *Let me guess. You went to high school with me, I tormented you in some fashion, and you're still slightly bitter.*

"You don't remember me?" The brunette takes her seat, and I do the same.

I stare at the nameplate on her desk. The degrees on the wall behind her.

"Of course I do, Danielle." Squinting, squinting. "Danielle Pierce, right?"

She doesn't look convinced. "Yes. Chapel now. I'm divorced."

"I'm sorry."

She slowly blinks. "For what?"

"For grades seven through twelve. Okay, now about Riley."

Danielle stares at me a lingering moment before taking her red nails and opening a manila file. "Yes, little Riley. Today she started a fight."

"In class?"

"Before school. On the playground."

"Why?"

Danielle lifts a dainty shoulder. "She said some girls were picking on a student named Sarah, but Sarah denied it, and so did the girl whose nose she bloodied."

"Anything broken?"

"No. Did you want it to be?"

I straighten at her viper's tone. I'll have to ask Beth what I did to this chick. "No, of course not. I was never into violence myself. I guess fighting was the one thing I stayed away from." That and head gear.

"The child will be fine, but obviously she went home for the day and her parents are quite upset."

"I'm sure they are."

"Riley has built quite a file in the month we've had her." Danielle thumbs through the pages. "She's pulled a fire alarm, let the class gerbil loose, tripped a boy, put glue in a substitute's chair, thrown chicken nuggets at a classmate, and run away multiple times."

I have no idea what to say here. "I'm getting familiar with her behavioral issues."

Danielle closes the file with a slap. "I know your father has gone back to work, so who is taking care of this child after school and the evenings he has to go in?"

"Um . . ."

"Mr. Montgomery mentioned you were coming for an extended visit to help out with Riley."

"Did he?"

"How long will you be staying?"

I swallow and meet Danielle's icy gaze. "Indefinitely."

One big lecture, a few warnings, and lots of advice later, I'm driving down the road with my niece, nauseated by the knowledge that I'm staying another week. *God, why me? Why now?*

"You missed your turn, Auntie M."

"Watch the tone, Rocky Balboa. *What* were you thinking, punching a little girl in the face?"

"I was thinking she needed to get her paws off Sarah. She's the one who's little."

"The principal said Sarah backed up the other girl's story that you attacked without any reason."

Riley huffs and stares out the window. "Whatever."

"No, don't whatever me. Give me the truth here."

"Nobody believes me anyway. What's the point?"

"Try me."

"Like you care."

I yank the car over on the shoulder and jerk the gear in park. "Riley, I *do* care. I don't want my niece knocking in people's faces or pulling fire alarms or whatever else it is you have up your sleeve." Tattered sleeve at that. "You cannot act that way."

She turns her head so that all I can see is the back of her curly red head.

"Look at me."

Nothing.

I take a deep breath and let out a sigh that could only belong to a woman out of her league with a kid. "I know things are hard right now."

"You don't know nothing about me."

"I know when your birthday is."

She tosses me a fierce look over her shoulder. "I know when Zac Efron's birthday is, but that doesn't mean jack diddley."

"I'm your aunt."

She laughs. "Lot of good that does me. I've seen you, like, three times in my entire life?"

I roll my shoulders and try to dislodge the guilt sitting there. "I sent you birthday and Christmas presents." Good ones too. Like a Wii and a scooter.

Riley whips her head around. "Yeah, thanks. Mom hocked them all. Maybe next time I could just get some socks or a few pencils—something she won't steal."

Oh. "I . . . I didn't know." What in the world has Allison put this child through? If I had only known, I—

Who am I kidding? I don't know what I would've done. My sister didn't really want anything to do with me, and I didn't fight it. It was always easier to just stay away. Stay away from it all.

"Riley, I don't know what your mom told you about me, but I'm not a horrible person. I do care about you." This is the part where I should say I love you. But I can't. We'd both know I'm lying.

"Can we just go home?"

"We're going to Target."

"Hello, I just slugged Megan Oberman. You're supposed to yell at me, take me home, send me to my room, then yell at me some more." She blows air out her lips. "Don't you know anything?"

"You know what you did was wrong. Even if Sarah needed taking up for, you don't hit someone. You tell an adult."

"I'll remember that next time."

"There won't be a next time. And we have to get you some clothes and a new bedspread. That purple one went out with the New Kids on the Block. So just tell your grandpa that I thoroughly yelled at you, and we'll call it good."

"Grandpa doesn't yell at me."

"Right." I've never known him to hold back on any man, woman, or fist-wielding child.

I can feel her weighty stare. "That's it?"

"Yep. As long as you cooperate and help me shop." I hit the exit marked Grapevine.

She chews her lip and considers this. "I'm not wearing pink."

"Fair enough."

"And if you get me a Hannah Montana bedspread, I'll pull every fire alarm in Target I can find."

"Deal." I stick out my fist, and Riley lifts a scornful brow. "Bump it. Come on."

A small giggle escapes, but she reels it back in. "You are so lame."

Chapter Eight

"Carley, I know it's bad timing. But my family is in crisis, and they need me." I pace my bedroom as my producer lists all the reasons why I need to be on a plane to Taiwan tomorrow morning. "Just a week. That's all I'm asking for. Plus it will be a great chance for that intern to get some more camera experience." Knowing I have an impressive collection of vacation days, Carley finally agrees. But her disappointment practically reaches through the phone to tap me on the shoulder and shake its head in shame.

Okay, God. You got me here. For a week. But that's all I can do. And I'm gonna need you to get me through every minute. You and SweeTarts. And Jolly Ranchers. And I might have to go to the hard stuff and get some Chunky Monkey.

I walk down the stairs to the smell of tacos.

"The principal says you have to apologize." My dad sets a plate in front of Riley.

Riley's upper lip lifts in a snarl. "The principal looks like she sucks lemons all day."

True. "Oh, just apologize and get it over with," I say, going to the silverware drawer. "And tomorrow keep your hands to yourself."

"Speaking of tomorrow." Dad walks back to the stove. "I have to go in to work early. I need you to take Riley to school."

"Why are you working, Dad?"

"For the fun of it. Get the kid something to drink."

"The kid wants a Dr Pepper," Riley says.

Dad looks at me over his shoulder. "Milk or water."

"Why isn't Maggie cooking?" Riley asks as I grab the two percent.

"Because she can't." Dad stirs the ground beef. "Just like her mama. Terrible cooks."

As the refrigerator blasts cool air on my skin, memories flash through my mind. Me trying to please my dad by making a pork chop dinner. I burned those chops, and all he could say was, "Can't you do anything?" I think I've been trying to answer that question all my life.

"Has my mom called?" Riley asks.

The kitchen falls silent.

Dad focuses on transferring the food to a serving dish. "No. I'm sure she will. She's just getting her head together."

"I'm going to church Sunday." My own announcement surprises even me. "Who wants to join me?"

Dad sits down at the table. "Have to work."

Riley grabs a taco shell. "Me too."

"I don't want to go alone, Riley. You can go with me." I'll call Beth and see where she goes.

"Nah."

"I took you shopping today."

Her green eyes narrow. "You gonna hold that over my head the rest of my life or just this week?"

"That new black skirt and rocker T-shirt would look great at church. There might be some cute boys there."

"Boys are stupid."

"There might be some new people to beat up."

"Maggie," my dad warns.

After a dessert of ice cream and chocolate syrup, Riley pushes her bowl away. "I'm gonna go up and watch TV."

"Do your homework first." Dad's voice leaves no room for argument, but Riley doesn't seem the least bit fazed.

"Homework is dull."

"So's working at McDonald's all your life." I tweak a stray curl and make a mental note to get her a hair appointment. "Go on up and get started on your school work. I'll join you in a bit and help you hang your new curtains."

With a sigh that comes from the tips of her toes, she squeaks the chair across the floor and shuffles out of the room.

"I've decided to stay for a week."

Dad looks up from his coffee, surprise lighting his eyes. "Um . . . good."

I guess that means thanks.

"I might not find your sister in seven days. Or another babysitter."

"I can't live here. I have to go back to work. I have a life in Chicago." And then there's John. He's left six messages in the last two days. I guess my deep, meaningful four-word texts haven't been enough to satisfy him. But I said we needed space.

At midnight I put my book down, slip on a light robe, and traipse down the hall in my bare feet. I turn the knob on Riley's door and slowly push it open with a creak.

Walking forward in the dark, I head for her bed and—*oomph!*

"Ow!" comes her voice from below.

I trip over a hard lump in the floor and careen into her

mattress face first. Getting my bearings, I switch on her bedside lamp. "What are you doing down there?"

She sits up. "What does it look like?"

"It looks like you're sleeping on the floor with your new comforter."

Riley stares at her hands and blinks at the light. "I'm pretending to have a campout."

"Why?"

"Because I just am. Go away. If I fall asleep over my multiplication tables tomorrow, it's going to be your fault. What are you doing in here anyway?"

I rub the knee I banged on the bed frame. "Checking on you."

"Why?"

"Because . . . because that's what adults do!" Isn't it? It just seemed right. Until I stepped on her and went airborne.

Eyes of fire look up at me. "You're not my mom."

"I'm not trying to be."

My niece flops back on her pillow and throws the comforter over her head. "Go away."

"Riley, I—"

"Try to walk around me this time."

I twist the knob on her lamp and carefully let myself out of her room. It's like I have no maternal skills. No child instinct. I need Mary Poppins.

Slipping into my own bed, I close my eyes and let sleep pull me under. And a familiar dream lures me further into the darkness.

"Maggie—"

I'm at the Ivy Lake pier. Moonlight spills out onto the water like light from heaven. "Mom?"

She stands on the top of the gentle waves and holds out a hand. "Come on out."

My feet are stuck to the worn boards of the pier. "No. I can't."

"What are you so afraid of?"

The water laps at the pier and splashes on my feet. "I'm sorry, Mom. I'm so sorry."

"Just step out here with me, Maggie." Her hair floats around her face, red and wavy like mine. Then she slips beneath the watery surface, inch by slow inch.

My breath hitches in my throat, tears pour down my cheeks. "I'll go for help. Just don't leave me. Please don't leave me." I run the planks toward the shore.

"You're going the wrong direction," she calls.

But I just keep running.

And running.

The next morning I wake up with a mouth of cotton and bags under my eyes big enough to carry a small child. I spend some time with my Bible before I even put my feet on the floor, searching the pages for some encouragement.

A few chapters later, I throw my hair in a ponytail, walk down the hall, and blast Riley awake with some off-key singing. "If you don't get up, I'm moving on to the one and only Hannah Montana song I know."

Riley's eyes pop open. "I'm getting up."

I give her my best go-team pep talk all the way to school, and I'm pleased with the submissive way she sits there and listens, quietly taking in my every word. It isn't until she opens the car door at Ivy Elementary that I notice she's had my iPod on the whole time. I reach for the ear buds and tweak them out of her ears. "I'll just keep this. And you look totally cute in your new outfit today. Keep your hands to yourself and no food throwing, alarm pulling, or teacher gluing."

"Fine. Don't forget to pick me up. School gets out at two-thirty."

"Nice try. See you at three." Which means I have to be in the car-rider line at, like, eleven a.m. I swear some of those moms must camp out the night before.

At two-fifty, I'm one of a string of adults at Ivy Elementary waiting to pick up a child. I've read a chapter in a book, filed my nails, and done the crossword in *People.* And there's still time left.

My door flings open and Beth jumps inside. "Hey, girl! I thought this was your car."

Yes! An adult to talk to. "I don't know how you do this every day."

She runs her fingers through her dark bangs. "I thought you were leaving today."

I shrug and sigh. How do I even explain this? "Riley's going through a really hard time. I just had no idea." My cheeks burn with guilt. "Allison and I were never close, but after Riley was born, she really shut me out. She made sure I had nothing to do with her. If I was home visiting, Allison would make sure she was out of town." I shake my head and look into my friend's compassionate face. "I don't even know my own niece. I'm the worst aunt ever."

"No, you're not." Beth grabs my hand and pats it. "You're here now, aren't you?"

"For a week. And then what?" So many questions. What if Allison doesn't come back? And even if she does, is she fit to raise her own daughter? "I really don't know what I'm supposed to do about any of this."

"You know what you need?"

"A vacation in Maui?"

Beth shakes her head. "Dinner at my house."

"I should probably stay home."

"No, come on. Mark's taking the kids to his mom's for the evening, and we can hang out. You have a whole week ahead of you."

Ugh. Don't remind me. A whole week with my dad. And in a town that won't let me forget that I bungee jumped off the water tower in the eleventh grade.

"I won't take no for an answer." Beth swats my shoulder. "We'll have fun. Besides, you've never seen my house."

"I don't know."

"If you come, I'll forgive you for not visiting one single time in the last decade."

My resolve crumbles like a stale brownie. "What time?"

After saying good-bye to Beth, I finally creep to the front of the line. Leaning across the seat, I open Riley's door and wave. "Hey there."

Riley stomps toward me and sticks her head in. "Mrs. Ellis needs to see you."

"Who?"

"My teacher. She's a cow."

I move the car to a nearby parking spot and climb out. "What's this about?" I ask Riley.

"I think she wants to get your permission to send me straight to Harvard. I'm freakishly smart, you know. I'm like one of them child prodigals."

When I sit down in the classroom, I find Mrs. Ellis neither a cow, nor wanting to discuss my niece signing up for the SAT.

"Here is a large stack of work that Riley has yet to complete." The older woman slides a thick yellow folder across a desk. "Maybe you could spend some time looking over it this weekend." She smiles warmly, and the thought occurs that she'd make a lovely Mrs. Claus at the mall for Christmas. "I'm so glad you're helping out. Riley needs someone in her corner." She winks at my niece, but Riley just stares at her with all the enthusiasm of one watching grass grow.

I spear Riley with a look. "She will definitely get this work done."

"Riley's grades are terribly low. And she just sits there while others are completing their work." She rests a hand on Riley's shoulder. "Obviously there's a sharp brain in there. I'd like to see her use it. She needs consistency. And some extra help."

"I'll do what I can, Mrs. Ellis." Maybe I can find a tutor before I leave.

Mrs. Ellis clasps her hands together. "You know, the more an adult is involved, the greater chance for a child's success."

Unfortunately that adult can't be me. "I do agree with you."

"Perfect! I knew you would." She waddles back to her desk and returns with a form. "We're having a field trip Monday, and Riley hasn't gotten her permission slip signed."

"Oh, well, that's easy enough." I rummage in my purse for something to write with.

"Actually, I was hoping you could go with us."

I drop my pen. "Huh?"

Mrs. Ellis's smile dimples her cheeks. "We're short on chaperones, and we really need the help." She lifts a well-meaning brow. "And I'm sure Riley would love to have your company."

Riley chews on a thumbnail. "Not really."

"Well . . ." Not sure how to get out of this.

"It would mean a lot to us." Mrs. Ellis tilts her head toward Riley. "I know you want to do everything you can to help out the school, as well as your niece."

"Um, absolutely."

"Wonderful! I think you'll enjoy it." Mrs. Ellis pats me on the back and beams. "We'll be spending the entire day at Ivy Lake."

Chapter Nine

Nothing can bring on guilt like finding two empty Twinkie wrappers in your room and not remembering them passing across your lips.

Deciding I need to burn a few calories right away, I slip on my running shoes, tell Dad and Riley good-bye, and walk the two miles to Beth's.

As I pass by the houses, buildings, and stores I used to know, I think about my high school days. What a punk I was. Didn't care about anyone but myself. Didn't know Christ then. Didn't know much of anything except the whole town thought I was as wild as my mom, and I wanted to live up to that legacy. I was determined we'd both be remembered. And one of us definitely was.

I turn into a subdivision that wasn't here five years ago and look for the fourth house on the right.

That's funny. There are at least five cars there. I dig into my pocket and check the address again. Number eight Nightingale Lane.

Before I can lift a finger to push the bell, Beth swings the door wide open. "Get in here!" She pulls me to her in a fierce hug. "So glad you came."

"Me too. I—" I freeze as I look up. Omigosh. A living room full of people. "What's going on?"

"Well, this is our class reunion committee. Three classes, actually. We already had a meeting scheduled tonight, and I thought it would be the perfect chance for you to see some old friends."

My eyes sweep the room, and my stomach goes south. The veterinarian stands there, arms crossed, looking like I just spit on his birthday cake.

"Hey, Maggie!" A large, bald-headed guy breaks from the pack and envelopes me in a bear hug. "Long time no see, eh?"

I laugh and pull away. "Chris Parsons." Quarterback of the Ivy Lions. Take away thirty pounds, add some hair, and he looks just the same. "How are you?"

"Good. Got two ex-wives, three kids, and a job as a Wal-Mart assistant manager."

For lack of anything better to say, I throw out a safe catchall phrase. "Wow." I try not to look at Connor Blake, whose droll gaze remains locked on my face. "Do you live in Ivy still, Chris?"

"Nah. Live with my mother in Grapevine." He nudges me with an elbow. "Between the alimony and child support, Mom's basement is all this guy can afford!"

Okay, moving on. "Beth, maybe I should come back another time. I don't want to interrupt your meeting." Must get out of here.

Connor leans a hip against the leather couch. "Afraid of a little time with some old friends?"

Shelly Frances, a girl who was a grade below me, laughs. "Oh, the stories we could tell about Maggie."

Chris snaps his fingers. "Yeah, like the time that—"

"I just remembered I left the oven on." And I might stick my head in it. "I really should go."

Beth stands near and puts an arm around me. "Let's all be nice. No need to bring up old dirt." She squeezes my shoulder. "Everybody gather round the dining room table for some lasagna and reunion discussion. Time's ticking."

We walk into the dining area to find the table all set. Ivory and blue plates, cloth napkins in an artsy pattern, and place cards made from mini picture frames.

"I have four kids, and we eat on Chinet. So I never get to break out the good stuff." Beth motions for us all to sit down.

Locating my name, I find myself beside Mr. Personality. The doctor of rudeness.

I ease into the chair and force myself not to sniff him. Do *not* do it. Do *not* even—drat! He smells nice. Totally doesn't smell like a jerk.

Beth brings out a big pan of lasagna and sets it in the middle of the table. Three more side dishes follow. Plates are filled and the conversation begins to flow. With each pass of a dish, I take a quick study of Connor Blake.

"Now, let's talk about this reunion. It's only four weeks away, and it will be here before we know it." Beth sits at the head of the table and leads the meeting with all the skill of a congresswoman. Or a mother of four. "We decided last time to spice it up and be different." She turns to me. "We want to have some activities at the dance. Like a quick ballroom lesson or some line dancing or karaoke. Something to give the night some variety and get people involved."

The doorbell rings, and Beth glances at Connor. "You want to get that?"

He rests his napkin on the table and walks into the living room. When he returns, he has Riley's principal beside him.

"Hello, everyone."

Beth smiles. "Hey, Danielle. Grab a seat, and I'll get you something to drink."

Danielle looks at me, her face pinched.

"I'm campaigning for reunion queen," I say. "Just wanted to get an early start."

The guys on the other side of me laugh, but Danielle does not. With a few soft words to Connor, she takes her place at an empty spot at the other end.

I wonder if Connor and Danielle are dating. They certainly look good together.

Beth returns with a glass of water for the newcomer. "We were just reliving some old times and talking about our dance ideas."

"Do you have any Maggie memories to share?" Chris asks.

"Yeah." Danielle glares at me over the top of her glass.

Oh boy.

"I remember the time she hid my clothes in gym class, and I had to wear my smelly track uniform all day."

This one I recall. "I'm sorry. I was terrible in school." This evening is just a thrill a minute. Can't wait to do it again in the next decade.

But Danielle isn't through. "And I remember you asked my prom date to go at the last minute, and he dumped me. And then you didn't show up."

"Yeah, I didn't go to prom that year." My mother drowned the day before prom. I spent the entire weekend in bed, so the furthest thing from my mind was my date. My mother had helped me pick out my dress. It was black and sparkly, and it made me feel like a princess. I didn't attend prom the next year either. It was just too much. That dress still hangs in the back of my closet, a beautiful reminder of the ugliest time.

"The girl's mother had died." Beth's tone carries a warning. "I'm sure it's hard to think about your updo when you've just lost a parent."

"Drop it, Danielle." This from Connor. "I just want to focus on the food," he says in a lighter tone, making me want to kiss his cheek and thank him. "Besides, if we were to list off all the things Maggie did wrong in high school, we'd be here all week."

Rescinding that thank-you now.

Beth consults a legal pad beside her plate. "Chris, you still gonna contact the DJ and try to get a better deal?"

"I'm on it."

She turns to a guy in thick glasses and a Star Trek T-shirt. "Michael, I need you to go check out that other band. I'm just not sure about the one we have."

"Going this week."

"Jermaine, you need to get me the bids from at least three florists by our next meeting."

"Sure thing, Beth."

She fires off jobs for every person, and my head spins with all the details involved with a simple two-day gathering.

"Now, I have the number for a ballroom dancing instructor, but everyone's delegated to something already." Beth turns to me.

I grin wide. "That look may work on your husband, but it won't on me. I'm just here for a quick visit. And watching my niece has become a full-time job."

"Oh." Her face falls. "I guess you're right. I'll do it. I mean, never mind that I have four babies to raise, a part-time job, and one depressed husband who spends all his time pounding the pavement for work." She stares at her lap.

The noose tightens around my neck. "Fine. I'll do it."

She perks up instantly. "Great! Now Maggie needs a partner." She scans the table as Michael and Jermaine raise their hands high. "Connor can go."

Danielle puts down her fork. "I'll go with Connor. I wouldn't want to impose on Maggie's vacation."

"No," Beth says. "Maggie needs something to fill her hours."

Don't I have a say in this? "But I—"

"And we all know if she gets bored, she gets in trouble." Beth's smile is so sweet, it takes out most of the sting.

I steal a glance at Connor, who butters his roll without saying a word.

I surprise myself by staying the entire time. In fact, when I next look at my watch, there are only a few of us remaining.

I stand up and stretch. "I should get home."

Beth hands me my purse and follows me to the door. "I'm so glad you came."

I look at my friend, the girl who stood beside me through every catastrophe I got her into. "Me too. I'm sorry it took so long." I open the front door, only to feel the mist of rain. "Oh great."

Beth glances in the driveway. "You walked?"

I nod. "After I lost a battle with Twinkies."

"Connor can take you home."

"No!" I pull on Beth's arm. "That's okay. What's a little rain, eh?"

Connor walks to the doorway, his henley stretching over his chest like he's a Gap model. "I'll drive you."

"Um . . . all right." We both say our good-byes and quickly walk to his truck.

Connor opens the passenger door and helps me in.

I barely click my seat belt in place before the man goes on the attack. "Beth's got a lot going on right now. Don't commit to helping her out if you're not going to follow through."

Watching the rain rivulets race down the window, I force myself to count to ten. In French. Then Spanish. "For someone who's smart enough to get his doctorate, it surprises me that you're dumb enough to think I'm the same girl I was at sixteen."

He navigates a turn. "Aren't you?"

"You've certainly changed. At least appearance-wise. But tell me, were you this much of a jerk back then or is this a new development?"

"I care about people."

"And I don't?" He shoots me a look I can't fathom in the darkness of the truck. "Why don't you just say whatever it is you want to say to me, Connor."

He pulls into my dad's driveway, and the only sound between us is the rain and swish of the windshield wipers.

"I'll pick you up for the dance class Saturday at six."

"Don't you trust me to be there?" I don't even let him answer. "I'll just meet you."

"I'll be here at six."

"Your chivalry is borderline obnoxious." I feel around the door for the handle and finding it, give it a good tug. "Good night."

"I knew your sister."

The rain assaults my face as his words stop me cold. "Beth said you were . . . acquainted."

He shrugs. "Your sister and I were friends. She confided in me sometimes."

The rain sops my hair, but I can't seem to move. "And the mystery unfolds. This is why you can't stand me."

He closes his eyes for a brief moment. "I don't dislike you. I just don't trust you. Your sister never had anything good to say about you. When I came back to Ivy to take over my dad's practice, she was still here. With a baby and a sister who wouldn't even give her the time of day." He shakes his head. "I know I'm not supposed to judge, and I'm trying, but Maggie, she was alone and messed up, and all she could talk about was you."

I brush the wet bangs from my cheek. "I—I . . ." How do I

explain this to a stranger? "She has a mental disease. She'd never take her meds. And you believe her over me?"

"Seeing's believing. You haven't been to Ivy in five years. Just don't get that niece's hopes up if you're not planning on being a permanent part of her life. She's had the wind knocked out of her too many times."

"You didn't know the real Allison."

"Maybe not." He flicks on his defrost. "But I knew you. And I know that little girl who's been nothing but alone."

I slam his door shut and run into the house.

That night I go to bed with my anger and dream of my mother. And the lake.

Again.

Chapter Ten

After all these years, math *still* makes my head hurt.

"No." I pick up the pencil and hand it to my niece. "Nine divided by three is what?"

As Riley stares at the worksheet, my mind wanders back to last night. Who does Connor Blake think he is? And the nerve of him to say, "I don't mean to be judgmental" right before he totally unloads his misguided opinions on me. Like that made it okay? Well, I didn't mean to eat all the strawberry Jolly Ranchers in the bag last night either, but that doesn't mean that I didn't do it. Or that the calories aren't circulating right now with a game plan to head straight to my butt. What exactly did my sister tell him about me?

"Done."

I pop back into the present as my niece shoves her homework toward me. "Let me see." I scan her math work and find it all correct. "You're great with numbers."

Her hazel eyes drop to her hands, but I see the pink bloom on her cheeks.

"Okay, let's move on to English. Did you read that short story last night?"

"Yeah, couldn't put it down."

Oh really? "All right, tell me about Helen Keller."

Riley stares at a spot outside the kitchen window. "She's a really great lady."

"And what else about her?"

Riley bites her lip and strikes a reflective pose. "I don't know. I read four other short stories after that, and it's all kind of running together."

"How is Helen Keller different from you and me?"

"She's a midget."

"A midget?"

"Yes, and she wants to play in the WNBA, but nobody will listen to her." Riley gives her head a mournful shake. "Nobody believes in Helen."

I flip open her language arts book to the short story and point my finger to an illustration of Helen. "She's deaf and blind."

Riley steals a glance. "Wow, that would be really hard with the height thing."

I straighten my spine and roll some tension out of my shoulders. "Riley, you didn't read this."

"I accidentally read the wrong one."

Her tone is desperate, but I'm learning not to buy into what this kid sells. "Let's just read it right now then. Aloud. You read a paragraph and then I will."

An inner struggle plays across Riley's face. She sits there for a full minute, flipping through the book, brushing crumbs off her shirt, crossing and uncrossing her legs.

"Today, Riley."

"I'm mentally rehearsing my character voices. Don't rush me." She takes a deep breath and stares at the first page. "There . . . was . . . was . . ."

"Once," I supply.

"I know! Once a girl . . ." Her eyes squint at the word.

"Named."

"Named Hannah."

"Helen."

"Helen Keller. And she was a difficult person."

I double-check the words. "She was a different child."

Riley shoves the book away. "This is stupid. How am I supposed to read something so boring when it's about to put me to sleep?"

Maybe she needs glasses. "Can you see the page okay?"

"Yeah."

"What's this word?" I put my finger under the word *friend.*

"If you don't know, I'm not going to tell you." Riley drums her fingers on the table. "With all this homework, I don't have time to teach you to read."

"What's the word, Riley?"

"Farmer." She slips off the chair. "I gotta go. I promised a friend I'd call and check on her. She made an A-minus on her spelling test yesterday and is threatening to OD on juice boxes."

"Freeze, short stuff."

She stops in the doorway but doesn't turn around.

"Is reading hard for you?"

"No!" She spins around on her new ballet flat. "I'm not stupid!"

"I didn't say you were." I stand up and go to her, but she takes two steps back. "Riley, it's okay if reading is hard. Math is difficult for me, but look how good you are at it."

"I can read." Her words come out with all the force of bullets.

"Sure you can. But I'd like to help you read even better. I think it would make all your homework easier." How can a kid read the directions to any assignment if she can't even decipher the words? No wonder math is her strength. She probably mimics the teacher's demonstration and just applies it to all the problems.

Tears pool in Riley's eyes, and she dashes them away. "I'm not dumb."

"Of course you're not. Who would say that?"

"Everyone." She sniffs loudly. "Everyone says I'm dumb, but I'm not!"

"Even smart girls need help."

"I don't need your help. I don't even like you, and I wish you'd never showed up. My mom was right—you're just mean and don't care about anybody."

"Riley—"

She runs through the living room, and the door rattles the walls on her way out. I watch her out the picture window, as she heads to the backyard. Guessing where she's going, I quickly run back to the kitchen in time to see her scale the rickety ladder up the tree.

Deciding to let her cool down for a while, I pick up my cell and call John.

"Hey," he says on the second ring. "I've missed your voice."

I never know what to say to that. "Yeah, I just wanted to return your call." I fill him in on the basics of the last few days.

"Does your dad know she can't read?"

"I don't know. He's at work. As usual. I think he still doesn't know what to do with a child, so it's easier to just stay out of the way." But what will he do when I'm gone? What will become of Riley?

"I thought maybe I could come see you."

"What?" Bad idea! Really bad idea. The script of my "it's not you, it's me" speech scrolls through my head, and suddenly it seems like the best possible solution to the mess that is John and me.

"I don't know if I can go without seeing you a whole other week."

Never mind that we go weeks without seeing one another all

the time. "John, um . . ." Here it comes. Time to get it out there. "I think I really need this space."

"Between you and me?"

"Yeah. Um . . . I don't think you should come down to Texas. I've got a lot going on right now, and I just can't think about us at the moment."

"What's there to think about?" Before I can answer he plods on. "Remember when we first started dating, and you warned me that when guys get close, you break it off?"

"Yes." I don't know why I was so honest with the guy, but I felt like he deserved to know what he was getting into. I come with my own warning label.

"I think this is just you running scared. And you know what?"

I'm afraid to ask.

"I'm not going to let you do that."

"No, really. I need some time to think and straighten some stuff out and—"

"I'm not going to let you push a good thing away, Maggie. I'm strong enough for the both of us."

Does the guy get his lines off Lifetime movies? "It's over, John. I can't do this anymore. I'm sorry."

"Just like that? You're walking away? Maggie, you're just stressed and overwhelmed."

"Yes, but it's more than that."

"Doesn't any part of you want to try?"

Sometimes being an adult is highly overrated. "No, I'm sorry. I don't." Because heaven forbid I be normal—have a real relationship verses a series of dates. "I wish I did. Maybe I just need to retire from dating, get a house full of cats, and call it good."

He sighs. "The right guy will make you want to stay and fight for it—"

"And . . . I'm afraid you're not him."

Silence on the other end. "I'm not going to talk you out of this, am I? You're going to give up on five months?"

"I do care about you—but it's not enough. You deserve more than that."

A long moment of silence passes. "I will miss you, Maggie. But . . . I guess I understand."

"Take care of yourself." I hang up and relief battles with the guilt. But I couldn't keep on seeing this guy. I'm relationship TNT. *God, what's wrong with me that the closer they get, the more I want to run? Why am I so afraid of love? And commitment . . . and circus clowns.*

I rehearse a few things in my head to say to Riley, then walk outside into the cool morning breeze of the day.

"Riley? I'm coming up." I test the first rung, then climb the rest to the very top. Pushing open the door, I find it unlocked and needles of apprehension prickle my skin. "Riley?"

I eyeball the entire space. She's gone.

"Riley!" With flashbacks of my first day in town, I yell her name as I canvas the yard. I check the spot where she keeps her bike, but find it barren as well. Great. Not only is she upset, but she's upset and mobile.

Jumping in the car, I make two sweeps of the neighborhood before cruising through the rest of town. I need one of those police bullhorns. Or the handcuffs, so I can chain her to her room. Forever. This kid is so grounded. I'm talking time-out for infinity. She'll see the light of day when the Jonas Brothers are on their twenty-year reunion tour.

Thirty minutes later, just as I'm trying to decide whether to give into screaming or crying, my phone rings.

"Yes?"

"Maggie, it's Beth."

"Beth! Riley's run away again and—"

"She's okay. Connor's got her. She found a hurt puppy and apparently put him in her basket, then road all the way to the Ivy Lake Animal Clinic."

"All the way out at the lake?" Is she nuts? Those roads are narrow out there.

"Connor wanted me to call you and let you know she's fine."

"I'm on my way. And, Beth?"

"Yeah?" Kids scream in the background.

"Thanks."

"That's what friends are for, Maggie."

I drive toward the lake to the vet clinic, not even bothering to look at the majestic trees or the changing scenery. *God, what do I say to Riley? And why would she listen to me? By this time next week I'll be gone. Not out of her life, but not a consistent fixture either. Where is she going to get the stability she needs?*

I spring from the Focus and open the lobby door, sending a bell to jangling. The sounds of yipping dogs greet me, and I walk by a woman with two cats hissing in a crate.

The same receptionist mans the front desk. "You again?"

"Is my niece here? I think she brought in a puppy."

"Just a minute. I'll page Dr. Blake." She picks up her phone and speaks into it. "He said to go into examining room number two." She points across the hall to a door with two red bones on the door.

Dodging a Labrador on the loose, I approach the door and give it a small knock before entering. I don't know why. It's not like the puppy needs any privacy.

"Hello." I look from Connor to my niece to the dog. "I hear you have a new patient."

A small cocker spaniel whimpers from the table.

"She's really hurt," Riley says, with eyes only for the animal. "I found her in a drainage ditch, bleeding really bad."

"Was this before or after you ran away?" I ask.

"Riley probably saved this dog's life." Connor places a gentle hand on the dog's dirty head. "There's some serious infection in her leg. If it had spread, she wouldn't have made it." His blue eyes fuse with mine. "As it is, it's going to be a pretty serious treatment."

Riley's bottom lip quivers. "He—he says he doesn't know if she'll get to keep her leg."

I stand transfixed as Connor puts a strong arm around my niece . . . and she lets him. She leans into his side and wipes a hand across her red nose.

"I'm sure if anyone can help your puppy, it's Dr. Blake here." The words surprise me as much as they do Connor.

"*My* puppy?" Riley asks. "I can keep her?"

"No, what I meant was that you found it and—" I watch the hope fade from her face. Pain returns. "Let's just see how things go, okay? I promise I'll make sure she's taken care of."

"I need to get the dog into surgery." Connor's voice is calm, but strong. "I wanted to make sure someone was with Riley first." He turns to my niece. "Running away was not cool, Riley. You should've had an adult bring you here. But I'm glad you trust me with this dog, and I'm going to do everything I can to help her."

Riley nods her head and loses her battle with tears. "I love this puppy."

I rest my hand on her shoulder. "How about we let Dr. Blake do his thing, huh? You and I need to talk, and Dr. Blake can call us at home with an update."

He smiles at Riley, and for the first time I see the dimple in his right cheek. "I'll let you know how it goes and tell you everything when I pick up your aunt tonight."

I fight the urge to squirm as his gaze lingers on me.

Riley says good-bye to the scruffy mess, and it occurs to me that this is as childlike as I've ever seen her. As broken and defenseless as she's ever been. No filter. No bull. Just Riley, a girl hurting for another wounded creature.

I put the car in drive and turn the radio off. "You can't keep running away, Riley. You can't ride away on your bike every time you get upset."

"What do you care?"

Back to that, are we? "I do care. You're my niece, and I don't like the idea of you by yourself somewhere in town. And it's crazy to just go shooting off every time something doesn't go your way. Big girls don't run. They stick it out and deal with the problem."

"Is that what you do?"

Well, no. But I'm a screwed-up mess who eats candy by the pound and breaks up with men as frequently as one spits out a piece of gum. But we're not talking about me here! "Why'd you leave, little missy? Spill it."

"I dunno."

I switch the radio back on and hit the scan button. "First polka station that lands on, I'm crankin' it up and singing along."

"Fine!" She snaps off the music. "Because I'm stupid. Okay?" She throws up her hands. "I'm dumb. My mom said I'm dumb, and I am."

I can't even breathe in this car. I roll down a window and let in some spring air before I Hulk out and hurt someone. "You listen to me. You are not dumb. I've met a lot of dumb people in my life"—dated quite a few too—"and you are *not* dumb. When I told you you were smart, I meant it. You are the sharpest little girl I've ever met. So if your mother said that, she was wrong." From the corner of my eye, I glance at my niece. Her face is chiseled in stone. "I know you don't totally understand this, but your mom sometimes doesn't know what she's saying. Her brain tells her to say and do things that it shouldn't. So I know she didn't mean what she said."

The lip trembles again, and Riley's voice drops to a whisper. "But I am stupid. I don't get anything in school. Everyone laughs at me when I'm called on."

My stomach in a pretzel knot, I reach for her hand and hold it tight when she tries to pull away. "Um . . . well, those kids are being mean, and I know you would never make fun of someone like that." *Though you wouldn't hesitate to rip someone's hair out.* "But we're going to show them how smart you really are. You and I are going to fix this, okay, Riley? I mean it. We Montgomery girls have to stick together, right?"

She sniffs. "Not really."

"Work with me here."

"Stick together. Like underwear with static cling."

I reach out and brush a tear from her cheek. "No more running away?"

"I can only promise so much in one day."

Chapter Eleven

The doorbell rings at ten 'til six, and I feel as skittish as a sixteen-year-old on her first date. Why didn't I insist on meeting Connor at the dance studio? It's not like it's a big deal or anything. Okay, I might've changed clothes four times, as evidenced by the pile of shirts and skirts on my bed. But, so? I like to look nice. That has nothing to do with a brooding, mercurial vet who happens to have a healing touch with animals *and* children.

"I'll get it!" Riley yells, sailing down the stairs and, from the sounds of it, skidding to a halt in the entry as her sock feet hit the hardwood. "It's Dr. Blake!"

God, help me to just calm down. This evening is a favor to Beth, and I can get through this.

Gliding my hand down the banister, I take each step slowly, giving my courage a little time to build. It doesn't work. Maybe I should ask Riley to go.

"What's the latest on the puppy?" My niece gazes up at Connor like he's a living, breathing Superman. "Did she make it?"

Connor runs his hand over Riley's unruly hair. "Of course she did. She's sleeping now." He spares me a glance. "But she did lose that leg."

Riley sucks in her lips. "How will she walk?"

"You'll be surprised. She'll be up and walking in no time.

Animals adapt surprisingly well after losing a limb. The puppy will still be able to run and play and have a normal life. She'll just be different."

Riley's brow furrows. "But who will want her now?"

I step forward, throwing my purse over my arm. "We'll worry about that later. I'll make sure she has a good home. Right now, let's just focus on the dog getting better. What do you say to Dr. Blake?"

Riley's frown doesn't budge. "Thanks."

"You're the one who saved a dog today, Riley," Connor says. "God must've known you were just the girl for the job."

Riley does a figure eight with her toe, and I can almost hear the wheels spinning in her little mind as she chews over Connor's words.

"Are you ready?" he asks, his intense eyes on me.

No. I want to puke. "Riley, Grandpa's cooking pizza for you in the kitchen. Why don't you go see if he needs help. I'll be back later. Or you could go with us perhaps."

She laughs. "Borrrring."

There went that idea.

"Don't do anything gross like kissing." Riley makes gagging noises in the back of her throat.

I roll my eyes and laugh with embarrassment. "Like I'd kiss Connor." Omigosh! Did I just say that? Out loud?

"I'll give you an update on the puppy tomorrow," Connor says to my niece, holding open the door. "Maybe we can arrange a visit."

Connor shuts the door behind us, and my shoes click on the side-walk. "Sure you don't want me to drive separately? I don't mind."

He says nothing until I'm belted in his truck. Connor puts the vehicle in reverse, his focus on the rearview mirror. "Any particular reason you're afraid to be alone with me?"

"I typically limit myself to hanging out with people who like me. It makes for a better evening."

"I don't dislike you."

"I don't really care what you think of me. This is a favor to Beth, so let's just put our personal differences aside and get this done."

"Fine."

"Good."

He turns up the radio and the piano-driven lyrics of The Fray fill the truck.

"So your dad tells me you're a cinematographer for a travel show."

I lied when I said I didn't care what he thought of me. It drives me nuts when people don't like me. Will the sixteen-year-old in me ever grow up? "Um, yeah. I am. We're working on the last few shows of the season. You talk to my dad?"

Connor turns the wheel onto Central Avenue. "I talk to most people in town. It's a shame he had to go back to work. Especially with things being so precarious at the factory. If it closes, it will hurt the whole town."

"Reliant Tires has been here for years. It *is* Ivy."

Sometimes I think about my job and how stale it's become. And then I feel guilty. I *have* a job. I have a paycheck. I should just be grateful, right?

We spend the rest of the ride in alternating bouts of polite small talk and awkward silence.

"Here we are." Connor pulls up to the Mansfield School of Dance. Turning off the engine, he turns his head and looks at me with civil resignation. "You ready?"

"Can't wait."

He holds open the door to the studio and lets me walk in first.

Five couples are already on the floor, twirling and swirling and doing all sorts of *Dancing with the Stars* moves.

When I turn around, Connor is introducing himself to an older couple. His smile presses deep into his cheeks, and his face is animated in friendly conversation. I guess he reserves the neutral mask just for me. What an honor.

The music begins, and Connor returns to my side.

"Okay, class!" The older gentleman claps his hands. "I'm Fred Mansfield and that's my bride of forty-five years, Martha." The woman does a sweeping bow. "We're going to quickly review the basics for the sake of our newcomers, then pick up where we left off last week."

Oh no. I can't ballroom dance! I can kick butt on some Dance Dance Revolution, but something elegant and refined? Nope.

"You have that look on your face again."

I'm startled to see Connor standing so close. I take a step back. "What do you mean?"

"That look that says you'd rather be sky diving than get close to me."

"I have no idea what you mean." Though a good freefall from the sky does sound nice right about now.

He holds out his arms, a smug look on his face. "Afraid to dance with me, Maggie the Fearless?"

I swallow and consider telling him the truth. "No. Just don't step on my feet. I'm sensitive like that." I offer him my hand, and he wraps his warm fingers around it.

"This one goes on my shoulder." He places it there. His other hand slowly slides to my waist, where it rests lightly.

"Right. I knew that." I want to go home.

Mr. Mansfield calls out some steps, grabs his wife, and they begin to demonstrate a waltz.

"Watch me," Connor commands.

"I want to watch the teachers."

He pulls me into the moves, and it's all I can do to keep up.

"Loosen up." He shakes my arm. "Your limbs are too stiff."

"Are you through criticizing me or is there more fun to follow?"

He leans close to my ear. "You don't know how to dance, do you?" His smile could make a nun blush. "That's okay. I'll slow it down for you."

"Don't do me any favors." My head comes to his chin, and from this vantage point, I can smell the sweet spot of his cologne. Like I need another distraction.

"Let's practice that turn!" the instructor calls out.

Oh shoot. Let's not.

Connor spins us around, and I trip over my feet, his feet, and our neighbor's. He pulls me tighter to his chest and counts out loud. "One, two, three. One, two, three . . ."

"So where did the veterinarian learn to dance?"

"Summer camp." He moves us effortlessly across the floor.

"Math camp? No? Maybe chess camp?"

The corners of his mouth twitch. "Nothing wrong with having different interests. I didn't need the in-crowd."

"Is that what you told yourself every Friday night when you had the boys over for Super Mario and pizza?"

"I had girlfriends."

"Inmate pen pals don't count." With a firm grip, he spins me again, and I hang on tightly to keep up. "That wasn't nice."

"You should be paying attention."

"So what about now? A fiancée? Any ex-wives in your past?"

"One ex-fiancée."

"Aw." I curl my lips in a pout. "Did your Lord of the Rings–themed dates bore her?"

He stops abruptly, and with a yelp, I'm dropped into a dip, forced to look straight into his eyes. "She got a grant to study nuclear physics in Ukraine, and we drifted apart."

Oh. So she was smart and stuff. She probably looked like the hind end of a schnauzer though.

"We tried to make it work, but after *Sports Illustrated* called her for the swimsuit edition, we just never could sync our schedules."

It's like *Revenge of the Nerds*.

"And how about you?"

His husky voice flitters over my skin, and I feel myself relaxing in his arms, moving with the music. "Um . . . What was the question again?"

"Boyfriends?"

"Oh, right. It's complicated."

"It's a yes or no question. And don't forget, you started this line of conversation."

One, two, three. One, two, three. "I can't say I've found *the one* yet. Dating's very hard with my job." And my personality. And my neuroses. And the fact that I'm still waiting for Orlando Bloom to show up at my door.

"If you love a person, distance doesn't matter. You move mountains to be there."

I watch the blue flecks in his eyes and see seriousness settle in. "You're talking about Riley."

Beneath my hand, he shrugs a muscular shoulder. "Not necessarily. Just seems to me you live a pretty isolated life. On purpose."

I press my feet to the floor and stop. Connor keeps a firm grip on my hand. "I've already told you, whatever Allison said about me, you can take it with a grain of salt. No matter what the situation, she sees herself as the victim. So before you go believing every word she said, know that this is the same woman who told Riley she was stupid."

The fine lines on his forehead deepen. "That kid . . . I can't imagine what she's been through."

"I'm not the monster here, Connor. I'm doing the best I can with Riley, but every day I learn something new about her situation." Or about her in general. "My sister kept her from me."

"But it wasn't hard."

Okay, I'll take that. "No, it wasn't. But what was I supposed to do, track her across the country and demand to see my niece? My sister and I were never close friends. Allison rarely returned my phone calls. Pretty much made it clear in a hundred different ways that I was to leave her alone."

"She blamed you for a lot of things."

My heart does a shuffle step, but I ignore his curious expression.

The instructors herd us all back together and begin teaching the foxtrot. Connor leads like he walked straight out of a Fred Astaire movie, and I can only bumble along. Pretty soon, my embarrassment is long gone, and all I can do is laugh.

Harry Connick Jr. croons a song about love as Connor's hand moves to my mid back. His knees brush my thighs as he forces me to walk backward.

"Look at me instead of watching the teacher," he says.

"I'd rather not."

"Quit trying to lead."

"Quit bossing me around."

He chuckles low and pulls me into a wide turn. I lose my footing and stumble, but he sweeps me tighter into his arms and keeps right on going, without a single comment as to my clumsiness.

"Go up on your toes," he coaches softly. "Glide with the music. Now we're going to turn three times."

"Once was plenty."

"You can do it."

"I stink at this. It's okay to say it. In fact, it's okay to give up and take me home."

His chin angles down as he studies my face. "Are you giving up?"

I huff out some air. "No." Well. Yeah.

"I guess the wild girl from high school has just gotten older."

A hot poker in the eye could not sting more. "Or maybe this is too tame for me."

He lifts a dark brow. "Really?"

"Yeah. Perhaps I'm used to something more exciting than slowly waltzing across a dance floor. In fact, I doubt *you* could keep up with *me*."

He throws back his head and laughs, a deep rumble that has me smiling. "I can go toe-to-toe with Maggie Montgomery any day."

My eyes narrow. "I doubt that."

"Want to bet?"

Alarm bells clang in my head. "No."

"I'll name the challenge. And you lamely attempt to beat me. If I don't do it better than you or can't go through with it, then I'll babysit Riley one evening so you can have the night off."

The old familiar lure of the dare reels me in like a trail of hundred dollar bills. "And if you win?"

His smile is chocolate–covered sin. "Not *if*. When."

"And if some freak twist of fate has you winning?"

His eyes dip to my lips and back up. "You spend a day on the job with me."

I lift my chin. "Name it."

"Monday afternoon. Out at the lake. There's a bluff we can jump off and then—"

"No."

He stops dancing. He brings our joined hands in front of him. "You can't turn down a challenge. That means I've already won."

"Pick another one."

"I picked the bluff. It's not as easy as it sounds. It's incredibly high and—"

I pull my hand from his grip. "I need to go. Riley's probably driving my dad nuts by now."

His eyes lock on to mine. "What's going on?"

"Nothing. Just pick another dare. Or maybe I should pick." I force a playful tone into my voice. "You aren't exactly the best judge of living on the edge. Why don't you let me choose?"

He watches me for one . . . two . . . three long seconds. "Okay. Throw down your best gauntlet."

I inhale and fill my lungs with air and relief. "I'm a little unfamiliar with what's available. Give me twenty-four hours to research your options for total humiliation, and I'll get back with you."

"I better be impressed."

I pat his solid chest. "Doc, I was born to impress."

Like an invisible white flag has been waved between us, we put down our animosity and actually enjoy the rest of the dance lesson. Connor entertains me with stories, but hedges when I question him about his former fiancée.

At ten-thirty, Connor puts the truck in park in my driveway and climbs out.

"I don't need you to walk me to the door," I say, walking by his side. "This isn't a date."

"Like I'd date you."

"And I'm not kissing you under the porch light, so you can just forget it."

He rolls his baby blues. "You couldn't keep your hands off me all night."

"Only because you dance like you're in the middle of a Tourette's fit, and it was my only option to staying upright."

Connor stops at the porch, one leg poised on a step. "You lie through your teeth when you feel threatened." His eyes make a lazy trail over my face. "What I can't figure out is why I make you so nervous. I'm just a reformed math nerd."

"I lived through six bomb evacuations last year." My laugh is girly and light. "And you think *you* make me nervous?" I give his shoulder a friendly squeeze. "I don't think so."

He captures my hand and holds it. Looks at it before releasing it, his thumb sliding over my palm. Did he mean to do that? But when I glance up, his face is a blank canvas of innocence.

"Tell your dad and Riley I said good night."

His eyes are the most amazing shade of azure. Like the Atlantic ocean on a clear summer day. "Er, right . . . I'll tell them that." Clasping the cold metal of the screen door in my hands, I pull it open. "See you later."

He walks off the porch, only to turn around, still in motion. "It's okay if you want to back down from the challenge. I won't tell anyone your daring days are over."

My mouth lifts in a slow smile. "And miss the chance to see a grown man cry?"

Later that night I slip into bed, rubbing my feet against the cool of the sheets and thinking about the evening. "She blamed you for a lot of things," he'd said. There'd been something in his words, his stare—something heavy, intense, questioning.

Just how much did Connor Blake know? What had Allison told him? With her mental state, it would no doubt be a whole lot of fiction.

Yet I know . . . it couldn't be worse than the truth.

Chapter Twelve

"I still don't understand why I have to go." Riley checks her hair in the visor mirror for the tenth time.

"Because it's Sunday. That's what you do." I took a pair of scissors to her hair this morning. Evened it out a bit. "You go to church and learn about God." That explanation sounded much better in my head. "Besides, you owe me for not outing you to your grandpa that you ran away. Again."

"I already told him."

I release a weary sigh. "It's kind of hard to hold things over your head when you do responsible things like that."

I turn into the parking lot of the Ivy Lake Fellowship church. Beth assured me last night that it had a good kid's program, as well as some contemporary worship music and a pastor who wouldn't jump on his pulpit or put me to sleep.

"There's Beth and Mark." I wheel in next to her white minivan and watch her two oldest pile out. Beth clutches the baby while Mark quickly grabs the hand of a two-year-old boy. And I can't even handle a pet rock.

"Do you go to school with her oldest?" I point to a tall girl in braided pigtails. "Josie, right? I think she's the grade ahead of you."

Riley chews on her thumbnail. "I dunno."

"Guess you can meet her then." I shoot her a look. "And no misbehaving today. I'm serious—give yourself just one day off." Even the Lord took a day of rest.

"Hey, girl!" Beth thrusts the baby into my arms. "Take Delilah for a sec, would you?"

"Uh . . . okay." I rearrange the squirming child and move a tiny hand away from my silver hoop earring. I watch her face for the coming tears. Babies do not like me. It's a curse. It's like they see me and get the instant urge to cry, throw food, or puke.

"I gotta get a Kleenex for Dalton's snotty nose." Beth digs around in her gigantic diaper bag. "He's been dripping green stuff for days."

"Ew." Riley crinkles her nose.

My friend catches up to her husband and hands him a tissue. "And I won't even tell you what's been going on at the other end."

Mark turns around. "She means Dalton's other end. Not mine."

Beth introduces her oldest daughter to Riley. Besides a "hey," my niece has nothing to say.

"Josie's going to take you to children's church, Riley," I say with a smile I hope is comforting. "I hear they have snacks." I consider asking her to snag one for me.

"I'd rather go with you," Riley whispers as we reach the front entrance. "Please."

"We sing totally cool songs," Josie says. "And the youth pastor is so funny. Come on. My sister Zoey's coming too."

Riley gives me a look that will probably stick with me the entire church service, but I don't cave. "I'll see you after church." I pat her back and bounce the baby in my arms. "And don't take any samples out of the collection plate."

She rolls her eyes and trods forward, lagging behind Josie and her sister.

"My girl likes you." Beth tweaks Delilah's nose, and the baby giggles and covers her eyes. "You go get us some seats while Mark and I check the kids in." She takes Delilah back and points me in the direction of the sanctuary.

I no more take my seat and open the bulletin before I hear my name. "Maggie?"

My head shoots up at that voice. "Hey, Connor." He hovers over me, immaculate in his pressed khakis and blue and white striped polo. Almost mature looking. "You go to church here?"

"Yes. I'm surprised to see you."

"Surprised that I'm in this church or surprised that I'm not one of Satan's minions?"

Connor gives me a half smile. "Why don't you bring Riley by the clinic late this afternoon? She can check on her puppy."

"It's not her dog, so don't even put that thought in her head."

"I think it would be good for her to watch the puppy's progress. She could even help. The dog wasn't quite weaned yet, so we're bottle-feeding her."

I stare into his tanned face and wonder at the weird butterfly sensation in my stomach. "Okay. I'll call you."

"Connor?" Danielle Chapel walks down the aisle in spiked heels that could do mortal harm. She curls her hand around Connor's arm. "Did you get us a seat?"

He pulls his eyes from me to stare at the vision in a gray pin-striped skirt and tight black sweater. "Down front. Danielle, you remember—"

"Yes," she clips. "How are you, Maggie?"

"Good. You?"

She waves at someone across the room and ignores me. Is she his girlfriend? But he talked like he didn't have one. Surely Danielle's not jealous of the fact that I went to a dance class with Connor.

This woman reeks of junior-high insecurity. And a little too much Chanel.

"We better go sit down." Connor gives my shoulder a brief squeeze. "I'll talk to you later."

I watch the two of them walk away, looking like the perfect couple. Not that I care.

Now free of children, Beth and Mark slide past me into their seats. The worship minister takes the stage, and a ten-piece band blasts out the first notes of a worship song.

Everyone stands up and begins to clap. This isn't quite like my church at home. Not that I get to go there much. My job doesn't really allow for much consistency. And we're a little on the traditional side. Hymnals. Order. Routine.

A man from the choir steps out front and wails some notes like he's the Justin Timberlake of Jesus music. By the last song, some of the culture shock has worn off, and I try closing my eyes like Beth as a woman sings. The tune slows down, and I let each note of the piano and violin weave through my spirit like a gentle whisper from God.

"I will be with you when you pass through the waters," the woman sings, holding her Bible like she's just giving melody to scripture. "And when you pass through the rivers, they will not overwhelm you."

The song wraps up, and I feel a sense of loss. I want to stand up and say, "Please keep singing. Please—just don't stop." *God, the waters do overwhelm me. Sometimes I wonder where you are. And where were you when my mom died? When my sister went crazy. When I left home. Alone.*

A tall African-American man takes the stage. His navy suit sits on shoulders that could single-handedly power through the Cowboy's defensive line. "What a great song. Thank you for coming today to the Ivy Lake Fellowship." He tells a funny story about his young daughter fixing his hair in bows last night, and everyone laughs. I feel myself relax into the seat, letting go of some of the tension of an unfamiliar place.

"I want to continue our series on fear. Last week we talked about David and all the near-misses he had with Saul. Can you believe how many times that poor guy thought his number was up?" Someone shouts an amen. "Today I want to tell you about three men in a furnace." The pastor goes on to paint the story of Shadrach, Meshach, and Abednego, the men who defied the king and were thrown in the fiery furnace instead of just bowing down to a gold statue.

"Who could blame them if they had caved in, huh?" the pastor asks. "Who doesn't want to avoid the fire? The heat? Doing the right thing is often the last thing we want to do. And sometimes . . . the most painful. Can anyone here relate?"

Hands go up all over the building. But not mine.

The pastor walks the length of the stage. "What's holding you back today? Every single one of us has fears. You know who eats that up? The enemy. He loves nothing more than to see you hanging tight to all those things you're afraid of. You know why?"

"Preach it!" the man beside me yells.

"Because you will never, *ever* have the life God's planned for you as long as you're holding on to that fear. You can't swim to shore if you never let go of that life preserver." He walks down a few steps and stands level with the congregation. "Brothers and sisters, those guys walked into a burning furnace not knowing what was waiting for them. But they walked in knowing God was in control. Whether they lived or died, they had surrendered all they had and put their full trust in God. Do you have something to surrender today? Do you need God to meet you in the fire like he did those three men? Because sometimes you have to step out on faith into something that's gonna scare you so bad, your hair's gonna stand

and you're gonna be crying for your mama before God pulls you through the other side. Does anyone hear me today?"

One by one, people jump to their feet. Applause breaks out all across the room. Hands go up toward heaven.

And I just stand there. Heart pounding. Mind whirling.

The soloist's voice rings out above the piano, her words pure and melodic. "Do not fear. For I have redeemed you. I have called you by your name. You are mine . . ."

Beth nudges me with an elbow. "We're going to pray at the altar. Would you like us to pray with you?"

"No." I shake my head. "Thanks, but . . . I'm going to stay right where I am."

"So how was church?" I ask Riley on the way home.

"S'okay. They gave us Fudge Rounds, so it wasn't too bad."

Little Debbies always turn my head too.

"How come Grandpa didn't come with us?" she asks.

Um . . . because he'd have to leave his recliner? "He's not really into church. When your mom and I were growing up, he always had to work. So our mother would take us sometimes." Mostly not. It wasn't until last year when a friend invited me to a Christian concert that I got saved. In that crowd of a few thousand, I was anonymous. It was just me and God.

"If my mom died, would she go to heaven?" Riley plays with the button on her zebra-print jacket.

"Jesus loves your mom, Riley. He loves you too." I stink at this stuff. I really do. "And I know he's looking out for you every minute of every day. Even when it doesn't feel like it." Even when it feels like you're totally alone and abandoned. A misfit in your own world, in your own family. When you're plunging off water towers and praying someone will notice you. Really notice you—just once.

The aroma of pot roast hits me as soon as I open the front door of the house. "Yum. That smells good."

"Wipe your feet," Dad snaps, staring at the hardwood floor. "You're tracking in dirt, Maggie."

Riley runs up the stairs, dirt specs trailing behind, but Dad doesn't say a word. I hold on to the banister and take off my perfectly clean heels. "Smells good in here."

"I hope it's not overcooked. It's been in the oven an extra thirty minutes. I thought you two would be back by now."

"Beth and Mark's service goes a little later than noon." I wander into the kitchen and survey the lunch progress. "Anything I can do?"

"Nope." Dad comes in and stirs the gravy. "Last time you were here and helped with dinner, I had to scrape burrito sauce off the ceiling."

I laugh at the memory, but my dad just shakes his gray head.

He turns as Riley reappears, wearing the new jeans and black T-shirt I got her. "You sure looked pretty in your church clothes."

She opens the fridge. "Thanks."

I stand there and count the times my father has told me I looked pretty in my entire life. That would be zero. None. Nada. Not that I'm jealous of my niece. I'm not. But I can't wrap my mind around how different he is with her. Maybe that's the magic of a grandchild, because I've never seen him treat anyone like he does Riley. At least when I leave, I'll know she's not in the hands of the father I was raised with. He won't try to choke out every ounce of her spirit with his cruel words and frigid indifference. But even then . . . will it be enough?

A few hours later, I'm sitting with Riley on her bed, helping her with her English homework, when my phone rings.

"Hello?"

"Hey, it's Connor Blake."

My heart does a weird little flip. "How'd you get my number?"

"Beth. I'm up at the clinic and thought Riley might want to see the puppy."

"Riley would like to do anything to get out of her homework. I guess as soon as we finish, I can bring her out."

"Let me talk to her."

"What?"

"Put your niece on the phone."

"Okay . . ." I hand the phone over. "Dr. Blake wants to talk to you."

Her eyes grow wide with all the excitement she *didn't* show her school work. "Uh-huh. Yeah . . . okay." She nods her head and concentrates on whatever Connor tells her. "Got it. I can handle it. Yeah, see you."

Riley sets the phone on the bed. "He says if I do my homework, I can feed the puppy."

I smile at her enthusiasm. "Then let's get to work."

Two worksheets and one short story later, Riley and I stand in the Ivy Lake Animal Clinic.

"Come on back in," Connor yells.

Riley leads the way straight to where her puppy lies in a caged bed. Other dogs and cats in various states of healing make their presence known.

"The puppy's just waking up from a nap." Connor motions Riley over. "She's still pretty out of it. There's where her stitches are. But she's going to be fine." Before Riley has a chance to tear up, Connor shows her how to use the baby bottle to feed the dog. "Easy. There, you got it. Doing great."

Leaning on a counter, I watch the two of them, their heads

together over the small animal. Every few minutes Connor leans back and takes in Riley's intense face as my niece whispers sweet, inaudible things to the puppy.

At one point Connor looks at me. And I look at him. And we share a smile.

Thank you, I mouth.

You're welcome, comes his silent reply.

"Matilda, you ate really good," Riley says, as the puppy goes back to sleep.

"Matilda?" I move closer to my niece.

"She has to have a name." Riley runs her hand over the puppy's downy head. "She needs to know we care about her, and we can't keep calling her 'the puppy.'"

I lift a shoulder. "I think 'the puppy' has a nice ring to it."

"Matilda went home with me last night," Connor says. "I kept her close by so I could feed her."

No wonder my sister was friends with this guy. He's so *not* a dork anymore. Aggravating, yes. But geek? No. If only I had known back then.

I walk through the room and stop and say hello to a Persian cat. Then a border collie.

"Your niece seems to be doing better," Connor says from behind me.

I coo to a toy poodle and turn my head. "She has a long way to go."

He looks at Riley as she talks to Matilda. "Every creature flourishes with some care and attention. It makes all the difference."

I straighten. "I can't stay in Ivy . . . but I know I want to be a part of Riley's life. I just have to figure out what that means."

He looks into my eyes and steps closer. "You're doing a good job, Maggie."

I shake my head and dislodge some hair from my ponytail. "I botch it up daily."

Connor reaches out a hand and tucks a wavy strand behind my ear, his finger a soft caress on my skin. "Don't sell yourself short."

I move until we're facing one another. Inches apart. I stand there, rooted to the spot. Drawn to his eyes like they hold the promise of a king-size Snickers bar and other sinful temptations. My breath grows shallower.

His focus dips to my lips. "You are . . . not what I expected."

"What am I?"

"You are—"

Ring! Ring! My phone trills in my pocket, sending both of us feet apart.

"Gonna get this." The phone is a wet fish in my hands, and I drop it twice before Connor reaches down and hands it to me in his large hand. "Um, thanks."

What am I *thinking*? I have to get away from this guy. "Hello?"

"Maggie, it's Dad."

"Oh, hey."

"I need you to get home."

"Ugh. I forgot to clean up the dirt in the entryway. Look, Dad, we're feeding the puppy Riley found. I'll sweep as soon as we finish here."

"Forget the dirt!" His voice is rushed, anxious. "Just hurry on back."

"Dad, whatever it is. I'm sure it can wait. We have to—"

"It's your sister. It's Allison."

My heart plunges. "What about her?"

"She's standing in my living room."

Chapter Thirteen

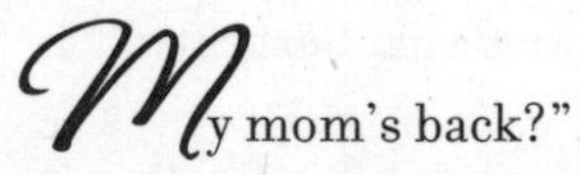

"My mom's back?"

The brakes squeak as I stop in Dad's driveway. "Yes." But who knows what condition Allison's in.

Slowly, as if neither one of us is ready to go inside, Riley and I walk onto the porch and inside the house. I place my hand on her back and give it a little bolstering rub as we stand in the living room.

"Dad?" I call.

"Up here," comes his voice from upstairs.

With Riley following behind me, I climb the steps and peek in each room. I find them in my current room, my sister curled in a ball on her old bed. Or what's left of her. She lays there, thin as any runway model, her light red hair now a mousy, frizzed mess.

Sitting in a nearby rocking chair, Dad's face is drawn and pale. "I put Allison in here. I can't get her temperature under control. She shakes like she's freezing, but she's dripping sweat."

I stand over the bed. "How'd she get here?"

"Friends," Allison says, her lips trembling. "I got friends."

"Dealers. Users." Riley steps forward and sits on the end of the bed. "When they get sick of her, they always send her back."

If my head could spin, it would fly off my neck. "She's left you alone before? Like for a long time?"

Riley shrugs. "A few days."

My eyes lock on Dad's. Guilt pierces me like a hot poker in the chest. "This has to stop."

"Go away," Allison mumbles.

"What did you take?" I ask her. "Allison, what did you—"

"I heard you." Her eyes are round as pie plates. "Just leave me alone." Her body jerks with each word. "It'll . . . pass."

I pull Riley's hand into mine. "Do you know what she's on?"

"Probably a bunch of things. OxyContin, Vicodin, Valium."

A ten-year-old knows these words. I close my eyes at the crime unfolding in front of me. In what kind of world is it okay that my niece can quote meds like a *Physician's Desk Reference*?

"I didn't know what to do." Dad leans forward and rests his hands on his knees. "I never do."

"You've seen her like this before?"

Her head falls in a silent nod. "I don't think it's ever been this bad, though. She was seeing bugs before you got here." Dad casts a furtive glance at Riley. "Maybe you should go downstairs and watch TV, hon."

Her laugh is small and bitter. "I do this all the time."

Oh, the hits keep coming. *God, why didn't I know about any of this? How could my dad just keep this from me?*

Allison opens her parched lips. "I saw Mama today."

Ignoring her, I look at Dad. "We should call an ambulance."

"She was swimming. At the lake." Allison laughs, and the high-pitched sound has my hair standing on end. "You remember the lake, don't you, Maggie? It always was your favorite place."

The goose bumps spread, and I rub my arms against the chill. *I am not doing this. I will not be swept under by her words. This is evil talking. A hallucinating woman is not going to drag me down.*

"That's it." I throw my purse on the floor and dig for my phone. "I'm calling 9-1-1."

Dad shoots to his feet. "No!" With a look at Riley he lowers his voice. "She can't have this on her record. The state department will—"

"I don't know how to deal with this!" I gesture to my trembling sister. "We can't detox her by ourselves. And Riley does not need to be around this."

"Please." My father's eyes plead with me, conveying words his mouth can't express. "Don't do this, Maggie."

I slide my finger over my phone and watch the screen light up. And hit redial.

"Maggie?" I feel a small sense of comfort at Connor Blake's voice. "What's going on?"

"I need some help. I mean, Allison needs help. Can you come over?"

Ten minutes later, he stands at Dad's front door. I step back to let him in. "Hey."

He studies my face. "You okay?"

"Yeah . . . but Riley." No wonder that kid is so tormented. Tears pool in my eyes, and I quickly swipe them away.

"Hey, don't do that." He pulls me into his arms, and I automatically stiffen. But he doesn't let go. "It's going to be okay."

"No. It's not."

His chin drops to my head, and I inhale his light tangy cologne before inching away, out of the warmth of his arms. "Thanks." I sniff indelicately. "I'm not much of a hugger. Don't know what got into me."

He rolls his blue eyes. "You are so weird."

"Says the president of the Ivy Nerd Alumni."

"Anyone ever tell you you're afraid of human contact?"

"Anyone ever tell you one day you're going to want to wear socks with sandals?"

Connor flashes me a quick and lethal smile before getting down to business. "Where is she?"

"Upstairs. She's really freaking out."

He nods. "Coming down off something."

"A few somethings." At least according to Riley, the ten-year-old narcotics expert.

We walk upstairs and Connor assesses the situation. "We need to get her to the ER."

Allison holds out a jerky hand. "Connor . . ."

He takes it in his and gifts Riley with a smile. "We're going to help you get better, Allison."

She throws her other arm over her face and laughs. "Uh-huh. Heard that before. Tried that before."

Connor turns to Dad. "Are you okay here with Riley?"

"Yes. But if Allison goes to the hospital—"

"We have to," I snap. "We're going."

"I want to come too," Riley says, looking younger than her ten years. "Take me with you, Maggie."

I drink in her misery. "We'll be back soon. Stay here and keep Grandpa company."

Connor leans down and scoops my sister into his arms, lifting her as if she's weightless, a light piece of fluff that could blow away in the breeze.

Allison murmurs to herself in the backseat of Connor's truck the entire way to Grapevine. I struggle for something to say to fill in the space.

"Want to play ninety-nine bottles of beer on the wall?" Connor asks.

"I would never put my counting skills up against the president of the math club."

"And they say Maggie Montgomery can't pass up a challenge."

Two excruciatingly long hours later, my sister is admitted, IV'd, and passed out cold in room 333 at St. Raphael's Hospital.

Connor opens the door and enters with two waters and some crackers just as I'm ending my call to Dad. What I wouldn't give for some SweeTarts right now. Isn't it funny how sometimes you can't stand the thought of food. But candy? Now that's totally different. I can always choke that down.

The vinyl of the chair squeaks as Connor eases his tall frame into the seat. I take the Dasani he offers, but pass on the crackers.

"You can go home," I say. "I'll be fine here. I'll have Dad pick me up later."

Connor leans his head back into the seat and lolls it my direction. "Nah."

"Seriously. Go home."

"Seriously. No."

I watch the second hand move for another hour, my thoughts keeping me quiet.

"Tell me about the night your mother died."

A semiautomatic fired in the room couldn't have shocked me more. "What?"

Connor lounges in the chair, his hands folded over his chest. Eyes closed. "I remember when we were in high school, there was an accident. At the lake."

If I were not wearing my Victoria's Secret push-up bra, I think my heart would flop out on the floor. "Yeah."

"Still difficult for you?"

A million answers shoot to the surface. "It was a long time ago."

The seconds tick by before he speaks again. "Allison said you were never the same."

My throat clenches. "I lost a parent that night. How could I be?"

He opens one blue eye. "Anything you want to tell me about that evening?"

That I'll never be free of it? That I relive it almost every night in my dreams? That I hear my mother's voice on the wind. On the subway. In a crowded street. "No. Can't think of a thing."

"Allison always had some crazy ideas about your mother's death."

"She drowned. End of story." End of life as I knew it.

"She says you're afraid of water to this day."

"Maybe I don't like getting my hair wet."

He trains both eyes on me for a long moment that has me dropping my gaze to the linoleum floor.

"You know, between you and your sister . . . I can't ever seem to get a straight story."

My head snaps up. "Then maybe you should mind your own business."

His mouth drags up in a lazy smile. "Maggie . . . that's getting harder to do by the minute."

Chapter Fourteen

"I think the school will understand if I don't go on the field trip today." Riley stands in her bedroom this morning, hands on hips, facing me down like a tiny Joan of Arc.

"No, you're going. We're both going. Grandpa is staying with your mom. It's all taken care of." Though I'm tempted to give in. A whole day at the lake? Mrs. Ellis said it's some natural science center. What's wrong with a nice, safe museum?

"It's not every day I can use the excuse 'my mom's detoxing.' It would be a shame to waste it."

Though Riley's tone overflows with sass, every time I got up to check on her last night, she was lying on her pallet on the floor, staring at the ceiling. Wide awake.

God, help me be the support Riley needs. Saying I have no idea what I'm doing right now is like saying Rush Limbaugh's a little *conservative. I have no* clue *what to do here.*

"What if my mom needs me?" Riley asks.

"She has more than enough help."

My niece shoves a foot into her shoe. "What if Matilda the puppy needs me? What if Connor forgets to feed her?"

"The man has a mind like a Mac computer. I don't think he's ever forgotten anything in his life." I push her toward the door. "Let's go."

We walk into Mrs. Ellis's classroom just as Riley's principal walks out.

"Hello, Danielle." *Looking prunish as always*. "How are you?"

"Fine." She glances down at Riley. "Miss Montgomery, we better behave today or else we will not be going on any more field trips. Do we understand?"

Riley scrunches up her face as she peers up at her principal. "We don't think that's correct grammar." She flops a dismissive hand. "But what do we know? We're failing language arts."

I pull my niece to me and dig my fingers into her scrawny shoulder. "So . . . Danielle, are you going with us today?"

She sniffs her perfectly straight nose. "No. I have too many responsibilities here. I can't just take off like some people."

"My aunt works for a TV show. She gets to do lots of cool things."

Somehow my hand finds its way to Riley's mouth. "Why don't you go check us in, *sweetie*." I pat her on the top of her red head. "Now." I give a nervous little laugh as Riley walks away. "Kids. Aren't they precious?"

Danielle stares back at me with nothing resembling maternal kindness. "I should warn you that Connor is a sucker for wounded animals."

"Uh-huh. Well, cool thing he's a vet then, eh?"

She crosses her arms over her tailored black jacket. "I mean he'll help anyone. Anything. I just don't want you to get the wrong idea about any time he spends with you."

"Oh." Awkward! Psycho!

Danielle steps forward on spiked heels. "You used to have all the boys dangling from your finger back in school, didn't you? Well, you know what, this isn't our senior year."

"Thank goodness for that."

Her eyes narrow to reptilian slits. "Some people tend to take advantage of Connor's generosity. I'm sure you won't be one of them."

"Connor isn't exactly doormat material. I bet he can take care of himself." *Calm down, Maggie. Ease the tone.*

"His fiancée all but stood him up at the altar six months ago. Left him two days before the wedding. I guess his friends and I are a little protective of him."

Well, Dr. Blake didn't mention that little facet of the story. "I'm sure he appreciates having a good friend, though, to look out for him. Everyone needs someone to watch his back."

Her left eye does this twitchy thing that has *me* squinting. "Just take care of your niece and your sister and leave the rest to those of us who actually care about Ivy."

Ivy . . . or a certain veterinarian?

"It was nice to see you again, Danielle." Nice like a mosquito bite on the butt is nice.

One bumpy, loud bus ride later, I'm *still* fuming over that woman. Who does she think she is? First of all, Connor has not said a word about dating her. And two, like I'm moving in on him anyway. I'm sure. I have four days left here.

I peek to the back of the bus where Riley sits with a small white-headed girl. Every time Riley turns to speak, the girl just bows her head and nods.

Decisions have to be made. I know I need to make arrangements for Riley's care. Her mom is not going to be in any shape to help. Dad said this morning he was calling a treatment facility in Dallas. Supposed to be one of the best in Texas. So Allison will be out of commission for at least sixty days. Maybe I should think about transferring to another cable network and forget National Geographic. Forget *Passport to the World*. Something that doesn't involve so much travel.

Like HGTV. Surely a network about home can't involve too many trips. And then I could fly in on long weekends to be with Riley. Maybe once a month. Every six weeks? And she could come visit during school breaks. *God, I want a chance to be the fun aunt. I don't want to be the loser aunt anymore. I really think Riley's warming up to me.*

I look back again, catch her eye, and wave big. She sticks out her tongue and turns toward the window. Maybe she'll perk up when she sees I brought my video camera to film our fun day.

Knowing her, she'll find a way to feed it to the fish.

The bus finally comes to a stop, and I put on my brave face and climb out. I can handle this, right? Twenty-five kids. Some animals. Piece of cake.

By noon I'm about ready to throw myself off the observation tower. I've had three girls glued to me for the entire three-mile hike, one mom who will not shut up about a Mary Kay makeover, and I'm pretty sure there is something crawling down my shirt.

The tour guide stops and identifies yet another plant species. The kids scribble the name down on their field trip journals, and I zoom my camera on my niece, who continues her routine of ignoring me. She's doing a really great job.

Mrs. Ellis catches up to me in her sensible Easy Spirits. "It's so nice of you to join us today. Riley seems to be coming out of her shell a bit."

Coming out of her shell or retiring the boxing gloves? "Actually I wanted to speak with you about getting a reading tutor for Riley. I'm going to be leaving this week, and I need to get some things lined up for her first." I explain my discovery about Riley's low reading skills.

Mrs. Ellis is not the least bit surprised. "I had spoken with her mother about it"—she drops her voice—"before she took off. But she told me quite plainly to mind my own business."

"Her mother is going to be out of the picture for a few months." I fill Mrs. Ellis in on the basics of Allison. "I'm only telling you this in case you observe Riley acting out." I pause. "That is, more than usual. Well, I mean if it escalates to a level you've yet to see." Like she sets a classmate on fire or takes hostages on the playground. "She doesn't say so, but I know she's scared. Things are so up in the air with her mom."

Mrs. Ellis holds back a low tree branch. "I'm sure it's a frightening time for all of you."

I grow uncomfortable as she spares me a quick, maternal gaze packed with pity and other variations on sympathy.

"I think I'll go find my niece."

"We're getting ready to cross the Little Sugar Creek bridge," our guide announces. "We ask that you grab your buddy's hand as you walk across. It's only wide enough for two, though, and it might still be a little slippery from this morning's rain, so please be careful."

I glance at Riley, but she quickly latches on to her friend Sarah's hand. The two get in line and cross the wooden planked walkway that covers the flowing creek.

"This also serves as a bike trail, as well as a nature hike," the guide says as he steps to the other side. "The water can get as low as four feet during the dry season. The water's a bit higher now—about five feet. We've had a lot of rain lately, so it's pretty close to the bridge. Please keep your feet out of the water, though. No dipping, no dangling. You don't want a fish to reach up and grab you."

The kids laugh. I do not.

I grab the hand of Lucy, one of the little girls who only moments ago was attached to me like a sock with static cling. "Ready to go?" I gently lead her toward the bridge. *Don't look down. Don't look down. You're perfectly safe.*

"Hey, I want to hold Maggie's hand!"

"Me too!"

Once again I'm surrounded by all three girls. "Now, Jessie, you grab Leyla's hand. I've got Lucy's. There's only room for two of us to cross at a time."

The girls press in closer until I'm standing on the edge.

"I want to go with Maggie."

"I do!"

"Ladies, please. Move back, Jessie. There isn't room. Leyla, step away. Get back before I—"

Fall.

With one push from Jessie's hip, I lose my delicate balance.

And tumble over the side of the bridge.

I sink beneath the surface, as voices mingle in my head. Shouts come from above. Have to get out. Can't breathe. Can't move.

I close my eyes against the sting, and see my father. *"Can't you do anything? I'm trying to teach you how to swim, and you won't even pay attention. Now paddle, for crying out loud! Look at your sister. She's already diving."*

"I'm trying, Dad."

"Try harder. You'd have to be stupid not to get this. Quit holding your nose like a baby."

My arms and legs finally move, and I paddle with all I've got. But it's no use. My limbs grow heavy. My mind swirls in a black fog. And I just give in and go lax.

So this is how it's going to be.

Water took my mother's life.

And now it's finally come for mine.

Chapter Fifteen

Death by field trip. What did I ever do to deserve this?

An arm belts around my waist. My head bobs as I'm pulled up, up. Toward the light.

We break through the surface, and I suck in air with my whole body. My chest shudders in spastic coughs.

"Hang on, ma'am. Almost got you out."

Did that seriously just happen? I struggle to open my eyes. I want to go home. I want to crawl in my bed and never see anyone again. I want this water out of my lungs. I cough until there's nothing left, as our guide in his Natural Science Center shirt lowers me onto the ground.

"Are you okay?" He leans down like he's going to give me mouth-to-mouth.

"Don't even try it." I push his face away and give into another coughing fit. "That bridge is not safe." I spit out some water. "Not safe for children especially. You must have hundreds of people fall every year."

"Actually in twenty years, you're the first." He shakes his head. "I kept waiting for you to stand up."

"Stand? I guess I was too busy fighting for my life."

"Ma'am, did you hear me say that river's only about five feet right now?"

I push the hair from my eyes. "No, I guess I didn't." My head was too full from all the plant species. And I don't even want to think about the condition of my video camera.

I rise to a sitting position and find twenty-five children staring at me with wonder. One claps hesitantly. As I'm helped to my feet, the applause grows until the forest resounds with the noise. I cover my face with my hands and groan. *Thank you for rescuing me, God. You saved me from the water . . . only to kill me with humiliation.*

It's everything I can do not to cry. My hands shake as I wring out my hair.

"Are you sure you're okay?" the guide asks. "We have a nurse on staff."

"No," I say a little too sharply. "I'm sorry. I'm . . . I'm not really a swimmer." Haven't been in the water in years. Never wanted to return.

By the time I drive us home, my hair is dried into a tangle of yuck, and my hands won't quit shaking.

I turn off the car and unsnap my belt. "I'm sorry, Riley." I scan my overloaded brain for something to say. "I know today was a little embarrassing."

She turns in her seat. "A little embarrassing?"

I bite my bottom lip. "Okay . . . a lot."

"Are you kidding me?" she squeals. "It was totally cool! It was like something from *America's Funniest Home Videos.* Those girls just butted you right off that bridge." She gives my hand an awkward pat. "You seriously rocked today, Aunt Maggie."

She springs out of her seat and into the house. I sit in the car for another five minutes.

Knowing Dad won't be home from work for a few hours, I go straight to the kitchen to see what I can make for dinner. I'll take Riley to see her mom afterward. And after my shower.

I peel open the refrigerator door. And just stand there. Seeing nothing.

Nothing but water. Blackness. I close my eyes, and I'm right back there. I hate that feeling of powerlessness. Out of control. Out of my hands. My body not obeying my brain. What is wrong with me? *God, why can't I get over this? I've conquered so many things, met so many challenges head-on. Yet today just proved . . . some things you can never leave behind.*

Deciding we can just do pizza later, I make my way upstairs and climb into the shower. I stand under the heated spray and let it wash away the grime, the bug spray, and eventually my tears.

People walked through fire in the Bible. And I can't even handle five feet of water.

Three shampoos and two body scrubs later, I sit on the back porch, my hair damp and free flowing. I sink into the deck chair and curl my legs around me, letting the lowering sun warm my chilled skin. I close my eyes and rest my head against the back of the chair and try to think calm thoughts. Kitties. Roses. Flip-flops. Strawberry ice cream. Tax refunds.

"Anyone home?"

I jump at the voice, my hand going to my throat. "Oh." Connor Blake steps from the grass onto the porch. "You scared me."

His eyes scan me over, miss nothing. "You okay?"

I run my fingers through my damp strands, foolishly wishing I had taken the time to dry it. Style it. Put on makeup. A good push-up bra. "Sure. How are you?"

In one step he's on the porch, grabbing the seat beside me. He rests his elbows on his khaki pants. "How did the field trip go?"

Horrid. Disastrous. A nightmare of epic proportions. "I think Riley had a really good time. It was nice to see her smile."

"That's it?"

"The bologna sandwiches at lunch were a little rubbery, but other than that, yeah. Good field trip for the kids."

He shifts forward until he's perched on the edge of his seat. Inches away. "You look like crap."

My eyes narrow. "And *that*, Connor Blake, is why you didn't have a prom date."

His smile tells me my arrow did not hit a weak spot. "Riley called me to check on the dog. She mentioned you were the highlight of the trip."

I press my eyes together. "I'm really tired. Keeping up with a gaggle of screaming, wiggly, sticky fourth graders has worn me out."

"What happened today?"

"Nothing." What is it about this guy that makes me want to blurt it all out? To just blab my life history and catch him up on the whirling disaster occurring in my heart.

He reaches out a strong hand, his healer's hand, and rests it on my knee. "You're shaking."

I know. And I can't stop. "Just chilly tonight, I guess."

"Maggie, it's practically record-breaking heat for April."

I take my eyes off his hand and look into his face. "Did you want something or is this part of some veterinarian outreach program? I'm sure there are other people in town who need your company."

His smile doesn't let up. "I'm sorry you had a bad day."

My eyes sting at his humongous understatement, but if I cry in front of Connor, it will be the cherry on top of a humbling, soul-crushing day. "Just back off, Doctor. I'm fine."

"You know what I think?"

"You hope pocket protectors will make a comeback?"

His face grows serious. "I think you're hiding—"

"Maggie?"

My head snaps up at my dad's voice as he pushes open the back screen.

"Hey, Dad." For once, I'm glad to see him. Perfect timing.

Connor stands up and shakes Dad's hand. "Mr. Montgomery."

Dad looks between us, but his face reveals nothing. "I'm taking Riley to get something to eat, then on to the hospital. Saw Allison at lunch today, and she looked a lot better. She was coherent, but tired."

"Okay." I tunnel my fingers through my hair and sigh with exhaustion. "I'll get my purse. Connor, thanks for stopping by." My tone is about as sincere as a politician's apology.

"Hope you get to . . . feeling better."

I'm saved from a response as my phone rings in my pocket. I check the screen. Work. "I'd better take this. Hello?"

"Maggie, we need to talk." Carley. Great. Just what I need.

"Just a sec, Carley." I put my hand over the phone and whisper to Dad. "You and Riley go ahead. I'll drive to St. Raphael's myself. This could be awhile." I wiggle my fingers good-bye to both men.

Letting myself back into the house, I talk as I climb the stairs to my room. "Did you get the footage I sent you?" Yesterday I finally got the nerve to send Carley a piece of my documentary file.

"Yeah, Maggie, but what is it? I thought you were sending me something for a new show idea. What I saw looked more like a Save the Children infomercial."

"I just . . . I know it's not right for *Passport to the World*, but maybe one of our sister networks?"

Carley laughs. "Why?"

"Why?" What kind of question is that? I finally break down and share it with her and *this* is what I get? "Because I think there's a story there, Carley. I mean, we go to all these places and report on the travel culture, but what about the dark side? What about some of the things we've seen and ignore or edit out? Child trafficking, poverty, child prostitution, kids who—"

"That's not what we're about. Look, I thought it was gripping stuff, but it didn't entertain me."

"It's not supposed to." I sit down on my bed and fall backward onto the pillows. "I sent it to you for your professional opinion. I just think . . . I don't know."

"I don't either. I mean, I *seriously* don't know about that footage. But I know our show can't use it, and I can't think of anyone who could. Who wants to see children in these circumstances? Maggie, consider our demographic. Consider what marketing would say. These are hard times for everyone, and people want an escape. That's what our network provides. They don't want to be depressed even further with images they can't do anything about."

"But they're not just images. They're people. They're children."

"What I want to talk about is next week's show. I'm flying from Taiwan to Montreal Friday. I'll need you to be ready to go as soon as my plane lands at two. What time are you arriving?"

"I'm not." The words slip from my tongue like they belong to someone else.

"What do you mean, you're not?"

I rub a knot at the base of my neck and accept my new reality. *This is what you want me to do, isn't it, God?*

"Don't do this to me again," Carley says. "Of course you're going to be there."

God, give me the words. Help me. I feel like I'm jumping into water again. "I'm . . . staying here."

"That's impossible. Do you mean you're quitting? After all we've—"

"No!" At least not until after my National Geographic interview.

"No, of course not. I, um, just have a lot going on here. My sister's in pretty bad shape and is going to be out of commission for a while. My dad can't take care of my niece by himself."

"Get a sitter. It's not hard."

No, sticking around and taking care of people is hard. "I can't. Carley, I need a leave of absence. There are two weeks left in the season before our break. I'll come back when we return in June."

I can hear her pen tapping on something in the background. "You have no idea what you're asking. We're down to the wire here. We're in Montreal for three days, then leave to film in Cairo. It's our—"

"Biggest show ever. Yes, I know." I can feel the chill of the water lapping over my head, surrounding my body. Taking me down into darkness. "I'll call corporate tomorrow, but I wanted to tell you first. I have to take care of my family. My niece needs me."

"You know your job is on the line here. This couldn't come at a worse time. And not only is it the season finale, but everyone's contracts are up for renewal. This will *not* look good."

"It's a chance I'm going to have to take."

"And besides, I need you to help me with my wedding dress. I can't find one anywhere. Not that I've had time to look."

This sounds more like Carley, my *friend*. "Maybe we can spend a weekend in New York when you get back from Egypt," I say.

She sighs. "I have to go. We're already behind schedule, and we have work to do before it rains. Take care of yourself, okay?"

"I'm sorry."

"Maggie, think long and hard about this. You decide if it's worth risking your career." She ends the call, and I let the phone slip from my hands.

God, is this the right thing? Why do I feel so out of place here at home, then? I have no idea what I'm doing with Riley. She needs stability, but my staying a few weeks isn't really going to provide that. And I can't afford to lose my job. I kind of need to eat. And pay for my apartment. And my candy habit.

My eyelids grow heavy, and I surrender to exhaustion. So tired. Just going to close my eyes for a minute. Or two.

An hour later, I bolt awake to the sound of screaming.

Then realize it's me.

Dreaming. Again.

Wide-eyed, I peer around the room, just to make sure of where I am, that I'm safe at home. On dry ground.

In the bathroom, I splash cold water on my face and twist my hair into a messy knot. Then I grab my car keys and drive to St. Raphael's to see my sister, the windows down the entire ride. Letting the wind carry away the dregs of the nightmare that was my day. And my evening.

A nurse in Tweety Bird scrubs points me to the right room on the second floor. I never was good at science, but what I wouldn't give to have elastic waistband pants as my work uniform. Scrubs must be the best.

I gingerly knock on the door and push on through. My dad and Riley are nowhere inside. Just my sister, who lies propped up with two pillows beneath her head, an IV in her arm, and skin pale as funeral parlor powder.

"You just going to stand there?" she asks, her eyes still closed.

I step into the room, walk past a flat-screen TV on the wall, and stop at the foot of Allison's bed. "Hey there."

She opens one bleary eye. "I knew you'd be by."

"Did you see Dad and Riley?"

"Yeah. They went for some snacks. Riley's pretty impressed with the cafeteria here for some reason."

I laugh. Sounds like her aunt. I've eaten food from all over the world, in some of the best five-star restaurants. But I have a deep, twisted love for cafeteria food.

"How are you feeling?" I move to sit in a faded blue chair beside her.

"Great. I was about to go run a 10k until you got here."

I offer her a wobbly smile. We're sisters . . . and yet I don't really know her. Don't know what to say.

"How are you really feeling?"

She rubs her eyes. "Old. Tired. Basically like death. But they've got me on some stuff to make detox less painful."

"Where've you been, Allison?"

She slowly raises her eyes. "I wouldn't just leave Riley, okay? I knew she was in good hands."

"With Dad?" I laugh and shake my head.

"He's pretty good with her."

I bite my tongue on the million and one things fighting to get out of my mouth. "I'm pretty sure when the state department steps in, things aren't going well. Riley needs her mother."

Her hair falls in straggly strands across her shoulders. The hospital gown hangs loose on her bony shoulders, and I can hardly call up the image of the girl she used to be.

"I just needed to get some stuff straightened out. Riley's fine. She's a tough kid. I knew she would be better off with Dad for a while."

"And now?"

"What about it?"

"Did you get everything worked out you needed to?"

"I'll get my kid when I'm good and ready." Allison turns her head toward the window and looks out at a darkened sky. "Like you care."

"You know I do." In that I'm-a-sister-to-a-maniac sort of way. "And I care about Riley."

"You don't give a crap about either one of us. It's all about you, you, you."

I try to keep my voice calm. "I'm still here, aren't I?"

"Let's just say I don't feel too guilty about you taking care of my kid for a few days. Family takes care of each other, don't they, Maggie?"

My sister pins me with such an open look of contempt, I have to avert my eyes.

Allison's fingers pick at the cotton blanket pulled over her legs. "You have no idea what my life is like, so don't sit there and judge me, big sister."

"Allison, I'm not—"

Tears spill down her cheeks, and she dashes them away with angry hands. "Everything's always come so easy to you. School, friends, work. Well, I'm not you. The only thing I've had going for me was Dad in my corner." Her lips curls. "And that drives you nuts, doesn't it?"

"No. I'm not jealous of your relationship with Dad."

"Isn't it funny? Look at all you accomplished, and you've still never measured up in his eyes."

My sister is crazy. Just flat-out crazy. But the barb still sticks. "Maybe I should go." I rise to my feet. "Dad said you were being transferred tomorrow to a facility in Dallas. I'll pray it—"

"Yeah, you pray for me, Maggie." Allison fluffs the pillow behind her head and lays back again. "You do that."

Despite everything telling me not to, I step closer to the bed and rest my hand on the rail. "I do want you to get better. Riley needs you. You have a beautiful daughter who wants you to get well. She's . . . she's got a lot going on, and—"

"Oh yeah." Allison chuckles to herself. "Riley told me about her field trip today. Nice of you to chaperone. I sure couldn't. I had to sign over guardianship, and Dad won't let me around her right now. Do you know how that makes me feel? You two can't keep her from me forever."

The walls in the room seem to shift closer, and I pull on the tight neck of my T-shirt. "I should go. I'm sure you're tired and—"

"All this time and you've never gotten over your little water phobia." She clucks her tongue. "Why is that?"

"I'll see you tomorrow before you check out."

"You were taught to swim, just like I was."

"Good-bye, Allison." I back up, unable to turn from my sister, transfixed by her words, her scornful face.

"Has coming back to Ivy made you remember anything? It's terrible how you conveniently passed out the night Mama died. Selective amnesia, the doctor said. Is that how it was, Maggie? Do you remember now?"

I hold my bag to my chest. "No."

"Do you remember what happened the night I lost my mother?"

Tears cloud my vision. My pulse pounds in my ears. "I have to go."

"I think you do, sister," Allison yells. "You watched her drown and did nothing. You took away my mother, then left me alone!"

I have to get out of here. Now.

I spin on my heel, desperate to flee.

And find Connor Blake standing in the doorway.

Chapter Sixteen

There's something about a man standing in my way that makes me turn into a Roller Derby queen; I use my elbows.

"Excuse me." I shove past Connor, only to be hauled right back to his chest.

"What's going on?" He looks down at me, and I drop my gaze. My teary, puffy-eyed gaze.

"Nothing." I sniff. "I have to go."

He loosens the grip on my shoulders, but holds me in place just the same. "Hang on." Connor holds out a finger to my sister. "I'll be right back, Allison."

"I'm not going anywhere," I hear her say as Connor pulls me out into the fluorescent-lit hall and into a small waiting area.

"What are you doing?" I wrench my arm away.

"Just give me fifteen minutes to check in on your sister, okay? Then I'll take you home."

I swipe my hand across my dripping nose. "I have a car. I'm not riding with you."

"Maggie, you're dead on your feet." Connor plants a hand on the wall beside my head, his blue eyes roaming over my face. "Are you even sleeping?"

"Yes," I snap.

He lifts a dark brow.

"Maybe . . . well, sorta." I push on his shoulder. "It doesn't matter. I don't need to be chauffeured home like some helpless female."

"I'll have someone pick up your car tomorrow."

"No." The elevator slides open, and I dart inside, punching the close button. "Good-bye, Connor. Go back to Allison."

"We're not through talking about this." The doors draw together, shutting out Connor, who stands tensed like a lion ready to pounce. To protect my sister? Me?

I head straight for bed when I get home, even though it's eight-thirty. And I didn't floss.

God, everything is such a mess. My job, my sister . . . my past. And I'm losing my grip on all of it.

My eyes flutter closed, and sleep finally finds me.

I wake up early the next morning, do my quiet time, then go for a run in the neighborhood. I return just as Dad is putting on his cap and grabbing his keys.

"Saw you coming down the road," he says as I walk into the kitchen. "Allison's getting discharged early. Gonna go pick her up, then take her to the rehab facility in Dallas. Can you get Riley to school?"

I pull out my headphones and wipe some sweat from my forehead. "Sure."

Dad walks to the dining room, then pauses. "Heard about the field trip yesterday."

I hold a glass under the faucet. "Yeah, I was a big hit. I got a standing ovation."

His hard eyes hold mine before breaking contact. The man

never can look me in the eye. "A woman your age should know how to swim. None of those lessons took?"

You mean the ones where you took me to the creek and all I learned was how to be bitter? Craziest thing, but no. "Next time I go to the science center, I'll bring floaties."

Dad walks out of the room, his work boots falling heavy on the floor until the moment I hear the click of the front door.

"How ya doing?" I ask Riley, as she buckles up beside me in the car.

"Fine."

A girl who was doing fine would not still be sleeping on the floor. With a ratty teddy bear and her shoes within arm's reach, like she'd be all prepared in case she needed to leave in a hurry in the middle of the night and just have time to grab the important things.

"You look cute today." I shoot her a reassuring smile and watch as she tries to shrug off the compliment. But the pink tinge on her cheeks gives her away. I don't think my niece has heard many compliments in her short ten years. A girl can't get too many of those.

"Are you okay with your mom being gone a few months?"

She shrugs the shoulder beneath her new Old Navy T-shirt.

"She's gonna get better, Riley. They're going to help her, and when she comes back home to you she—"

"She's not going to get better!" Riley slaps her hand against the armrest. "Do you know how many times she's done rehab? Guess how many times it stuck?" My niece forms a zero with her fingers.

I turn onto Main Street and join in the equivalent of rush-hour traffic for Ivy. "She's been before?"

"Tons of times."

"Did Grandpa know?"

"Of course. He'd either come stay with me, or if it was in the summer, I'd stay with him."

It's like my family has lived on this separate planet from me. A place I was not even slightly a part of. And now, that explains Dad's going back to work. Rehab isn't cheap. Especially when you're paying for a return customer.

We pull into the drop-off line, and I put the car in park. "Riley, I—"

She swings open the door. "I know. She's gonna get better. She'll come back and be supermom. I've heard it before." Riley picks up her backpack and slings it over her shoulder. "Bye."

She slams the door, and I watch her walk up the sidewalk. One child in a sea of many. Yet so alone. And way too young to be all out of hope.

I wheel out of the parking lot and see a familiar minivan and wave.

Beth rolls down her window, and I check behind me to make sure no one is coming as I stop.

"Hey, girl," she says, pulling her hair into a ponytail.

A Peppy's Pizza sign sits atop her van. "Um . . . Beth? What is that?"

My friend rolls her eyes. "My new part-time job. The convenience store didn't work out. That night manager is a real hag. My kids came by one night and rearranged the peanut-butter cracker section, and Mr. Denton went ballistic. Plus, guys kept asking me to air up their tires."

"Mark okay with you doing pizza delivery?"

She twists in her seat. "Dalton, if you don't give your sister back that toy, I'm gonna give you the biggest time-out when we get home." The mom face drops and the friend smile returns. "For now, Mark has no choice, but he doesn't like it. He's working part-time at his uncle's seed mill. But my job's got bennies. Free pizza from the no-pays, you know? Been eating like a queen." She laughs, and I find myself smiling right back at her. Oh, how different we are from the high-school days of cutting class and kissing boys in the back row of the movie theater.

"So you're still here, huh?"

"Yeah, gonna stay a bit longer." I give her the update on Allison.

"The reunion committee is meeting at the Ivy League Diner. Go with us."

An image of Connor trips through my mind. "Um . . . I better not. I have to do some film editing today."

A car behind Beth toots its horn. "You can buy me lunch. I'm too poor to pay for the lemon in my water."

"Are you using guilt to get me there?"

"Yes." She hoots with laughter. "See you at noon." And with a casual wave to the vehicle behind her, Beth drives away.

When I return home, the house is still, save for the call of the birds outside and the hum of the ceiling fan in my room. Putting it off as long as I possibly can, I walk upstairs and call Erin Valentine, executive producer of *Passport to the World*. I have the same conversation with my boss as I had with Carley. Yes, I know contracts are up. Yes, I understand this is crunch time for the season ending. When I remind Mrs. Valentine of my enormous reserve of sick days, she acquiesces.

Feeling my load lightened, I open my laptop and fire it up, my fingers itching to piece together more footage. There were those two sisters in Cambodia whose faces I'll never forget, who, like Riley, were ten going on forty. And the boy in Angola who lost his leg in a landmine while collecting firewood for his family. Or the teen girl from Darfur, who, according to our guide, faced terror after terror on the necessary trips to get water. Where are their voices? Chills race up and down my skin each and every time I look at their faces, their stories, stored on my hard drive. Trapped in my computer until someone frees them.

And I think sometimes that person should be me. I mean, I do feel this pressing urge to push this project. But I like my job. I do. I don't love it right now, but I like having a paycheck. And traveling. And knowing that I got out of Ivy.

But these faces haunt me. Their lives float to the surface of my mind throughout the day. I'll be doing dishes or boarding a plane and see one of these forgotten children.

God, what do you want from me? What am I supposed to do? Even Carley thinks it's a ridiculous idea. Maybe I should just pass this off to someone who knows what she's doing. Because it's sure not me.

Two hours later, the front door opens and shuts with a force to shake the walls.

"Dad?" I call. Pushing my MacBook off my legs, I slip off the bed and scurry down the stairs. "Dad?"

I find him in the kitchen, pouring a glass of tea the color of rusted nails. Strong, easy on the ice. Just like my mom would fix.

"Dad?"

His head bobs like it's about ready to blast off his neck, and his fists clench at his sides. "What"—he rasps—"did you say to your sister last night that set her off?"

I blanch at his raw anger and take a step back. "I . . . we . . . we just talked. She got upset, got irrational." Got crazy.

"*What* did you say?"

"She—" Blamed me for Mom's death, her life, the state of the economy. Every problem in the universe. "She started saying stupid stuff about how Riley was fine and not really a concern. I could only listen to so much of that." She told me I watched my mother drown.

My dad's face pinches in anger. His neck is flushed scarlet. The dad I grew up with and learned to fear stands before me. "I asked you—I specifically asked you—not to upset her. And you couldn't do that one little thing? Is it really that hard to just keep your mouth shut? You were with her for, what, thirty minutes?"

"She doesn't even care about her daughter. And believe me, I held back. I didn't so much as raise my voice at her." *Your golden child. The one you could tolerate. The one who got away with everything, while I lived grounded every second I breathed in this house.*

Dad plants his hands on the counter and leans back, glaring fire that could melt the Ivy fountain in winter. "Allison is gone."

"What? Where?"

"Do you think if I knew where I would be standing here? Where do you think I've been the last few hours? I've looked all over town. I've called everyone I know. Your sister has disappeared, and all the nurses know was that they'd heard an argument last night."

Fear and guilt bounce on my gag reflexes. "I'm sorry. I didn't intentionally upset her, but Allison said some horrible things."

"Of course she did!" he yells. "She's mentally and chemically imbalanced. She's disabled, for crying out loud. She's bipolar and schizophrenic! Are you proud of yourself, Maggie?" Dad runs his hand over his mouth, his eyes wild. "What has she ever done to you?"

"She accused me of killing our mother!" My voice pierces the air and hurts my own ears. "Allison may never be able to do anything wrong in your eyes, but she has always been perfectly hideous to me. And you have never cared. You'd let her get away with murder if you could, and somehow find a way to blame me. Well, you know what, Dad? I'm not responsible for the fact that she doesn't take her medicine. And I'm not responsible for the fact that she eats painkillers like M&Ms."

"That's not her—"

"Fault? It's not her fault?" I feel the heat spread across my face. "Is that what you were going to say? Because it is. We're all stuck with the lives we got, and it's what you make of it. And *this* is what she's making of it."

"Is that what they teach you in church?"

This stops me cold. Deflates me like a popped balloon.

He walks past me, the air hanging with the scent of his soap and aftershave. "I'm going to work."

I don't say another word. I'm all out of them.

The front door slams again, and when the truck starts, I'm still glued to the spot. Unmoved. Unblinking. Barely breathing.

Who says you need water to sink?

Chapter Seventeen

At ten after twelve, I'm sitting in the parking lot in front of Ivy League Diner, staring at the pink fluorescent open sign and wondering why I'm here.

After Dad stormed off, I got in my car and just drove. Cranked up the radio, sang old eighties hits until I was hoarse, and stopped and bought some SweeTarts. Eventually I found myself at the cemetery, sitting in front of Mom's grave with my legs tucked beneath me. I brought her some wild flowers and rested them on her stone. I didn't have a single thing to say. Found myself talking to God instead. He was just as silent as the cemetery.

With a sigh reserved for tax filing and Pap smears, I push on the metal bar of the door and walk into the diner. While I scan the crowd, my mind whizzes with stress-fueled thoughts. What am I doing here? What if Beth's the only one who wants to see me? Why reconnect with people when I'm only passing through?

I feel the draw of Connor's eyes before I see him. My skin prickling, I turn to my left and there in the corner is Beth and her committee. And Connor. Watching me.

I weave in and around the tables, inhaling the scent of sirloin burgers and homemade fries. And doesn't that just take me back? Dinners after home football games. My mother bringing my sister and me here for lunch, letting us order dessert for the main course. My first part-time job in high school.

"Maggie!" Beth throws her hands in the air like I just scored a touchdown. "Look who's here, guys. Chris, pull up another chair so the girl can sit."

"Hey." I squeeze into the available seat between Beth and Connor, relieved to see Danielle isn't present. She's probably too busy harassing small children. "I hope you don't mind if I crashed your meeting. I promised my old best friend I would buy her lunch if she'd let me tag along."

Beth curls her arm around me and gives me a squeeze. "I'm so getting that pie now."

I hang my purse over the chair and accidentally bump Connor's shoulder in the process. "Sorry."

He leans toward my ear, his breath brushing my cheek. "We have a conversation to finish."

"No. We don't."

Beth taps my hand and pulls my attention back to the table. "Did your sister get all taken care of?"

I unroll my silverware from the white napkin and set my utensils on either side of my plate. "Um, no." I dart a glance at Connor. "Allison . . . she left the hospital this morning on her own. We have no idea where she is. Haven't heard from her."

"How did she do that?" Beth asks.

"One of the nurses thinks she saw her walking the halls with a man. Probably her old boyfriend or something. I don't know."

"Oh, Maggie," Beth says. "I'll pray for your family. And poor Riley. How's your dad taking it?"

Right up there with the Spanish Inquisition. "He's hanging on." To his twisted principles. To the idea that it's all my fault.

"Well, on to happier things then, right?" Beth pulls out a notebook from her industrial-sized diaper bag. "Okay, so the dance instructors passed the test. Connor and Maggie both told me they had an excellent time."

Connor lifts a brow. "You did?"

I shrug. "It was an okay evening. Beat staying home and watching public television."

Beth continues, "So now we need an update on the caterer, the DJ, the band . . ."

As Beth conducts business, the waitress comes by the table, pops her hip, and rests a tray on it. "What can I get you?"

"I'll take the—"

"My, my my. Lookie here."

Oh no. I take in the woman's white beehive, wrinkled smoker's pout, and see time stand still.

"If it isn't Connie Montgomery's daughter."

"Hello, Mrs. Nicklebock." My gosh, is the woman *still* working here? She was the first person I showed my new driver's license to fourteen years ago. She gave me a free slice of coconut cream pie. And a job.

"I hear you're a big-shot TV girl now."

I smile. "More like just a girl who heaves around a camera. No big deal."

"You remember that time you got all mad at the boss and quit?"

"It was so long ago and—"

Connor rests an arm around my chair. "Let's hear this."

Mrs. Nicklebock snorts. "Mr. Clydes, the owner, wouldn't agree to donate some food to a needy family. Maggie got so mad, she stood on the counter and told the whole diner that Mr. Clydes was buying everyone's dinner. We sold out of pie and pot roast in five minutes flat."

Connor looks at me, his mouth quirking.

"Mr. Clydes called it robbery, but our Maggie here claimed it was a random act of kindness." Mrs. Nicklebock slaps her tray and cackles.

"Well, it sure was nice to see you." I quickly give her my order and study the napkin in my lap like it's the coolest of inventions.

"So that gives everyone a job," I hear Beth say. "Which leaves me with needing someone to check out that new band I heard about. Any takers? Thursday night? No. Okay, Jermaine and Maggie, I'm putting you on this one."

My head pops up. "What?" I look to Jermaine O'Dell, but he just shrugs.

"Yeah." Beth consults her list. "Everyone here is already committed to other things, except Mark and me. But I promised I'd go with him to that job fair in Dallas."

I stir my drink with my straw and give in. "Okay."

"Great, let's talk about the picnic for that Saturday . . ."

I eat my burger as the group makes plans. I can't take a breath without being aware of Connor near my space, invading my extra-large bubble. When the table conversation turns to old high-school times, I find myself finally relaxing. I sip my tea and laugh at Beth's animated tales.

"Do you remember when Jermaine caught that Hail Mary pass at the finals?" Beth asks. "Ran right into Susan Flanahan, captain of the cheer squad. Knocked her out cold."

"Knocked her flat too," Jermaine says. "She lost the stuffing in her bra on the impact."

We finish our meal and return from the trip down memory lane. I hug Beth, tell everyone good-bye, and walk outside into the sunshine toward my Ford.

I just get the car unlocked when I hear that deep voice behind me. "I think by default, I've won our bet."

I turn around, my hand on the hood. "I've been a little busy."

Connor sticks his hands in his jean pockets, the dark denim hanging on him like he uses the same stylist as Brad Pitt. His button-down oxford is untucked, the sleeves rolled up to the forearm. It's altogether a preppy work of art.

"Just forfeit and be done with it." He steps closer, and I see the hint of stubble on his face.

"I don't back down, Dr. Blake."

"In that case, tell me about last night at the hospital."

My face falls. The lights go out. "I have to go." I swing open the car door, only to find his hand in the way.

I stare into his face, so close if I just moved mere inches, our lips could touch.

"I need to know, Maggie. I'm just trying to get my stories straight."

"What does that mean? Have you talked to my sister?"

Connor rubs the back of his neck and nods. "Yes."

"Did you help her leave this morning?"

"Of course not. Look, I know you don't know me, and you definitely don't trust me, but I'm trying to help."

"Well, don't. Nobody asked you to."

He pauses. "Allison did."

The breath stalls in my chest. "Just what exactly is going on between you and my sister?"

"Why don't we go talk somewhere?"

"I have a better idea. Why don't you just tell me now."

The phone on his hip vibrates, and he grabs it at once. "It's the clinic. I have to go."

"Connor, I need information. What do you know about Allison?"

He clips the phone back in its place. "Bring Riley out to see her puppy after school. We'll talk."

"Connor—"

"See you then." He walks away, full of confidence and purpose. Comfortable with his place in this town and in the world in general.

And I stand there, clutching the door of a Ford Focus, never more uncertain in my life.

When I pick up Riley at school, her face tells me she didn't have a very good day. Like a girl who doesn't know which direction her world is spinning. Like her aunt.

"Hey, kiddo." I give her a brief hug, even though, predictably, she squirms right out of it. "How was school?"

She shuts the car door and buckles up. "The best," she drolls. "I'm in a stupid play about history."

I take a swig of my bottled water. "Seriously?" I wave to the crosswalk guard and drive on. "That's awesome, Riley! What's your part? Martha Washington? Mary Lincoln? A Constitutional go-go dancer?"

"A horse's butt."

I spew water all over the steering wheel.

"See?" She throws up her hands. "It's stupid."

I wipe my mouth. "No. No, it's not. Just um . . . well, I'm excited about it. I can't wait to see it."

"Like you'll be here."

"Actually I'm going to stay for a few more weeks."

I don't know if I was expecting my niece to burst with unbridled happiness, but she simply stares.

"I'll see your play. I promise." As soon as the words are out of my mouth, I want to grab each one back. I promise? I can't just throw out promises. What if I get the National Geographic job, and they need me immediately?

"By the way, my teacher said to tell you thank you for volunteering to make the costumes for our class play."

I blink. "What are you talking about?"

Riley shrugs. "She asked if any of our parents or guardians would want to help, and I told her you were all over it." My niece hands over a folded note from Mrs. Ellis. I scan the lines with dread as I read the costume requirements.

"What were you thinking?"

"It was either you or Megan Oberman's mom, and I'm not wearing anything she makes."

"You did this to me on purpose, didn't you?" Some sort of weird, twisted, elementary school punishment. "I don't even know how to sew."

"Good thing you have three weeks to learn." She traces a path on the window. "So how's Mom?"

Crap. She still doesn't know. "Why don't we go get some ice cream and talk about it. I think we could both use it."

Her finger stills. "She didn't go to rehab, did she?"

There's just no way to soften this. "No. She decided to get away and spend some time with a friend instead."

Tired, wary eyes blink back at me. "She's on the run. Again."

"We'll find her." I reach out my hand and rest it gently on Riley's, but she shoves it away with an angry huff.

Two chocolate chunk scoops later, Riley and I walk into the vet clinic. The receptionist doesn't even speak. With her ear pressed to a phone, she waves her hand toward the back.

My hand on Riley's shoulder, I lead her to her puppy. Matilda whines in her warm bed, and Riley reaches out her hand to rub it across the dog's damaged body. I dig into my purse and pull out my smallest camcorder.

"Are you seriously gonna use that thing?"

I look at her in the screen. "Yep."

She rolls her eyes as she checks a nearby chart. "Time to eat,

Matilda." She walks into another room, like she's perfectly at home, and returns a minute later with a bottle. "Here you go."

"You can take her out."

Riley and I both turn at Connor's voice. I lower the camera.

"Why don't you sit down and spend some time with Matilda?" With eyes only for Riley, he gestures to a chair in the corner. "Lift her out gently. There you go. You're a natural with her."

I begin filming again as the puppy curls into Riley's waiting arms. A smile spreads on her face that I find myself mirroring.

A few minutes later, I tug on Connor's sleeve. "Can I see you for a moment?"

"Follow me." He opens a door, and I trail behind him into another hall. Shutting us inside, he leans against the wall, arms crossed.

"Did my sister call you this morning?" I ask, my voice a soft whisper.

His blue eyes fuse into mine. "I've already told your dad all I know."

"Well, enlighten me."

He stares down that perfect Roman nose at me. "Allison called me from somewhere on the road. A number in Dallas. She said she was fine, and she'd come back when she got things straightened out."

I focus on a spot on the tile floor until it's a blur in my eye. That is so like my sister. How is it *I* get called the selfish one? "And why is it she's calling you, Connor?"

"Because we're friends."

"Want to expand on that?"

His lips quirk. "Jealous?"

"Oh yeah," I sass. "Just eaten up with it. Can you just save me some time and level with me?"

"We became friends at church about four years ago when I came back home to Ivy."

"Allison—at church?"

"She just showed up one Sunday. Sat in a back pew, and I would always stop and talk to her. She came faithfully for about two months. I guess we kind of formed a bond. She trusted me, and eventually began to confide in me."

"Anything else?"

Connor lifts an arrogant brow. "Are you asking me if we dated?"

"Just answer the question."

"No. We did not date." He pushes off the wall with his foot and steps closer. I'm suddenly aware of the lack of space. "Now, it's your turn to do the talking. What did you and your sister talk about last night at the hospital?"

"I didn't go in there to intentionally upset her, if that's what you're getting at." The blood pumps through my angry veins. I'm so sick of being on the defense.

"Anybody ever tell you you're a little overly emotional?"

"Anybody ever tell you you're too confident for someone who can probably converse in Klingon?"

He has the nerve to laugh. "About last night?"

I count to five and begin again. "She started getting all weird." I relay everything Allison said about Riley. "I couldn't just sit there and listen to it. But other than defending Riley, I did not antagonize her."

"Anything else?"

You watched her drown and did nothing. You took away my mother, then left me alone! "No." I put my hand on the doorknob, ready to go back inside, but his fingers move to cover mine.

"Not so fast."

Connor leans on the door, his Spearmint breath fanning my cheek. "I was honest with you. Now you come clean with me. What else did you two talk about?"

Knots twist and tighten in my gut as Allison's cruel words about the night of my mother's death replay in my head. "I got upset over her blasé tone about her daughter and just left."

Connor studies me like one of his lab samples under a microscope. Seconds pass before he speaks. His hand flexes over mine. "It sure must get old."

I watch the flecks in his eyes, how the light plays with the color. "What?"

"Hiding from everything like you do."

With the charge of a cattle prod, I'm snapped back to reality. "I have no idea what you're talking about."

There's that lazy smile again. Makes me want to tear it off his pretty little nerd face. "You're forgetting I was there. I walked in on your conversation with Allison."

I lift my chin. "Some of us stopped eavesdropping in junior high."

His sly charm slides from his face. Steel replaces it. "I'm not the enemy here, Maggie. I want to help your sister, but sometimes it's hard to know where the truth ends and the lies begin."

"The lies begin with her." My voice echoes in the sterile hall. "But I'm not going to stand here and try to explain myself to you. If you have information, Connor, then pass it on. If you hear from my sister, have the courtesy to let us know. But otherwise, you and I have nothing to say to one another about this topic." I twist my hand beneath his and walk out the door.

Chapter Eighteen

My hands roam over the keyboard as I edit footage of a young girl from Ghana. Her story would be the perfect contrast to the boy solider who secretly let me interview him in Darfur. I scribble some notes on a legal pad and stick my pen back into the messy bun on top of my head.

It's two hours later when the front door shuts, and I notice the time.

Rolling the tension out of my shoulders, I close my laptop and barely miss getting mowed down by my niece on the stairs.

"Kinda late getting home from school. Did you stop and see the dog?"

"Yeah." Riley sidesteps me and walks to her bedroom with enough force to give the foundation a shake.

I look to my dad for an explanation, but all he does is grunt and hand me a note. He and I have hardly spoken since our last big blowup. He pretends to be polite in front of Riley, but as soon as she's out of earshot, it's the total cold shoulder. Nothing like feeling sixteen again. And not in a low body fat, eat all you want, giggle all day, and dream of Brad Pitt sort of way.

Opening the paper, the Ivy Elementary School letterhead greets me. As does a blow-by-blow of Riley's escapades at school today, including throwing glue at two girls during art and "accidentally" nailing these same girls with a kickball during P.E. At the bottom is the neat and efficient signature of the principal, Danielle Chapel. With her letters perfectly spaced and evenly looped, even her signature is snotty.

"She had a bad day today." I fold up the note. "She's clearly acting out after yesterday's upsetting news."

"I talked to her a little bit, but you know I'm not good at that stuff."

"What did you say?" My voice rises as high as a Justin Timberlake solo.

"I didn't yell at her," he growls. "So quit looking at me like I beat her with a switch. I never laid a hand on you girls."

Didn't have to. "What did you tell Riley?"

"Not much. I'm the grandpa. I've raised my kids. I'm supposed to be the one who hands her quarters for the gumball machine and gets her exactly what she wants for Christmas."

Since the man totally detonated all his parenting attempts, his take on being a grandpa has me sticking a finger in my ear to make sure it's all clear, and I heard that right. "With Allison gone, you are the parent."

Dad pinches the bridge of his nose. "Just talk to the girl, would you? She needs a female in her life, and you're the closest one."

"Your inspirational words are making me all misty-eyed."

Dad points a finger toward the stairs. "Go talk to your niece. I'll fix dinner."

I knock on Riley's door and find her flipping through an old JCPenney catalog. "Gonna do some shopping?"

"It wasn't my fault."

The bed sinks as I sit down beside her. "Tell me what happened."

"They were picking on Sarah. Again. But she won't ever stand up for herself. And those girls have her so scared she always denies it when the teacher comes."

"And no one else ever sees this?"

"They're good."

I pull Riley's hair out of her face and try to think of something motherly and wise. "At least you didn't depants anyone."

She lifts her head. "What's that?"

"Nothing," I say quickly. "Riley, maybe you should let Sarah take up for herself. Because all this is accomplishing is getting you in trouble. A lot."

"They say stuff about her." She lowers her voice. "And her mom."

I know that feeling. Lived with it for years. "You can be her friend without lobbing glue and kickballs."

"Never mind." She snaps the catalog shut. "Just forget it."

"I know you're upset about your mom, but—"

"Just leave me alone."

Deciding to let it go, I kiss her on the top of the head, whether she wants me to or not. Reaching for a stack on the floor, I pull out a first grade–level story book and set it in front of my niece. "Ready to read?"

She sighs and dumps her chin in her hand. "Okay. But this time, I'm turning the pages."

"I'm not a page hog."

"Yeah, you pretty much are."

That night I dream of the lake.

My mother calls out to me. "Maggie, get help. Please . . .won't you get help?"

"I'm trying!" I yell back to her, my voice broken by sobs. "Please don't leave me."

Allison appears by my side, her voice cruel and taunting. "You know what happened, Maggie. You were with her when she died, and then you left home. Taking your secrets. Maybe if you went in the water yourself you'd remember."

"No," I cry. "Get away from me."

Allison steps closer. And closer, her arms extended.

"No!"

But I'm powerless to fight her. She pushes me toward the lake, and I teeter on the edge of the pier, my arms flailing for balance.

"It's time to remember," Allison says. And with one final shove, I hit the water. And sink straight to the bottom. The water fills my lungs, my ears, my head. I open my mouth—

My own gasp wakes me up.

I sit up, clutching the sheet, sweat bonding my T-shirt to my back. My breath coming in gasps.

The clock on my phone reads 2:00 a.m. Four more hours 'til daylight. And I couldn't be more awake.

I have to get out of here. Out of this bed. This house.

The old restlessness gnawing at me, I punch a button on my phone and wait as it rings.

"Hello?" comes a groggy voice.

I take a deep breath and rest a hand over my pounding heart. "Meet me at the fountain on the square in ten minutes."

I hear the rustle of Connor Blake's pillow. "Are you nuts?"

"Given my genes, it's almost a certainty. I'm feeling a little daredevilish. Are you in? Or is the math club president too scared?"

"This better not be illegal. I prefer doing illegal stuff when I've had a full night's sleep."

I laugh and throw on my running capris. "See you in ten. Oh, and bring a flashlight."

"If this is all part of your plot to kill me, you should know I have lots of friends in this town." Connor shuts his truck door and zips up his light jacket.

"Probably because you pay them." I pat his chest. "Just like high school."

He grabs my hand and holds on. "I had plenty of friends, thanks. Just not the fast-moving crowd you were in."

I take back my hand and shove it in my windbreaker pocket. "The librarian doesn't count."

He yawns and regards me with open curiosity. "Yesterday you couldn't stand me. But now I'm your two a.m. phone call?"

"I felt the need to do something crazy, and you said at the dance studio that you were up for a dare. I just thought I would finally deliver."

He rubs his hands together in the early morning chill. "Want to tell me what's going on?"

"Boredom."

From his expression I see he doesn't buy that for a second. But I don't care. My skin itches for adrenaline. To be reckless. To challenge God or gravity, I don't know which. But I want the thrill of tempting it all.

An hour later, I stand shoulder to shoulder with Connor and question my brilliant idea.

The flashlight illuminates his face and the narrow wall around us. "So how is it this cave's been here forever, and I'm just now finding out about it?" he asks.

Somewhere in the distance drops of water fall on the hard

ground. "Legend has it, this cave is haunted." I shine my light on the rock. "So my friends and I never got too far inside."

"It doesn't make it any more appealing that you have to scale a mountain to get to it."

"That's the fun of it."

"Not in the black of night."

He's so close, I can feel his body radiate heat. I catch myself sniffing his air and turn my head. "You did pretty well. For a nerd."

"Bill Gates and I are not offended by that term."

I shine my light over our heads and look at the dark shadows above. Probably bats and who knows what else. I should be scared. But I'm not. Kind of numb. Until his finger intertwines with my pinky. I jump at the contact.

"Want to tell me what this is about?"

"Want to move your hand?"

I hear that obnoxious smile. "I'm scared. Only thing keeping me from crying." He continues staring straight ahead, making no eye contact. "Start talking." He squeezes my finger. "My bed's calling my name."

"Just woke up and wanted to cut loose a little . . . being in Ivy brings back the wild impulses I guess."

His laugh is quiet. "Words that would thrill most guy's hearts. But I've had enough human psychology to know something's spinning in your head. Watched you in the last week or so enough to understand this is just another diversion for you. Another coping tactic."

"Stick to the cows and dogs. Don't analyze me."

"Want to tell me why you couldn't sleep tonight?"

"Thinking of all my boyfriends back home. I know I'm going to have to pick one soon, and I do so hate breaking hearts in multiples of ten."

I hear the slap of skin as he swats something on his leg. "This was the dumbest dare ever."

"I'm sorry it didn't involve calculators. So tell me about your fiancée."

"Ex-fiancée," he corrects. "Nothing much to say. She couldn't handle the distance between us and eventually decided she couldn't live in Ivy."

Two days before the wedding, I mentally add. "I'm sure that was a difficult time for you."

"Taught me a lot." His voice echoes in the hollow of the cave. "I learned high-maintenance girls are a waste of my time. I want someone with simple values. Someone who'll care about her home, her family, puts others first. Isn't going to bolt at the first sign of trouble. Low on drama."

I bite back a laugh. "Good luck with that."

"Sweet-tempered. A nice kindergarten teacher maybe. Someone who likes kids. Teaches Sunday school."

"Don't forget likes to hunt, fish, and watch NASCAR. Connor, this woman does not exist. God didn't make perfect people."

"She'll know how to make a mean apple pie too."

"To smash in your chauvinistic face?"

He gives a lopsided grin. "I'm just saying the person I'm going to settle down with will be peaceful. Calm."

"An android."

We slip into a companionable silence as the flashlights are shone all around. The cave is filled with crunchy, scratchy, drippy noises, but after a few minutes, I call it for what it is. "Sadly there are no ghosts here. Just childish folklore."

"I think you have all the ghosts you can handle in your own house."

A chill sweeps over me that has nothing to do with the

temperature of the cave. My dream comes back to my mind in vivid color and stereo sound. And in the dim of the cavernous space, with a man who's practically a stranger, my tongue loosens up. "I had this dream." I lick my lips and start over. "I have this dream." I wait for Connor to throw out a witty barb, but he doesn't speak. Doesn't move. Stares straight ahead at the wall in front. "I don't know what my sister has told you, but I was with my mother the night she drowned. And I don't remember what happened. A fisherman dove in and pulled me back to the pier where I passed out, and when I came to, my mother was gone." They found her body the next day.

Water plops near me and splashes on my calf. Connor's whole hand envelopes mine. And like Riley accepting my quick kiss tonight, I let his hand remain.

"Allison never forgave me. She's always thought there was some big mystery to that night, but if there is, I don't know what it is."

"And your dream?" comes his quiet voice.

I shrug at the silliness of it all. "I don't know. Same thing every time. We're on Ivy Lake. My mom's there, and she's calling out to me. But I can't get her." My throat thickens. "I can't ever get to her in time."

"Maybe that's how it happened."

"Perhaps. But I don't think so. It doesn't feel right. It should fit in my mind like a missing puzzle piece."

"So this is why you're afraid of water?"

"I'm not afraid of it."

"It's okay. I'm afraid of some things too."

"Like what?"

"For starters, whatever's crawling up my leg right now."

"We should go." I smile in the dark. "Before the vipers wake up."

I pull away from the wall and take a step toward the gaping entrance.

"Maggie?"

I stop and turn around. "Yeah?"

"I've been praying for you. And your sister."

"Thanks." I stare at the ground, uncertain what to do with this. "Allison told you a bunch of bad stuff about me, didn't she?"

"You were pretty much right up there with terrorists and mimes."

"And now?" The question floats off my tongue before I can edit my thoughts.

"You've totally changed my mind."

"Oh. Well, good."

"Now you're only up there with telemarketers and the bowling channel."

I give him the instant view of my perfectly straight spine and lead us out of the cave. We stand at the top of Piney Hill, the tallest point in Ivy. All the town is blanketed in dark as it sleeps. Like normal people do.

"So how do we know who won this challenge?" Connor stands beside me, his arm brushing mine. "I think I do. You got me up at two, and I met the dare."

"You are such a whiner. No wonder you didn't play football." I shine my light straight down the rocky path. "Now that you know the terrain, we race. Whoever reaches the bottom first without breaking a limb wins."

"Is this honestly the best you could do?" His smile is tight. "I mean, seriously?"

I throw up my hands. "It's not like I have a lot to work with in this town."

Connor's eyes find mine. "Or at two a.m.?"

"Ready? Should I give you a head start since you and your type are not known for athletic prowess?"

His expression turns cat-that-ate-the-canary. "See you at the bottom. Where I'll claim the victory."

I return his smile. "Go." And I shoot off down the hill, my muscles remembering some of the hidden nooks and crannies.

I hear him behind me the whole way, his feet sending rocks flying all around the path. An eternity passes, and I see the end in sight, my flashlight trained on the uneven ground. Not much further. And I'm winning! I can smell the victory.

Out of the corner of my eyes comes a flash of movement, and Connor shoots past me. No! His long legs take two strides for my every one, and like an unwatched eBay auction, I see the prize slipping away in the final seconds. There's only one thing a self-respecting girl can do.

"Ow!" I drop to the ground. "Oh . . . oh no."

Connor jerks his body to a stop, grabbing on to a large rock for balance. "Maggie?" He's by my side in two leaps. His hands are on my shoulders. On my legs. Then my ankle. "What's wrong? Where are you hurt?"

"I think I twisted my ankle. It's okay. You go ahead."

His fingers are a light caress on my ankle, and I close my eyes at the touch. A single girl will take what she can get.

He presses on one spot. "Does this hurt?"

"Just a bit. I'm okay. Really." I start to rise and come back down with a gasp. "Maybe you could look right here." I touch a spot on the bone above my shoe.

He angles his flashlight and leans in.

And I shoot up. "See you at the finish line!" Laughing, I hustle the rest of the way, my hands outstretched for balance. Smelling the sweet scent of a win once again.

Level ground is in sight. The grassy end looms before me. Mere steps away.

And suddenly I'm being lifted high in the air. I give a squeal and kick out my legs. "Put me down!"

Connor laughs and keeps running.

"No fair!" I try to wiggle out of his arms, but he holds me with his iron grip.

"Don't even talk to me about fairness," he says on a winded breath. "How can you look yourself in the mirror?"

Just as he steps away from the end, he sets me on my feet, none-to-gently, then takes the victory jump onto level ground.

I stand there and watch him watching me. I shine my flashlight near his face and see squinting, gloating eyes. "You rat."

"Do you need a moment to pull yourself together?" He tugs on his shirt. "Need my sleeve to dry your tears? Your loser tears?"

I stomp forward and punch my fingers in his chest. "I was winning the entire time."

"Whatever. I stayed behind on purpose in case you fell."

I open my mouth to refute it, but I can't. "You and your stupid manners!"

"You owe me a day on the job. Tomorrow. Bright and early." His laugh is deep and husky as he gazes down at my shirt. "Don't wear anything that can't be peed or puked on."

I step closer to see him better in the dark. "You really know how to show a girl a good time." And stumble over a rock.

His strong arms reach out to catch me. Pull me to him. Our flashlights, angled to the ground, send up just enough light to see the intensity in his eyes.

Connor's fingers tip up my chin. His thumb skims a path down my cheek. "Why'd you call me tonight?"

I stare at his mouth and tell myself to breathe. "I don't know."

"Face it, whether you want to or not"—his gaze locks with mine, dares me to not look away—"you're beginning to trust me."

Of its own will, my hand comes to curl around his arm. "Like a wolf in a chicken coop."

His head lowers. "It's a start."

The night wrapping around us like a cocoon, I open my mouth to his. His arms move around me, draw me closer. And I just hang on.

His hands slide up to frame my face, and he kisses me with a slow tenderness that has tears stinging my tired eyes. I lean into it and sigh. Connor presses his mouth to my cheek, my temple, then seizes my lips again.

From somewhere in the fog of my head, panic starts to invade. Can't breathe. Can't think. "Stop." I peel my hands from his back and push him away. "Stop." My skin tingling, my face flushed, I take a step in retreat.

His eyes flash fire in the light's glow.

"That can't happen again."

Connor inhales the night air. Nods. "You're right. It can't. I'm through with complicated girls."

"And that's what I am?"

He rakes his fingers through his dark hair. "You're their mascot."

I ignore his smug arrogance. "You never answered my question."

He crosses his arms, his Nike jacket stretching tight across his chest. "Remind me."

"What are you to my sister?"

"A friend."

His answer is too simple. Too easy. "I don't believe you." Bile rises in my throat. You do not take your friends' boyfriends, and you do not make out with your sister's exes. "I think you were something more."

He kicks some gravel with the toe of a running shoe. "Trust me—friends. That's all you need to know."

I tilt my head back and watch the stars above me. So much bigger than me. "Forget the dare. I won't be at your office tomorrow. I think it's best we not run into one another again."

He advances and puts himself right back in my space. "Just like that? You're going to give up just like that?"

I swallow and force myself not to step away. "I don't need one more secret in my life. And I definitely don't need you." I hoist up my light and walk off, letting the breeze dance over my skin as I leave him there.

"She called me."

I stop at his voice.

"I worked for the church crisis hotline."

My feet twist in the ground, and I face him.

He holds the light in the crook of his arm. "She called me the night she tried to take her own life."

My stomach plunges south.

"All three times. Over two years when she'd pass through town."

"It comes with her disease. Especially if she's not on her meds. Usually she has someone to blame. Who was it? I need to know."

He lifts his gaze toward the crescent moon. "You."

Chapter Nineteen

"Do you have an appointment?" the school secretary asks me Thursday morning.

"No." It takes everything I've got to pull my cheek muscles into some semblance of a smile. I feel like I just got off an all-night flight to Europe, missed my eight hours of sleep, and landed in a time zone where daylight shines and I must participate.

"No appointment," she repeats, like my appearance is the equivalent of standing on a tabletop and yodeling in the library.

"Danielle and I are old friends. She'll be totally okay with it. In fact," I stare past her shoulder. "I think I'll just show myself back there and surprise her. I know you're busy."

As the woman harrumphs and sputters, I walk myself straight to Riley's principal's office. I do knock, though.

I don't like to be rude.

"Hey, Danielle."

My former classmate shoots me a death look, then goes into principal mode. She holds up a manicured finger and finishes her call.

"Yes, *Connor*, I'll see you at seven on Friday."

Connor? Is it just me, or did she deliberately emphasize his name? Like that bothers me. I'm sure. How old are we, twelve?

"Looking forward to it." She giggles like a giddy prom queen and hangs up the phone. "Let me just pencil something into my social calendar." With a ridiculous smile still on her face, Danielle types something into her phone before giving me her full attention. All traces of nice gone. "Did you have an appointment?"

"This will be quick." I scoot into one of the chairs in front of her mahogany desk. "I think my niece is getting a raw deal."

Danielle pooches her lips like she's checking for lipstick on her teeth. "Your niece is a menace to the fourth grade. Starting next Tuesday, she'll be spending an hour a week with the guidance counselor discussing her anger issues."

Maybe that's not such a bad idea. But it's the *way* the woman says it. Like Riley's just this unexplainable terror. Like she's the kid most likely to bring knives and pipe bombs for show-n-tell.

"Counseling is probably an excellent approach. But I still think there's something to Riley's belief that these girls are bullying Sarah."

Danielle leans on her perfectly organized desk, her fingers intertwined. "Maggie, if Sarah were being harassed, she would speak up, and we'd take care of the matter immediately. She's had plenty of chances."

"What if she's too shy? What if she gets knocked around at home and has already learned that nobody's ever going to believe her?"

She taps her thumbs together. "That's a bold statement we don't take lightly here. Do you have knowledge of abuse in her home?"

"No." I am flunking this conversation. "Of course not. I just think Riley is smart enough to recognize—"

"I have a meeting to get to." Danielle stands up and smoothes her black skirt. "Your niece is spending the day in our in-school suspension room today. But the next time it happens—it's a few days home, and I call the state department."

"That won't be necessary." That heifer. "Oh, one more thing. You know Riley has had her life torn apart. So our family has really appreciated the kindness and concern of Mrs. Ellis, her teacher." I pick up my purse and hang it over my shoulder. "She should really be commended. What a heart for children she has."

Danielle's eyes harden. "I'll pass on the compliment."

"Have a lovely day."

I spend the rest of the day on my laptop, playing around with footage from my travels. *God, is this just a hobby? Just something I've collected like the shoes in my closet? If I need to let this go, just tell me. Otherwise, I have to know what to do with this feeling that I'm supposed to share these children's stories.*

I close my eyes and just wait and listen. Like God is going to whisper the answer in my ear. But no answer. Again.

The afternoon passes in what's become our normal routine. I pick Riley up from school, we stop and see Matilda, we eat peanut-butter crackers, we read a book together, then do homework until Dad gets home to fix supper. Yet tonight he called and said he would be a bit late, so dinner's all on me. Alert the health department.

Yeah, I can do this. No problem.

"Riley!" I call at five-thirty. "Dinner's ready! Come and get it!"

She sits down just in time for me to plop down my hard work on her plate. "Hot Pockets?"

"What?" I rest my fist on my hip. "According to the news, schools have gone all nutritious, so I didn't want to overdo it."

She pokes a stubby finger into the crust. "This doesn't look good."

"Well, of course it doesn't. Not like that." I slip it from its microwave sleeve. "There. Much better. Mmmm!"

"Dude." Her voice is as dry as sandpaper. "You're an adult. You can't fix me things like this."

"Who says?"

She rolls her eyes heavenward. "You're supposed to, like, have food groups and stuff on my plate."

"It's not like I'm forcing you to eat brussels sprouts here. I thought you'd be happy." I'm such a reject mother figure. It's a good thing I didn't go with my side dish of mini Snickers bars I've got tucked away in my purse. "So does this mean you're not going to eat it?"

"Got anything else?"

"My other specialty is popcorn."

She shoves her plate aside. "I'll take it."

When the doorbell rings at ten 'til eight, I stick my head in the living room and tell Dad good-bye. "Make sure Riley brushes her teeth."

"Uh-huh."

He's barely spoken to me all evening, acting as if words bigger than one syllable are just too much for him to bear. One thing I did get out of him is that he hasn't heard from Allison.

I wrench open the door without even checking the peephole and find not Jermaine O'Dell standing on my front porch, but Connor Blake.

"What are you doing here?"

"Good evening to you too."

I just stand there and stare holes through the man.

"You're starting to hurt my feelings." He glances at his watch like he's bored.

"I'm supposed to go to Club Retro with Jermaine."

"Jermaine got a case of food poisoning, and I have the distinct pleasure of filling in."

Connor says this as if he'd really rather have a root canal. It's very uplifting to a girl's confidence. "Maybe I should just reschedule." I reach into my purse. "I'll call Beth."

He stills my hand with his. "Afraid of a night out with me?"

"At the moment food poisoning sounds more fun."

He shakes his head in mock shame. "You are such a sore loser."

"You are such a cheat."

"Me?" He laughs. "I lead a Bible study. I heal sick animals. You're the one who pulled the whole sprained ankle thing and—"

"Fine. Let's go." I breeze past him and walk toward my car.

"My truck's already running." Connor tugs on my arm and guides me to his waiting vehicle.

I slide in and pause, my hand on the handle. "No funny business tonight."

His laughing eyes hold mine. "Do you always think about making out? We're just going to listen to a band. So don't even try to beg me for a repeat of last night." His gaze drops to my lips. "Though you know you enjoyed it."

I shut my mouth on a futile protest as the door closes in my face.

Connor gets in and flicks on the air, kicking up the scent of hay, Tide, and the faint citrus spice of his cologne.

He entertains me with small talk as he drives past the Ivy city limits. He doesn't make another reference to our kiss, and though it feels like the elephant in the backseat, I eventually find myself relaxing, even laughing at his stories.

"That's a shame about Jermaine's food poisoning," I say, after listening to a funny tale involving some pro bono work he did at a pig farm last week. "I know that can be miserable." I take a quick assessment of his features, searching for any hint that Jermaine's sudden illness isn't of the fake variety.

"Yeah, it stinks," is all he says.

"He seems like a nice guy."

"He is. So's his brother Michael." He shoots me a wry look. "You don't remember him, do you? Grade younger than us."

"The guy at the reunion meetings. Of course I remember him. Sure, he was the guy who—" Connor's face says he's not buying it. "No, I don't."

"Michael O'Dell? His brother, Jermaine. Had another brother named—"

"Tito?"

"Richard."

"That's a disappointment."

The flashing lights of Club Retro greet us as Connor pulls into the parking lot. Instead of seeing a bunch of college kids as I'd feared, there's a mix of ages making their way inside.

As I open my door, Connor stands there waiting. Frowning.

"What?"

"I was going to open your door for you. Let me guess, you're too independent for that?"

I pat his shoulder. "If you think that's hot, you should see me balance my checkbook."

He shuts the door, leaving his arm on the window frame, staring down with those laughing eyes. "I should probably warn you now I'm going to buy your dinner tonight." His voice is so low, it sends off clanging bells of warning in my head. Like the kind that accompanies a melting nuclear reactor.

"That's sweet how you want to make up for all the dates you didn't have in high school." I give him a wink of my own, duck under his arm, and sail right for the entrance.

Inside a rock song pours from the speakers. Posters of singers who span the generations adorn the walls, as well as layers upon layers of artistic graffiti that pays homage to the art of music. We settle into a table next to a signed photo of Jon Bon Jovi. I ogle it with the appreciation it deserves, because at one time I was shot through the heart for that man.

A candle flickers in a globe on the table, casting soft shadows on Connor's face. We make quick work of ordering, and then settle in as the band sets up on a stage across the room.

"How much longer are you in town?" Connor asks.

"I'm not sure. I still have some things to get straightened out with Riley. Tutors. A babysitter." But I'm dragging my feet. Why?

His blunt fingers empty sugar packets into his tea glass. "Cinematographer. That sounds exciting. Tell me about your job."

I describe the basics of being in charge of the film crew. The travel. The unpredictable schedule.

He leans closer, his elbows propped on the table. "Do you realize you just told me about your job with all the enthusiasm of one reading her grocery list?"

I flip my napkin and lay it over my jeans. "I like my work."

Connor tilts his dark head. "Do you? Is this what gets you up every morning? Where your passion is?"

"Yes." I bristle at the knowing challenge in his eyes, that look he wears that says, *I see right into your head and can read you like a book*. He doesn't know me.

"I don't believe you."

I do my own leaning in. "I don't care."

The band begins to tune their instruments, a mix of whining guitars and honking brass.

"Beth said the band is pretty bluesy," I say by way of changing the topic. "I hope they're good." And quick. Because moving this outing along seems like the safe thing to do.

"Good evening," the lead singer says into the microphone. "We're the Funky Cold Medinas, and we're glad you're here."

They launch into their first song just as the waitress brings us our meal. Connor takes my hand as he blesses the food, but immediately lets go at amen. I nibble on a Cobb salad because Connor and I are not at the I-can-eat-hot-wings-in-front-of-you stage. Though Connor's spaghetti looks ridiculously good. Darn men and their ability to eat without any care or concern for things stuck in the teeth or dripped on shirts in places that really don't need attention.

Connor takes over the conversation again, and we discuss everything from politics to movies to his tight-knit family. Whatever dork components made up the man in his youth, they are long gone. I find myself laughing more than once at his outrageous stories, from childhood moments to his more recent animal escapades.

But then as Connor describes the community basketball league he started, I find my mind drifting to other places. I set down my fork and stop him midsentence. "I never mistreated my sister."

He rests his elbows on the table and gives me his full attention. "All right."

"No, it's not all right. That's what you think. That's what she told you."

"Don't you think I'm smart enough to consider the source and determine the most likely truth?"

"No." I throw up my hands. "I mean, yes. But Allison—she can be convincing."

"Why'd you stay away so long?"

"I don't expect you to understand. You with your *Cosby Show* upbringing."

"What about Riley?"

Anger pulses at my temples. "I didn't know things were bad, okay? My father never said a word about Allison's . . . decline. I live in Chicago. I'm on the road three hundred days a year. It's easy to disconnect."

His fingers wrap around his straw. "If that's what you want to do."

My eyes narrow. "Is this dinner or a therapy session?"

"I think you're running," he says. "I think you've been on the run ever since you left Ivy after graduation." The taut lines of his face soften. "Or since your mother died."

"I got out of this town so I could become something. Staying here would've been the worst thing I could've done. You have no idea what it was like in that house."

"Why don't you tell me?"

"I appreciate that you were my sister's confidante, but you're not mine. You think I don't feel awful coming home and seeing how neglected Riley's been? I do. But I don't know what I could've done." I press the napkin to my lips and throw it down. "I'm ready to go. I'll meet you at the truck." Before I can get to my feet, Connor's hand manacles mine to the table.

"Maggie, hold on, I—" The phone in his pocket rings. "Just a minute." His eyes shoot me a warning and his fingers tighten. "We haven't even ordered dessert. Sit down while I take this. Please." His attention turns to the call. "Hello?"

I focus in on the band as he talks, but it's a little hard to determine the quality of a blues song in the haze of my anger. Not to mention his fingers are making absentminded little strokes on the inside of my wrist. I study his face for signs of foul play, but Connor's totally engrossed in the call. Maybe he thinks I'm Danielle.

Connor pulls the phone away from his ear and rests it against his shirt. "Here." He hands me a menu. "Order us something for dessert. And none of that fancy stuff. I like ice cream. I like pie. Don't get froufrou on me."

"I'm ready to leave."

He angles his head and gives me that charmer's smile. "Babe, we're just getting started. I have to take this call outside. Can't hear a thing in here." He points to the phone. "I need to walk Jack Anderson through foaling a colt. It's his first." Connor takes a step, then doubles back. "Only a chicken would take advantage of this and run out." He leans down; his lips hover near my ear. "And we both know that's not you, right?" With a laugh he saunters away. "Okay, Jack. Now just calm down. No, I don't have horse epidurals."

I rip out my own phone and punch some numbers.

"Hello?"

"Beth, I am on to your game."

"What's that, Maggie? I can't hear you for all that music in the background."

I press the phone to my lips. "Jermaine O'Dell had better be puking his guts up."

"Now, what an unkind thing to say." She tuts like an old Sunday school teacher. "I'll be sure and pass on your get-well wishes."

"You do that. But your matchmaking days are over and—"

"Girl, the feedback is terrible. I'm gonna have to hang up now. You two have fun."

"Beth—" But she's gone. I slip the phone in my purse, raising my head as a shadow falls across the table.

"Maggie Montgomery?"

A woman stands there, arms crossed, frizzy ponytail. Trouble in her eyes.

"Yes?"

"You remember me?"

Can I just stick up a billboard downtown? *No, I don't remember you. I'm sorry I left at least one twisted and torched memory for everyone in the town of Ivy.*

"Debra Linden. You stole my boyfriend in the eleventh grade." Her fists clench at her sides, and I wonder if she and Allison might share the common bond of crazy.

"Wow, that was a really long time ago."

She takes a pull from her beer bottle. "David Paulsen."

"Refresh my memory."

"David," she spits, swaying on her feet. "Blond hair. Captain of the baseball team. Drove a Miata."

I roll my eyes. "David Paulsen. What a loser he turned out to be." The woman steps forward, her face red, her neck a patchwork of splotches. "I was doing you a favor. That boy couldn't keep his eyes on one girl, he flunked study hall, and his breath always smelled like eggs. I mean, can you say 'reject'?"

She pushes up her sleeves, her nostrils flaring. "David Paulsen's my husband."

Chapter Twenty

The woman wobbles as she takes a menacing step closer. I have to say, of all the stuff I've done, I've never been in a bar fight. *God, don't let this be the first time.*

"Debra, I'm sure he's now a wonderful—"

"And he *still* talks about you."

Ew. "That means nothing. Probably just leftover loyalty from science class." I curl my fingers around my fork just in case I need a weapon. "I let him peek at my final."

"I hear that's not all you let him peek at."

I shoot to my feet with a gasp. "Now that is *not* true! That lying little—"

"Excuse me for interrupting," says a smooth voice.

Behind the bleating shrew stands Connor, a hint of a smile on those full lips.

Debra cuts Connor with her drunk-girl eyes. "Maggie and I were just chatting. Catching up on old times."

He forces his big body in front of her and pulls me to him. "Maggie had her heart set on a dance with me, and I can't put her off any longer." He stares down into my face, his gaze glowing with love and other fallacies. "Come on, sweetheart. But if you start crying on my shoulder during the love song, I'm not wiping your nose this time."

His fingers lace with mine and give them a squeeze.

"Yes, dumplin.'"

Connor leads me onto the floor where other couples move in time to the raspy ballad coming from the stage. He pulls me flush with his chest, resting one hand on the small of my back, the other keeping my fingers captive.

I try to take a step back, but his arms don't budge. "I leave for two minutes." He smiles at a couple we pass. "Two minutes and you're about to come to blows with Ivy's meanest librarian."

"*That* woman's a librarian?"

His hand at my back rubs a slow circle. "You should see her when you have overdues."

A giggle escapes and I look into his face. As the band sings about a love that makes the sun rise, my eyes meet Connor's. Something flutters in my chest, but I ignore it. Probably indigestion from my altercation with Debra.

"I'm not kissing you tonight," I whisper.

"I swear that's all you think about." His smile is wicked. "I'm not just a piece of meat, Maggie."

He pulls me so close, my head has nowhere to go but to his shoulder. I rest my hands behind his neck and listen to the sound of his heart beating. Inhale his light cologne. Close my eyes and pretend this is someone I know. Trust. And for the first time ever—I feel safe.

"I'm sorry if I upset you." His chest vibrates with each word.

I give this some thought as the music lulls my weary brain. "Sometimes I don't know what you want from me."

He pushes air out his mouth. "I don't know either."

A saxophone takes a solo and wails a soulful melody. Connor and I fall into an easy quiet as the music does all the talking.

This man scares me. I stand next to him, and the fireworks in my heart are like a Fourth of July finale. But there's always this question in his eyes that I can't put words to. And definitely can't answer. Besides, I can't get involved with anyone in Ivy. I'm leaving. I'm temporary. I'm a vapor. Gone like shoes in the summer. Like a pack of Rollos in my purse.

"It's okay to be scared of everything that's going on," he says.

Spell broken. "I'm not."

His chin rests on my head. "Then why were we in a bat cave at two-thirty in the morning?"

"There's never a wrong time to observe nature."

"I'm glad you think so." He stops. Reaches into his pocket and checks his vibrating phone. "Yep. I figured I'd get a text soon. Jack needs some help."

"The guy with the horse?"

Connor keeps his hold on my hand, his eyes sparkling with unfiltered challenge. "I'm calling in my bet. Time to go to work."

"Me?"

He glances down at my black patent flats. "Hope those aren't your favorites."

"Connor, you really know how to show a girl a good time."

He rests his warm hand on the back of my neck and points me toward the door. "I read a lot of *Cosmo*."

"So what's the problem?" I ask as Connor starts the truck.

"Jack." He shifts the truck in gear, then rests his arm on my headrest. "He's new at owning horses. I guess when he bent down to take a look, things went bad."

"For the horse?"

"Nah." He rips into a pack of gum and hands it to me. "For Jack. He passed out. Hit his head. His wife took him to the emergency room just in case."

Connor picks up the speed, and we're in front of Jack Anderson's stable in no time.

"Let's go check it out." He grabs things out of the compartment in the truck bed. "You're not squeamish, are you?"

"No, but I'm also not participating. I'll be moral support."

We walk into the stable, and Connor makes a beeline for the back stall, humming a little tune as he goes. Settling down beside the quarter horse, he puts on elbow-length gloves as he croons soft words for the animal. "Hey, Harry."

"Harry? That's a boy's name."

Connor inspects the animal's hind quarters. "Jack's three-year-old son named her. He didn't really know the difference." He rubs his hand over the horse. "That's a girl. Hang in there, sweetheart."

"You like this, don't you?" I move back as he adjusts to get a better view.

His eyes, so intense, so direct, meet mine. "I *love* this. Helping people. Saving animals. I can't imagine doing anything else." With a frown, he checks the horse again. "Maggie, in my bag there's a flashlight. Move nice and slow and grab that please." He caresses the horse's coat. "Harry, my intern here is going to help us out. She's an okay girl, I guess. Kind of hardheaded. A little bit of a snob."

I hand him the light. "Harry, Dr. Blake hasn't had a lot of experience with women." Though that kiss blows that theory out of the water. "So don't listen to him. The closest he got to a girl in high school was the Princess Leia figurine in his Star Wars collection."

Connor's forehead wrinkles, and his entire focus is on the horse. "Come a little closer and shine that light on the business end."

I swallow back apprehension and do what he says. I'm really not into this kind of thing. I don't even watch Animal Planet.

"Harry, I'm going in."

At the sight of Connor's gloved hand easing into the horse, I turn my head and stare at the opposite wall. Ew!

"Just about got it." He mumbles encouragement to the struggling horse. "You're doing awesome, Harry. What a good girl. Almost done. You okay up there, Maggie?"

"Uh-huh." I press my lips together. "Great."

"Cause you look a little green. Might be the dim lighting, though."

Connor returns to humming, and I try to focus on that. And not the gooshy sounds from the horse. My stomach does a full rotation.

"What's going on down there?" I ask.

"Why don't you look and see?"

"Harry needs her privacy."

"Foals have to come out feet first. But this one has a leg caught. Just gonna"—he gives a grunt of his own—"try and pull it out. Easy, girl. Hang in there."

The horse moans. "Is she okay?"

"Could be better. Need some more light."

At that, I brave a look. Connor's face is strained, the fine lines around his eyes tightened as he focuses on his task.

Connor reaches in deeper. "Got it. Gonna help you pull this baby out, Harry. Work with me."

After a few heart-stopping moments, the hooves appear. Then thin, fragile legs. And finally the head. And tons of other stuff I try not to look at.

Finally the baby is delivered into Connor's strong arms. Tears gather in my eyes. *Lord, you make the coolest things. I am in awe.*

Connor rests the foal beside its mother, who immediately goes to licking. "Good job, girl."

"She did do great," I say on a relieved sigh.

"I meant you." He stands up, a grin splitting his face. "For a second there, I thought I was going to have two patients. You ready for part two?"

I blink. "There's more?"

He slips off his gloves. "Yeah. Mrs. Button made me a strawberry pie when I set her cat's broken leg yesterday. Come back to my house and have some."

"I can't. I need to—"

"Get home. Right." Connor looks unimpressed. "You're still on the job as a vet. And eating other people's baked goods in lieu of payment is just part of it." He gives the horse another glance. "I spared you the hard part."

"The gross part."

"I'm proud of you, Maggie. You were a big help."

"Anything for a girl named Harry." In the muted light of the stable, Connor holds my gaze until I feel my cheeks glow pink. "Your dream girl probably wouldn't have helped you tonight."

"No?"

I shake my head. "She'd be home. Watching PBS and getting a head start on her yearly Christmas letter."

Against my better judgment, I find myself being driven to his house.

"Did you always want to be a vet?" I ask.

"Except for a brief stint where I entertained the idea of being a ninja, yes. I grew up helping my dad. I practically lived at the clinic. I always knew I'd take over the practice."

"Was it expected?"

"No. My parents raised my sister and me to be whatever we wanted."

My dad raised me to be a neurotic stress ball.

"Whatever I would've chosen, I would've had my parents approval. But Ivy's exactly where I wanted to be." His eyes slide toward me. "Not like you, I guess."

"Where are we?" The question comes out with a little squeak.

But as the trees grow thicker along the road, dread completes the picture. "You live on the lake?"

He turns onto Lakeview Drive. "Yeah. I love it out here. I have a great view. And it's only about five minutes from the clinic."

We pass three houses before Connor pulls the truck into the driveway of a two-story modern log cabin. Lights glow all around in the landscaping and from the large wraparound porch. Tidy shrubs mingle with flowers and decorative rocks.

He nudges my knee. "You ready?"

I can do this. It's not like he's asking me to go *in* the lake, for crying out loud. Just because I haven't been out here since that night my life fell apart doesn't mean I can't handle it. I am tough. I am woman. I held a flashlight during a foal's birth.

Connor unlocks his front door and holds it wide open with his hip. "Make yourself at home." He throws on some lights. "Give me ten minutes to shower and change."

"This better not be the point where you come out wearing something more comfortable."

"You wish." He tosses me the remote, then hustles upstairs.

Log beams hold up the tall ceiling above me. A stone fireplace takes up most of one living room wall and stands ready to warm up the entire cozy home. I pad across the shiny oak floors and collapse onto one of the oversized leather couches. Flicking on the TV, it soon becomes a drone in my ear as my head lolls back into the cushions. Grabbing a burgundy throw pillow, I wrap my arms around it, burrow deeper, and close my eyes.

My own scream wakes me up. I fight with a blanket, desperate to get it off my body.

"Maggie." My eyes struggle to focus as Connor's hands shake my shoulders. "Maggie, wake up."

I shoot to a sitting position, my chest heaving in ragged

breaths. Dragging my knees up, I rest my head on them and just try to gather my wits.

His hand caresses the back of my head. "You okay? I was just coming to check on you when I heard you yelling."

I sniff and pull together a smile. "I'm fine." My laugh is nervous, forced. "It was just one of my mom's little visits again." *Lord, swallow me up now. How embarrassing.* "Really, I'm okay." My mother. She was there. Again.

The couch sinks as Connor settles beside me, his leg against mine. "Want to tell me about it?"

"It's nothing." But this *nothing* is consuming my life. I'm afraid to go to sleep. I've been watching TV until the wee hours of the morning just to avoid it. And I'm nights away from succumbing to those infomercials and buying a Boflex, hair removal cream, and a magical potato peeler.

"You called out for her," he says quietly.

I shrug and offer a wobbly smile. "I'm fine." I hold up a corner of the plaid blanket. "Where'd this come from?" How long was I out? Was I snoring? Drooling?

"I covered you up about thirty minutes ago. When I came down from my shower, you were passed out."

My face flames with instant heat. "I'm usually a little more fun on a date."

His heavy gaze drops to my mouth, then slowly travels back to my eyes. "Is that what this is? A date?"

"No! Not a date. Totally not a date. Just you, me, dinner, drunk Debra, the band, one dance, no dessert, some horse business, my nap, and you taking me home." I pause for a breath. "Definitely *not* a date."

A lock of my hair flutters out of place, and I watch as Connor's fingers reach out. Feel his whisper touch on my ear as he tucks it in place, his hand sliding down the length of my curls. Electricity snaps between us as time suspends. Chill bumps race up and down my skin. Though he's inches away, I can't seem to move.

"Good thing." His voice is low, hypnotic. "Because if this were a date, I'd probably have to kiss you at this point."

"Yeah." I can't take my eyes off his. "I wouldn't want that."

"You did seem a little rusty last time."

"Rusty? I am not—"

With a laugh, his mouth captures mine. "Why can't I leave you alone?"

I twine my arms around his neck. "Wish you would." And then I prove just the opposite, allowing myself to fall into his strong embrace, letting his mouth settle over mine.

My fingers thread through his thick hair as I press my face closer to his, change the angle of the kiss, and let passion weave its way into the locked-tight spaces of my heart.

Long moments pass before Connor pulls away, resting his lips above my eyes, rubbing them across my temple, then drawing me in for a hug. I wrap my arms tightly around his back and feel the slow, lazy circles he rubs against my shirt.

And as my pulse begins to recede, reality seeps back in. This cannot be happening. I don't have time for this. Why now? Why this man?

His gentle fingers massage the base of my neck, keeping me tucked tight. "We should probably slow things down. I'm a guy with boundaries."

Dude, I live and die by boundaries. "That makes two of us."

"At least we agree on something," comes his low reply.

He keeps up the gentle caress, and my eyes shut with each relaxing sweep of his hand.

"Want to tell me about the dream?"

"No." I don't want to talk. Don't want to move. I feel like if I stayed here forever I could actually sleep. Could feel safe. Sheltered from everything that presses down on me.

"Do it anyway."

I try to lift my head, but he won't let me go. I can feel the curling of his smile against my cheek as he shifts, sitting back into the couch and settling my body under his arm.

Somehow in the warmth of his arms, with his sharp gaze not on mine, the words spill out, like water trickling from a swollen brook. I can see her face even now, my mother's hand reaching out to me. "I'm standing on the pier down by the lake. And I can't get to her. She's in the water, waiting for me to help her." I tell him the rest, not sparing him a single detail. And when I'm done, instead of feeling like an idiot, like I've vomited up the craziness of my life, all I feel is relief.

"I've never told a soul all that," I whisper. Not sure why I did just now. But it doesn't seem wrong.

The seconds tick by as I wait for Connor's response. Finally he presses a kiss to the top of my head. "Thanks for telling me. I'll pray that you get the closure you need and can let this go." And he does. Right there and then.

At his amen, the thoughts still bubble to the surface. "Sometimes I think my mom is trying to tell me something. Or maybe God's wanting my attention."

"Maybe."

I duck out of his arms and scoot to the end of the couch, facing him. "I think I'm here for a reason—in Ivy."

Connor tucks his leg under the other and angles his body my way. "Are you ready to face what happened that night?"

"I think making sure Riley's provided for is that closure I need."

"But what if it's finding out the truth of your mom's death?"

"No." I shake my head, my throat thickening. "I don't think so."

His hand reaches out, slides across my calf, gives it a light squeeze. "You sure do have the world fooled. Isn't it tiring to keep up this tough-girl routine?"

I pull away from his touch, my tone cracking with fire. "What is that supposed to mean?"

Connor throws an arm around the back of the couch, an A&M T-shirt stretching taut across the hard planes of his chest. "You're so transparent, you're see-through."

Gone is my seductive, dark-haired angel. Now he's a doctor, lecturing a client on not taking care of a pet. "Everything's big about you—your job, your pastimes. And you use it, Maggie. You use it to send out a message to everyone who gets close to you that you're not afraid of anything. You can scale a mountain. You can travel the globe. You're always up for a good time, as long as it's dangerous and gets your adrenaline pumping. And as long as you can fly away for a few weeks afterward."

I unclench my jaw. "That's not an act."

"Isn't it?" He stands up, disappears into the kitchen, then returns with two glasses of water. He hands one to me, but remains standing. "Everything you do is surface level. When you get right down to it, I don't know if I've met anyone more afraid of life."

With a gasp, I shoot to my feet. "I *love* my life. You've only been around me a few times and suddenly you're an expert?"

His eyes pierce mine. "I know you, Maggie. And that terrifies you."

"I need to go." I bend down and reach for my purse.

"You don't even have the guts to talk this out."

"What's there to discuss?" My volume climbs. "You seem to

have this all figured out. Why don't you just type up a summary and e-mail it to me. Save us both some time."

"Your water phobia, your mother's death, your sister, even your relationship with your father. You're running from it all. You'd go hang gliding off a cliff at midnight if I asked you to, but your personal demons—those are the things that really bring you to your knees."

I take a step toward the door. "Do I need to call Beth to pick me up? A taxi? Take off walking?" Should only take me all night.

"If you leave Ivy without resolving this, it's never going to go away—the nightmares, your wanderlust—"

"I'm leaving now."

"And what about all the people you left behind in this town? Friends?"

"What about them? Are you seriously going to blame me for losing touch with people from twelve years ago? Would you like to blame the economic downturn of the town on me as well?"

"You're disconnected. Distant. You're scared to death of investing in anyone. And *that's* why you had no relationship with Riley. Not because your sister kept her from you."

My throat tightens. "That's not fair."

"We fight for the things we care about. And you let Riley go. It was too easy to stay away."

"I've already said how much I regret—"

"I know, Maggie." Those compassionate eyes hold me in place. "But what else are you staying away from? You've come a long way with Riley, and you're helping her face her ghosts. But now it's time to deal with yourself."

"And what about you, Mr. I-Want-to-Marry-June-Cleaver?"

"She's a little old—"

"You've got this checklist for your ideal woman. Well, you know what? As long as we're offering unsolicited advice, I've got news for you—Miss Perfect is going to bore you. And who can measure up to your impossible standards anyway?"

His lips quirk. "Are you saying you're trying?"

"In your nerdy little dreams."

"Strange." Connor steps closer until he's a touch away. "You're just passing through. So why does it sound like you care?"

"I don't. But Danielle Chapel does." My cheeks lift in a grin. "And by the way, she's the *definition* of high maintenance."

A frown mars Connor's brow. "What does Danielle have to do with any of this?"

"I was in her office when she accepted your date for Friday evening."

He rolls his eyes. "I had promised her months ago to attend a fund-raiser gala."

"I don't care." I hold up a hand. "I seriously do not care. Maybe you can analyze Danielle the whole night and list her every shortcoming. It seems to be a big turn-on for you."

"You are ridiculously complicated."

"So obviously we'd never work."

He grins. "Obviously." And then I'm in his arms again, crushed against his chest. His mouth descends on mine, blocking out my angry protest. He kisses me until I can't breathe. Can't think.

And then he steps away, calm as you please, his face impassive. Reaching into his pocket he pulls out his keys. "Something else to keep you up tonight."

He holds open the door, and I pass by him with a glare that could evaporate Ivy Lake. "That will be the last time that happens."

Connor's infuriating laugh follows me outside. "You keep telling yourself that, Maggie Montgomery. You keep telling yourself that."

Chapter Twenty-One

"Saturday morning at the spa." Beth admires her flamingo-pink nails as a woman wraps a chunk of hair in foil. "Just the thing to make my world a better place." She beams at me. "Thanks so much, Maggie. After all the work I've put on you, this is the last thing I deserve."

"Would that be the reunion work or the countless times you've deliberately put Connor Blake in my path?"

In front of us her oldest two daughters and Riley soak in a foot-bath up to their ankles, giggling and sharing little-girl secrets. My niece—finally acting her age.

Beth laughs. "I don't know what you're talking about. But I saw Connor yesterday when I stopped in at the clinic, and he was in quite the bad mood." Her eyes cut to me. "Would you know anything about that?"

"Maybe he missed Shark Week on the Discovery Channel." Despite the stylist's frown, I train my video camera on the girls.

"Uh-huh."

"How's the job search going for Mark?"

Beth lowers her voice so the girls can't hear. "There's just nothing in Ivy. And the plant's already talking about cutting twenty percent of second shift, so the odds of Mark getting back on there even temporarily are about as good as him winning Mr. America. Plus, who wants to be hired on at a sinking ship?"

The stylist clips at my hair, touching up the layers around my face. "I'm really sorry."

"Hey, none of that. God's in control. That is the only thing Mark and I *are* sure of." Her dark eyes sparkle. "He blessed me with this unexpected gift today."

"How can you not be scared, Beth? With the economy the way it is, four children, a house payment." I know later I'll regret reminding her of her bleak picture, but for now, I just let the words roll. "I have no idea how you stay so joyful and positive."

"It's like Pastor Thomas said at church Wednesday night: when Jesus called Peter out of the boat and onto the water, Peter was doing fine. Until he took his eyes off the Lord and focused on the wind. Then that boy went straight south. That's like Mark and me. It's too easy to take our eyes off God and start focusing on the bills, the shoes the girls need, the groceries. I don't want to sink. I want the grand prize, you know? I want to know the thrill of stepping out onto the water or whatever it is God's got planned for my family."

Images, thoughts, memories scroll through my mind. "Do you ever just falter—get scared? Do you ever have those moments?"

She quirks a brow. "Are we still talking about Mark's job?"

I nod, a little too eagerly.

Beth closes her eyes as the woman paints color onto her hair. "Sure, I have those moments where I get overwhelmed. But then I just remind myself that when Peter sank, the first thing God did was swoop out his big hand and pull him up." She laughs. "Jesus has to pull me up just about every day."

"I know it must be hard." I think about my mother's death, my gifted ability to not stay in a committed relationship, my desire to take that video footage on my computer and make something of it. And Riley. I still have no idea what to do with her. I feel like she needs me, but I can't just stick around indefinitely. Yesterday I hired a tutor from the local college. She'll start when I leave, taking my place beside Riley and the homework at the dining room table. Now to find a nanny.

"What's hard is not having that hope," Beth says. "I can't imagine going through bad times without that peace. Without that surrender, life just eats you up. Spits you out. Wears you down to nothing. You know what I'm saying?"

"Yeah, I—"

"Josie, you hit your sister one more time, I'm gonna knock you upside the head with this lady's blow-dryer. Yes, ma'am, I'm looking at you. Don't you make me get up from this chair." Beth reclines back in her seat and shuts her eyelids again. "What was I talking about? Oh yeah—keeping your peace. So important."

Later Beth and I sit in the pedicure chairs as the three girls get their hair cut and styled.

Riley eyes me in the mirror as the stylist combs through her wet locks. "If I come out looking like a French poodle, I'll never speak to you again."

"Like you could go two minutes without talking," I say. "Besides, thanks to me you don't have to ride the bus."

"Thanks to you, I eat Twinkies and Cool Ranch Doritos every day in my sack lunch."

Every mother in the joint stops and stares in astonishment. "What?" I throw up my hands. "So I've got a little bit of work to do in the nutrition department. It hasn't hurt her yet."

Riley leans over to Josie. "Actually, all the chemicals in the processed foods she gives me makes me violent." Her stage whisper can probably be heard all the way to the massage rooms in back. "I get in trouble all the time at school, and it's not even my fault."

"Oh, somebody's gonna get *her* peace. When she eats bean sprouts and tofu every day for the rest of her fourth-grade year."

Our eyes meet in the mirror, and Riley's tough-girl pout pulls into a smile. Then a giggle. I laugh with my niece, wanting to hold on to this memory and etch it on my heart forever.

Riley's eyes widen as something comes to mind. "Oh, Mrs. Ellis said she wanted to meet with you Tuesday. About the costumes for the play."

"Costumes?"

"Yeah, remember the ones you said you'd take care of?"

Completely blocked that out of my mind. "Um . . . yeah. I'm totally on it."

"You forgot about it, didn't you?"

I flop my hand in dismissal. "I'm so sure. Like I'm dumb enough to do that." I am so dumb enough to do that.

"I know that look." Beth waits until Riley is enmeshed in conversation with the girls again. "That's the look you got before you painted the water tower pink or freed the rival team's mascot."

"Yeah, and somebody should've told me it was a *real* skunk."

"That wild-eyed look is what you get when you're in a panic."

I prop my elbow on the armrest. "I have to come up with twenty-five costumes. Mrs. Ellis wants Gucci outfits on a garage sale budget."

"You can borrow my sewing machine. That'd probably be the easiest thing."

"Me?" I bark with laughter. "Sew? I can't even make boxed mac and cheese without something going horribly wrong. Maybe I can find something on eBay or in some thrift shops."

"How much time do you have?"

"About two and a half weeks."

"You're dead."

"See!" I drop my head into my hand. "It's hopeless. And Riley's counting on me."

"You know, with Mark home more, I've got some extra time," Beth says. "I could help."

"Are you serious?" I grab her hand and hold it tight. "You would do that for me?"

Beth's lips part in a giant smile. "Gotta take your eye off the wind, girl. Worry makes you sink. But hope?" She holds out her feet for the pedicurist. "Hope gets you twenty-five hand-sewn costumes."

We topped the day off with lunch at local pizza place, where the girls showed off their nails to everyone who walked by. And though Riley pretended to be completely unimpressed with her haircut, I caught her reaching her hand up to feel her short new bob more than once.

On the ride home, I'm totally jamming out to some Carrie Underwood, taking the solo as loud as I can.

Riley holds her polished fingers over her ears. "You're killing my brain cells!"

"Dare you to sing along." I crank up the volume.

"No. That's stupid."

"Bet you can't do it."

"What do I get if I do?"

I take a moment to play drums on the steering wheel. "After dinner, we'll do whatever you want. Movies, games, go for ice cream."

"Deal."

And I watch in amazement as my niece not only sings along but adds hand motions and wonderfully awful facial expressions. She continues her Vegas lounge act through the next two songs. I provide backup as she belts out the lead.

Bored by the time we hit the Ivy city limits, Riley comes up with another plan. "Hey, let's go see the puppy. I haven't seen her in a while."

"You were just there yesterday."

"But Matilda misses me." Riley messes with her seat belt. "She gets scared there all by herself. She needs to be reminded that someone cares about her."

"She has Dr. Blake."

"It's not the same. I like her the best."

Riley turns her big, Precious Moments eyes on me, and I'm lost. "We'll try. But it's two o'clock. The clinic closes at noon on Saturday, so I doubt anyone will even be around." At least I hope not. Maybe one of the kennel cleaners will be, and we can get in.

"Let me call him."

"Let's not."

"He said I could call and talk to him anytime. He's so nice."

I grip the steering wheel. "Isn't he though."

We arrive at the Ivy Lake Animal Clinic and find Connor walking out to the lone truck in the parking lot. Squinting his eyes against the sun, he throws up a hand in greeting.

Riley waves back like he's the adult equivalent of a Jonas Brother. She shoots out of the car before I can even get the key out.

"Hey, Connor!" she yells.

At what point did he stop being Dr. Blake? Does everyone just instantly fall for this guy? That would explain the confidence he wears like cologne.

He pulls her into a quick side hug, and she doesn't even squirm. That rat fink, double-crossing vet. Does he think he can lure her over to his side with his friendly demeanor and little needy dog? Yeah, well, I have a purse full of gum and other teeth-rotting delights, and I'm not afraid to use them.

"Hello, Maggie." Connor's smoldering eyes fall on me, and I have to look away.

"Riley just wanted to check on Matilda. But obviously you're busy, so we'll come back another time."

"Busy? Never too busy for Riley. Come on in. Matilda's been asking for you."

Riley spins to face me. "See. She's probably been crying. I was needed."

I have to smile at that. "You're needed all right."

I look up to find Connor watching me. My skin warms, as I remember those full lips on mine. His strong arms around me. *No! Stop thinking about it. What is* wrong *with me?*

He sends me a knowing wink, breaking the moment, causing a blush to spread across my cheeks. That boy knew exactly where my mind was. Shouldn't he be winking at some prim, sweet thing who loves nothing more than using her Crock Pot and avoiding drama in her well-ordered life?

"This way, ladies." He leads us through the clinic doors, weaving Riley a tale about the many friends Matilda has made.

"She's grown so much in the last few days!" Riley squeals as she gets her hands on the puppy. "Hey, Matilda. How you doing?"

"You can put her on the floor," Connor says. "Let her show you her new moves."

As if the tiny cocker spaniel is made of the finest glass, my niece carefully lowers Matilda to the tile. The puppy promptly falls on her butt, and Riley goes for it with a gasp.

"Leave her alone for a second," Connor says. "Have a little faith in the girl."

The puppy takes her time, sniffing the floor, scratching her ear. Then finally, on three wobbly legs, she takes three awkward steps toward Riley. Then three more.

"She did it!" Riley scoops up the dog and presses her to her cheek. "You did it, Matilda!"

Connor moves beside me, his voice low. "You're not crying, are you?"

I sniff and blink back the sheen of moisture. "Nah." I so need a Kleenex. And my camera. "It's strange, but anymore I just live for these moments. Where my niece is happy. Completely, lost-in-the-moment happy." My sigh blows my bangs off my forehead. "Why am I telling you this?"

He just smiles.

Before I can toss out a barb to take the edge off that infuriating arrogance, he walks back to Riley.

"I like your new haircut, Riley."

My niece glows under Connor's compliment, but keeps her focus on the dog. "Thanks. Maggie took me to a day at the spa." She shrugs. "It was okay."

Okay? How many times have I caught that girl looking at herself in the mirror?

"You've got an awesome aunt," he says.

"She feeds me Hot Pockets."

He looks at me and lifts an eyebrow. "I'm sorry, Riley. Sounds like you're in need of a good meal then. How about you and your aunt come out to my house tonight? We're having a family fish fry. You can even bring some friends."

"No," I'm quick to say. "We've already got plans."

"But—"

"Sorry," I interrupt my niece and cap it off with an innocent smile. "Maybe another time." Like never.

Riley crosses her arms. "You said I got to pick whatever we did tonight. You promised."

She lays her cards out like a Texas Hold 'Em champ. "I meant ice cream or—"

"Never mind." She picks the dog up and nuzzles it to her cheek. "Go ahead. Go back on your word. I'm used to people doing that."

Connor looks at me as if to say, *Do you want to beat the dog while you're at it?*

"Fine. I'm sorry. You're right, Riley. I—"

"Yes!" She punches her fist in the air, her face totally triumphant.

I just got had by one short scam artist. "But I'll just drop you off for a bit. I have work to do."

Connor nudges my niece. "I don't think that was what you wanted, was it?"

"No," she says. "Is a little quality time together too much?"

He gives his head a sorrowful shake. "*I* sure don't think so. But there will be plenty of adults at my house who'll be glad to spend time with you."

"Okay, fine! I'll go." It's like tag-team harassment. "But we can't stay long."

Riley's face is as solemn as a funeral mourner. "I'll be happy with whatever bit of time with you I can get."

I make a leap for her, snaking my arm around her neck and tickling her ribs with my other hand. "You are so full of it." She collapses into me, her giggles filling the room.

The puppy's small *yip* brings us all back to attention. "Oh, she's so cute, isn't she?" Riley says wistfully. "What will you do with her when she's healed?"

Connor bends down and rubs the dog's silky head. "Actually, I have a family interested in taking her next week."

"What?" Riley's face pales. "No. You can't. She won't know them."

I rest my hand on her back. "You knew you couldn't keep the dog."

She shrugs away from me. "That is so unfair! Nobody's gonna love Matilda more than me. She needs me. She needs someone to love her."

My heart crumbles into a million pieces. Riley might as well be talking about herself. "I'm sorry. But you can visit her until she goes to live with the new family."

Tears stream down her cheeks. "It's not the same. Matilda needs a real home—with me." She dashes her hand across her face. "I'm going outside." She hands the wiggling puppy to Connor and runs out, the sound of her growing sobs making me want to grab my niece and promise her the moon, the stars, and every dog in the universe.

I stare at the door. "That was a mood spoiler."

"Riley's really attached to the dog. She's taken great care of her when she comes in to help."

"It has been good for her."

The dog licks Connor's finger, and he scratches beneath her chin. "Have you asked your dad if Riley can keep Matilda?"

"That's pointless. He'd never let her have a pet. He hates animals." And most people. And most family members.

"You could try."

"No, I couldn't. And I'm not. I know the man. Besides, we don't have any idea where Riley will be in six months. Who's to say she'll be living with my dad then? If my sister can't handle a child, she sure can't handle a child *and* a cocker spaniel."

Connor steps closer, and I can't stop my hand from reaching out and petting the dog. "What will you do if your sister can't take care of Riley? Do you and your father have any plans in place?"

"Panic?"

But the good doctor doesn't so much as crack a smile. "I know you'll make the right decision."

"Why is it I feel like you're waiting for me to come to some big epiphany? And that anything less than taking Riley home with me is what you're waiting for me to say?"

"You have to do what God puts on your heart. Either way, it's going to take a lot of guts."

I huff and roll my eyes. "Which you don't think I have. Well, thank you, Dr. Phil. I appreciate the parenting advice. If only it were that easy for the rest of us." I walk toward the door, my shoes slapping the tile.

It's hard to make a dramatic exit when you're wearing flip-flops.

"See you at six. Come hungry."

"Yeah." I stand in the entryway. "Thanks for manipulating me, by the way. Nothing like forcing a girl to hang out with you."

He places the dog back in the cage. "Wear something hot."

Chapter Twenty-Two

Riley slams the door as we walk into the house. Her Cons pound on the stairs as she runs to her bedroom.

"Something wrong?" Dad asks from his recliner.

I take a seat on the couch and let my head fall back. "She's just getting attached to that puppy at the vet clinic. But other than that, we had a really good day." I tell him all about our adventures at the spa with Beth and her girls. "Riley was great with Beth's daughters. Totally behaved herself. She laughed the whole day." Well, until Connor's news pushed her over the edge.

He flips the page on his *Field & Stream*. "She cares about you."

His words hang in the air, weighted, searching. Like he wants those four words to stand for a hundred. Why can't men just say what they mean? I guess Connor does, but he's different. Sometimes I'd rather he didn't talk at all.

"I care about Riley." I stare at a petal-shaped crack in the ceiling. "What are we going to do about her?"

Dad turns another page. "We wait and see what Allison does."

"Dad, you've been playing this game for years. Allison hasn't straightened up yet. And Riley's the one suffering."

"You think I don't know that?" His eyes peer over the magazine. "I'm doing the best I can."

Isn't that the same thing I told Connor? But hearing it out of my dad's lips, I know—it's not enough. "Riley needs consistency. She needs to know where she sleeps tonight is where she'll sleep tomorrow night."

"Well, you're the smart one." He reaches for the remote and flicks on the TV. "When you get it figured out, let me know. In the meantime, I guess I'll just keep doing what I'm doing."

"And what's the plan when I go back home? I leave Monday for my interview with National Geographic. If they offer me a position, I could start in a few weeks."

He scrolls through the stations, stopping at a John Wayne movie. Ignoring me.

"Nice talking to you," I mumble and get up from my seat. "Riley and I will be going to Connor Blake's for dinner."

He keeps his eyes on the Duke. "We can ride together then."

I nearly fall out of my flip-flops. "What do you mean?" Foreboding prickles my skin.

"Connor called just before you came in the door. Invited me to join his family fish fry." Dad pulls a lever and props his feet up. "Nice guy. Told us to be there at six. Said to tell you to take a nap so you wouldn't still be cranky." Dad chuckles, and it takes me a moment to realize he's not laughing at the movie. He's laughing at me. Like he and Connor have this secret joke. And it's nothing to share fish and hush puppies together. Connor *knows* I don't want to hang around my dad. If there was any perk at all to going to this stupid outing, it's that it gets me away from the house. Ohhh. There better be pie there.

Upstairs, I sit on the bed and pull out my laptop. Opening my documentary file, I edit for a few minutes before shutting it down and signing on to Facebook instead.

God, every time I look at these faces in my video footage, I feel as lost as they are. Defeated. I can't be a documentarian. Who am I kidding? I run a camera. For other people. I have a great job with Passport to the World. *What kind of ungrateful person couldn't be satisfied with that? Sometimes I look back at the events that make up my life, and I wonder if I'll ever be happy with anything. At some point, I've got to quit trying to prove myself . . . and just live.*

At a quarter 'til six, I join Riley and Dad in the living room.

"Grandpa's going with us." Riley opens the front door, her sour mood a distant memory. "Isn't that cool? And I called Josie and Zoey."

Neato. "Let's go get your friends." And like one awkward, ill-fitting family, we get in my car, buckle up as if we're perfectly normal, and go to a fish fry.

The girls chat the entire way, as Dad listens to baseball on the radio. And me? I keep the lid on an anxiety attack as we drive closer to the very lake that swallowed up the only parent who loved me.

My stress accelerates as I pull into Connor's driveway. Apparently this man has one big family, because I count at least twenty vehicles.

As soon as I open the car door, I hear the bluegrass music. I tug up the top of my hot-pink sundress and wish for the millionth time I'd put on that little white jacket. Dad, Riley, and I follow the music to the backyard, where I see practically the whole town of Ivy. Kids run all over the place, throwing Frisbees, firing squirt guns. A group of adults toss a ball across a volleyball net. Men gather around a smoker, surveying the steam rising, as any self-respecting man would do.

"Hello there!" A woman who could be Cinderella as a senior citizen greets us, her blonde-highlighted hair bouncing in a style worthy of any Hollywood starlet. "I'm Mary Katherine."

"Hi." I introduce my father and the girls. "We're, um . . . that is

. . ." I can't even talk. The crowd is totally overwhelming me. So many people. "Connor invited us. Family dinner?"

She laughs, her vibrant blue eyes crinkling at the corners. "That's Connor. Everyone's family to him."

Danielle Chapel's words float back through my mind. How Connor picks up helpless strays. Maybe that's what I've become to him. Just a friend in his giant collection. Someone in need. But does he typically make out with good buddies?

"What beautiful girls you are," Mary Katherine says. "Look at your pretty nails." She inspects the hands of each girl. "And you must tell me where you get your hair done." The girls giggle and let the woman fawn all over them. "What a gorgeous dress," she says to Josie.

"My mom made it."

Beth is such a superwoman. In Chicago, all I do is work. I don't even clean my own apartment. But Beth sews, works, raises four kids, and is about the most chipper person I know.

It's disgusting.

Dad waves at some men playing horseshoes. "I'll see you in a bit. I'm feeling lucky."

Mary Katherine leans down, her hands perched on her knees. "Girls, if you go over to that picnic table over there, I have it on good authority there's some excellent lemonade to be had."

Riley gives me a cautious look, as if asking permission. "Go on. I'll catch up with you." The three all but skip away. "Don't drink out of the pitchers!" I laugh at the woman's face. "My niece is a little unpredictable."

She winks. "I used to know a girl like that."

I frown. "Excuse me?"

"I worked at the Ivy Drug store years and years ago—back when they still had one of those old-time soda fountains. Your momma would come in and bring you and your sister at least once a week. She'd buy you candy and shakes and let you spin on the bar stools until you were about ready to puke up your ice cream."

Warmth blooms in my chest. "You knew my mother?"

"I don't know that anyone *knew* her. But we all were familiar with her. While she took care of business in the drug store, you'd stir up some trouble of your own. Unscrew salt shakers. Do cart-wheels down the aisles. Talk Mrs. Brewster into letting you try out her cane. Seems like we had to peel you out of the front seat of the delivery car once or twice."

A rush of memories floods my mind. "I had forgotten all about that place. We were in there a lot, weren't we? Probably where my sugar addiction was born." That drug store is long gone. I think there's a bank in its place.

"Will you be staying in Ivy long?" She hooks a strand of hair behind her ears, setting the gold bangles on her wrist in motion.

My eyes roam toward Riley. "I don't know. I'm probably here for a few more weeks. I have some details to settle before I go. Chicago's where I live now."

Her face goes wistful, like she sees something more in me. "Sometimes home has a way of calling you back." Mary Katherine reaches out and pats my shoulder. "I hope you get everything taken care of."

A man with a full head of silver hair approaches. His smile is contagious, and I find myself returning it.

"William, this is Maggie—Connor's friend." Mary links her arm in William's. "Maggie, this is my husband."

"Nice to meet you." He shakes my hand enthusiastically. "We think a lot of Connor Blake."

"Do you know him well?"

Mary laughs. "Yes, he takes really good care of our poodle. Oh,

I was supposed to bring ketchup outside to the picnic tables." She flutters a hand toward the back door. "Would you be a dear and go get that for me?"

"Sure."

Her pink smile is winsome. "I hope to see you again."

I slide open the screened back door and step into Connor's gourmet kitchen. With his back to me, he stands at the stove, a huge skillet of fish frying on the burner. I take a moment to appreciate the view. His broad, strong back. His slightly faded jeans matched perfectly with a gray Abercrombie T-shirt.

He turns around at that very moment. His eyes light on mine, and he smiles.

"Hey." I stop staring and make a beeline for the fridge. "Um, some woman named Mary Katherine sent me in here for ketchup." Sticking my head in the door somewhere between some potato salad and a Jell-O mold, I let my face cool off.

Connor says nothing as I scan the shelves. No ketchup. Maybe it's in a cabinet. "Hey, where's your"—I spin around and bump right into his chest. My hands brace on him for support—"ketchup?"

Not moving an inch out of my space, he peeks around me. "I don't see it anywhere." His mouth sits near my ear, his breath sending a frisson of heat across my skin.

I slide to the left to get some distance. "Don't let me get in your way."

Shutting the refrigerator door, Connor watches me as he returns to the sizzling pan. "Mary Katherine, you say?"

"Yes. Blonde woman. Ridiculously beautiful."

The corners of his mouth kick up in a smile as he flips a fish. "I'll tell Mom you said so."

Oh. Well, of course. "So . . . the ketchup?"

"It's already out there. She took it out about half an hour ago."

"Maybe she wanted something else."

I hear him mumble something that sounds like "more grandchildren."

"I'll, um, just go on outside."

He scoops up the fish and piles it on a blue Fiesta plate. "I'm glad you're here."

"I don't like to see desperation in a man, so what choice did I have?"

Connor balances the plate on one hand, kissing my cheek as he walks by. "Pride is overrated."

"So are overly confident vets." I rub my cheek with my fingers. "Why did you do that?"

He shrugs, his face serious. "I have no idea." With his hand on the screen door, he pauses. "Maggie, you're here. Enjoy the evening. Eat some fish. You can't solve any of the world's problems tonight, so just relax and try to have a good time instead."

"You invited my dad." My voice is toneless.

"I also invited a Republican county judge and our Democratic sheriff." Connor shrugs. "That's the fun of being in charge of the guest list."

He walks outside, calling out to some friends, and leaves me standing alone. In his kitchen. Mulling over his weird attitude and the remnants of his cologne.

Fifteen minutes later, Connor calls for everyone's attention, and Pastor Thomas, the preacher from church, says a blessing over the food. The children go first, and I watch Riley weigh down her plate as she talks to Josie and her sister, Zoey, plus a few kids I've never seen before.

After dinner, a group of old men pick up some stringed instruments and their music floats through the air. Pastor Thomas starts another volleyball game, and though he asks me to play, I decline.

Connor watches, but doesn't say a word. Pulling my camcorder from my purse, I follow the kids and catch their every laugh and giggle.

The tiki torches are lit as the sun sets, and I find myself at odds and out of place. I don't really know anyone. I long for my laptop and a quiet house. Feeling a magnet's pull, I stand up, smoothing my skirt around me, and slip across the backyard and make the long trek to the edge of the property. To the water's edge.

A dock juts outs, bobbing slightly with the currents. The light from the house casts an eerie glow, as if warning me to stay away. Though this isn't the pier where my mother died, it's too close for comfort. The public access spot is a few miles away, and I've never returned. Never wanted to. Never could.

I wrap my hand around the metal railing and wait for my breath to slow. Resting my leather sandal on the dock, I step all the way up. And just stand there.

Water swishes all around me, quietly slapping at the sides. My stomach lurches as my sense of gravity is challenged by the motion. I hang on to the railing with both hands, clutching it until my fingers hurt.

But I can't go any farther. I can't walk to the end and look out at the water. And I'd rather strip naked and sprint across Connor's backyard than stick my legs in and let the coolness lap at my calves.

In the distance, a boat slowly sails to its destination, fearlessly surrounded by the vast lake. And I can't even move from this tiny spot. "Why can't I remember what happened that night?" I whisper in the dark, my voice shaking. "God, please help me. What's it going to take?"

But there's no answer. Just the call of a frog. The faraway motor of a boat. And once again, God says nothing.

Holding on to the rail like a lifeline, I turn around to leave.

And find Connor standing behind me.

Chapter Twenty-Three

I nearly jump out of my skin as I see him standing there. "Would you *quit* doing that?"

"What?" he asks, his hands stuffed in his pockets.

"That lurky, creepy, there-every-time-I-turn-around thing."

The comment bounces right off of him. "I couldn't find you and got worried." His eyes roam to the lake, then back to me. "You okay?"

"Yes. Just . . . relaxing. Like you told me."

"Relaxing?"

"Uh-huh." I inhale and exhale on a forced happy sigh. "I could stay here all night. So lovely." My teeth grind behind my smile.

"You want to take your hands off the rail?"

I blink. "No. I'm good." I give it a little tug. "Besides, I wanted to test its sturdiness—in case one of the kids came down here."

Connor takes another step closer. "I dare you to let go."

I fake a yawn. "I'm too tired for dares."

"You ready to hop off there then?"

"Yeah, you go on ahead, and I'll be along shortly." I tilt my head toward the sky and let my hair fall over my shoulder. "Just want to take in some nature for a moment."

"Maggie?"

I study the faint stars above me. "Yes?"

"I'm proud of you for getting this far."

He walks away, and I stare at the ground his feet just left. Loosening my hands a little, I stand for a few seconds and take one quick peek at the dark water below.

Okay, good enough.

I jump down and run the rest of the way back.

I check on Riley, who's screaming her head off in an intense game of water-gun tag. My dad sips on lemonade and lobs yet another horseshoe at a stake. Everyone is doing something. But me. I could join the volleyball game. I could squeeze into someone's conversation. I could just sit and listen to the men playing bluegrass.

I go to the kitchen instead. Give a loner a job, and she's a happy girl. The dishes sit in tall, leaning stacks on the granite countertops. I run my hand under the tap until it's hot enough to scald some caked on-baked beans, then fill the sink with soap and get to work, humming as I go. Sometimes there's just something comfortable about menial tasks. Even if it gives me prune skin.

An hour and a half later, I'm elbow deep in suds and ready to dry the last batch of dishes.

The door slides open and Connor steps inside. His hair is wind-blown, his cheeks pink from the cooling night air. "You just can't relax, can you?" He walks to me, pulls the dish towel out of my hand, and throws it on the counter. "What are you doing?"

And *he's* the one with his doctorate? "Dishes."

"Well, stop. You should be out there with everyone else."

"Not when there's baked-on grease to tackle."

He leans against the hard counter, inches away. "You are one messed-up woman, Maggie Montgomery."

"I don't know anyone out there."

"You know me."

"Too tempting to brain you with a horseshoe."

"You met my mother. My dad. There was Pastor Thomas and his family." He lists off a dozen people. "It's okay to get to know some of these folks. They're not going to hog-tie you and force you to stay in Ivy."

At that, we both fall silent.

Connor picks up a serving tray from my hands and takes it to a nearby cabinet. "Your dad and the girls went home already. My parents took them."

"Why didn't they come and find me?" I would've jumped at the chance to leave.

He shoots me a knowing smile. "I guess my mom offered first. Your dad said as long as you were with me, you could stay out an extra hour past your curfew."

"Oh, you're just oozing with charm tonight."

"Remind me of that when you're walking home."

I laugh and hand him a bowl. "You throw a good party."

"And you know this according to your view from my kitchen window?"

"Look, Connor, I'm leaving soon. There's no point in establishing connections here."

He steps forward, his face looming over mine. "You've got issues like I've got stray dogs." His forehead rests on mine as he pulls me to him. "Life's boring without people in it who care about you. Not everyone is going to suddenly leave you like your mother."

I move away. "She didn't leave. She drowned."

"Yeah, and you've been waiting for everyone in your life to disappear just as suddenly. But if you don't get attached, it won't matter as much. Won't hurt like it did all those years ago." His eyes hold me in place. "Like it still does."

"Right back at you." I reach for another towel and twist it in my hands. "You're the one who's still bitter from your last breakup."

He snorts. "Bitter's for girls. Besides, just because you don't like my plan doesn't mean it's not sound."

"Is this how you thank everyone who does your dishes?"

He grabs the towel and draws me to him. "Talk to me." His words are soft, entreating. Makes me want to spill it all—thirty years of things I've never shared with anyone. But I can't.

Desperate to break the moment, I scan the kitchen for something to focus on. I pull away and walk to the fridge. "What's this?" I point to a picture of a young child.

At first, I think he's not going to answer me. Then finally, he sighs and joins me. "That's Lutalo. He's my sponsor child from Uganda."

I run my fingers over Lutalo's one-dimensional face. "He's beautiful." I can almost hear him whispering his story to me.

"His parents both died of AIDS. He helps raise his three younger brothers and sisters. He has an uncle who watches out for him, but mostly I think he's on his own. World Vision, the organization that brought us together, came in and changed his life. They can go where I can't."

Lutalo's face smiles back at me, and once again, I feel tears press against my eyes. I don't know why. But something in his face calls to me. Begs me to look longer. "How did his life change?"

Connor moves behind me, his chest against my back. He reaches across my shoulder and lifts the boy's picture off the fridge and hands it to me. I hold it with both hands.

"They brought in a water collection system, a latrine, some agricultural help—things we totally take for granted. Then he got money to go to school. You know what he said in a letter?"

I shake my head slowly, unable to take my eyes off the picture.

"He said that in all this darkness, God showed up and brought him hope."

I turn around, my back to the fridge, so close to Connor I can feel his breath. "I . . . I have this video footage. Hours and hours of it. It would take days to watch it all." I swallow and listen to the pounding of my own heart. "I've been collecting it for the last couple of years."

He makes no move to touch me. Just watches me intently. "Of what?"

"Children. Probably close to a hundred of them. Everywhere we go on location, we see the best and the worst of a city. But normally we only show the best, the reasons to travel there. Make the place seem like paradise. But I began to notice this flip side. God just began opening my eyes to the darkness out there for all these children." I blink back tears. "Hunger, prostitution, land mines, terrorism, assault." Sniffing, I wipe at my cheeks. "But we don't show that. Who wants to see that side?"

"But you saw it. And you couldn't let it go."

I nod and look at this child's face in my hands. "Someone needs to tell their stories. They're dying to be heard—literally. And they have no one to stand up and be their voice."

His voice is soft as the evening breeze. "Then maybe that's what you do."

"I can't. I mean, I thought I was supposed to. Thought God was telling me to do something. But I've pitched it and been turned down five times. No one's interested. Even sent it to my producer, and she told me there was no market for it. She thought it was the dumbest idea ever."

Connor reaches out his hand and caresses my cheek. "You're going to let that stop you? You're Maggie the Fearless. Maggie the Bold."

I lean into his hand and give a watery smile. "We both know that isn't true. I retired those titles a long time ago."

"Maybe it's time to reclaim them."

"It's not a good time now anyway. There's so much up in the air—with Riley, with Allison."

"If this is the call God's placed on your life, you have to see where it leads." He presses a kiss to my forehead, keeps his lips there for a moment. "I believe in you. Wish you would."

"It's not that easy." I close my eyes and drag in a breath. "It's just not that easy."

"It's not supposed to be. Besides, since when have you liked easy, Miss I-climb-mountains-at-two-in-the-morning? You obviously feel strongly about this project. You have to keep looking for the right person to see your vision."

I wrap my arms around Connor and hug him close. "It's kind of hard to stay mad at you."

Connor's fingers smooth over my hair. "Go out with me, Maggie." I start to lift my head, but he puts it right back down. "You, me, dinner. No fighting. No reunion errands. No bats hanging overhead."

"I'm not the girl you're looking for. I'm never going to be that sweet domestic princess, you know."

"It's dinner."

I search his face. Is that really all it is? "I don't know, Connor. I leave Monday morning for that interview with National Geographic. Why start something we can't finish?"

"I didn't want to resort to this." He sighs deep.

"Don't say it."

"I dare you."

"That's not playing fair." I smile as I lean back and stare into his playful gaze. "Okay. Fine."

"Sunday night. There aren't any evening services this week. And you clearly need a night away from everything."

I roll my eyes and laugh. "I swear I've never shed a single tear in front of a guy before. I don't know what's wrong with me."

"I don't know whether to be honored or uncomfortable."

"Thanks, Connor." I rest my hands around his neck, like that's where they belong. "Thank you for . . . I don't know   just being you. I wish I hadn't been such a snob and had known you in high school."

The heat from his smile could light the Vegas strip. "You're not gonna start scribbling my name on your notebook or anything?"

"Um, no."

"Tattoo my name on your butt?"

"Definitely not there yet, either."

"Ask me to make out with you in the back row of the movie theater?"

"So cliché."

Connor leans in, brushes his lips across mine. "Then I guess I'll have to settle for the kitchen."

Chapter Twenty-Four

Riley studies her plate Sunday morning. "You call this breakfast?"

"Eggos? Breakfast of champions." I hold up the waffle box. "And it even has bits of blueberries in it, so don't tell me I'm not hitting some additional food groups these days."

She rolls her eyes, but I see that smile she covers with her milk glass.

Dad walks in and glances at the table. "Waffles?"

I wait for his caustic remark.

"Seems to me those would be better with eggs." He puts the paper down in his chair. "Who wants some?"

I choke on a sip of Folgers. Did he get beaned in the head with a horseshoe last night? Who is this man?

"I like mine scrambled," Riley says.

I cough and try to clear my throat. "I guess that sounds okay."

"With cheese," she adds.

"Now you're talking." We are so related.

Dad reaches below the stove and pulls out a pan. He sets it on the burner, then rubs his shoulder.

"Working six days a week is getting to you." I scurry to the bathroom and come back with some Tylenol. "Here. You should take it easy today. I don't know how you do it." My father should be fishing and puttering around like other men his age who've already put in their forty years of work.

"Thanks." He sets them aside and pours the whisked eggs into the skillet. "I don't mind working. I kind of like knowing I'll be there when the place closes down, just like I was there when it opened."

"You've worked hard, Dad. It's something to take pride in." Minus the part where you filled your every waking hour with work and left your family alone all the time.

In a few minutes, the three of us are gathered around the kitchen table, eating steaming scrambled eggs and cold toaster waffles. And somehow it tastes just right.

Riley tells us a story about Josie tripping a boy who chased her with a frog, and she and I burst into giggles. "You don't mess with Josie," she says with awe in her voice.

"Her mom was the same way. Hard to believe my motorcycle-riding best friend is now the sweetest mom in town."

Dad clears his throat and lays down the sports section. "I've been thinking about something."

"Hurts the head, doesn't it, Grandpa?"

My eyes widen, and I start to defend my niece's attempt at humor, but Dad's face splits into an uneasy smile. He reaches out and tweaks Riley's nose.

I rub my eyes and replay the image in my head. Yep, tweaked that kid's nose. What is going on here? Did I wake up in a parallel universe?

"I talked to Connor last night, and I thought I'd go pick up that puppy this afternoon."

"What?" Riley and I say at once.

"Dad, do you have a fever?" I move my hand toward his forehead, but he swats it away.

"Of course not." He studies his coffee mug. "But if the dog means that much to Riley, then she should have it."

Riley clasps her hands to her chest. "Oh, Grandpa! Do you mean it?"

"I said so, didn't I?"

"But, Dad"—my brain sputters like a dying train—"she wants to *keep* it. Forever. You know, take it with her *wherever* she goes." And we don't know where she's going to go. "And you don't like animals."

"I like animals okay."

"When they're on your plate."

"Ew." Riley scrunches up her face.

"Riley, do you want this puppy?" he asks.

"Yessss." She draws out the word like she's savoring it on her tongue.

"Then I'll go get it."

Squealing in the upper decibels, my niece leaps from her seat and throws her arms around my dad. With a small smile, he pats her back.

I guess if Jesus can help Peter walk on water, he can do a miracle in my dad too.

Because that's all that can explain this.

I help Riley with her hair, promise her ice cream after lunch to get her in a skirt, and finally, we're out the door for church.

When we get there, Riley sees Josie in the lobby. As I shake a deacon's hand, my niece hesitantly approaches Beth's oldest daughter. Riley contemplates her shoes as Josie finishes her conversation with another girl. Yet when she sees Riley, Josie's face splits into a wide grin and she pulls my niece to her in a big hug. The two dissolve into giggles. As they walk toward children's church, Riley looks back over her shoulder and waves good-bye.

"What a difference a few weeks make."

I turn around and find Connor standing near.

Glancing back at my niece, I can't help but smile. "She's slowly learning not everyone is going to reject her."

His eyes level on me. "Good lesson to learn."

I quickly change the subject. "Why'd you ask my father about the dog?"

"Why didn't *you* ask him?"

"I told you."

Connor's fixed smile is a sharp contrast to his challenging tone. "Is the issue that I asked him anyway or that he said yes?" He waves to a church member passing by.

I stare at the small emblem on the pocket of his button-down. "I don't like you butting in."

"We can discuss it tonight. Over dinner."

"I think I feel a headache coming on."

"Wrong thing to say to a doctor." Connor darts a quick look at my tush. "I've got a shot that could take any pain away."

"I better grab a seat." I step past him, only to be caught by the hand and reeled back to his side.

"I'll pick you up at six." He sniffs near my neck. "And wear that perfume."

Strangely addled, I move out of his loose grip and manage to find my way through the double doors of the sanctuary. Imagine. Trying to seduce a girl in church.

And imagine . . . me liking it.

"Hey, girl." Beth moves her purse out of the empty seat beside her, and I sit down.

She and her husband look so happy. Mark has his arm wrapped around her, leaning into her side, smiling like he doesn't have a care in the world. Like he didn't just lose his primary means of supporting his family. Like his wife doesn't have to deliver pizzas at night. How do you get that? That peace, that sense of knowing God's gonna take care of things so you might as well not even worry about it? If it were a drug, I could bottle it and make billions. Not to mention I'd down them on a regular basis myself.

"The girls had a great time at Connor's fish fry." Beth elbows me and wiggles her eyebrows. "Want to tell me what's going on?"

"Nothing's going on." Her face tells me she's not buying it. "We're just . . . hanging out, I guess. Plus he's still searching for Miss Perfection."

"Maybe he's changed his mind. You know, it's all over town that he's pursuing you."

The girlie part of my brain takes these words and seals them with a lipsticky kiss. The logical part of my brain—the dominant part—feels the old fears closing in. Shutting the gates down like a mall shop at nine o'clock.

"I have a job interview tomorrow with National Geographic. I'm too mobile for a relationship right now."

"That's probably what the people on the ark said, but they seemed to have made it just fine. Girl, you do not toss someone like Connor Blake away. He is the real deal."

I flip open my bulletin and pretend to read it. "Yeah, real arrogant, real bossy, and real nosy."

"And *real* hot." She swats my hand and laughs. "And your eyes just followed him to his seat just now, so don't tell me you haven't noticed."

"I'm not sticking around in Ivy. Connor knows that. We're just—"

"Hanging out." Beth purses her lips.

He eases into the seat next to Danielle Chapel and a few other people. She hugs him tight and laughs at something he says.

Beth points in their direction. "He and Danielle are in a Bible study together. They're just friends."

"Does she know that?"

Beth throws her head back and laughs. "Maggie, when you do fall, you're gonna fall hard. I just hope you don't let it pass you by and decide to go bungee off a water tower instead."

"That is the most ridiculous bit of—"

I'm cut off as the worship minister grabs his mic and the band explodes into jubilant song. The congregation stands, and everyone begins to clap in time to the beat. Beside me, Mark and Beth Sterling lift their hands up high and praise the God they cling to. The God they're believing will deliver them from debt and foreclosure. The God they're expecting to keep their babies fed.

The next few songs keep me on my feet and wind my brain down, letting me shut out the things pressing down and focus on the Lord. I block out thoughts of Connor, my parents, my sister, even Riley. *God, help me to keep my mind and heart on you.*

Pastor Thomas takes the pulpit, and I grab a pen to fill in the sermon notes on the back of the bulletin. But when I flip it over, there's just an empty page with today's date.

"Brothers and sisters, I don't have blanks for you to write in today. Don't have my thoughts outlined out all nice and neat." He slowly walks from the left side of the stage to the right. "You know why? Because I want you to just listen. Because I have a message that every person here needs today. And you're gonna let the Holy Spirit personalize it for you. He's gonna tell you when you're being spoken to. And *that's* when you write something down."

A woman behind me shouts an amen. I settle into my seat and prepare to listen. Though I'd rather have notes.

"Do you remember the story of Jonah and the whale?"

A low rumble of uh-huhs go across the room.

"Maybe you heard this story in children's church—back in the day when we used puppets and felt boards." I laugh at the old visual. "I want to tell you that story again. Now, God told Jonah to go to Nineveh. And Jonah said, 'No way am I doing that.' So he thinks to himself, 'I'll just leave. God can't catch me. I can't go to Nineveh if I'm on a boat headed somewhere else.'"

I doodle a star on my blank page. Then I turn it into a flowering rose.

"So Jonah hops on a ship, and what does the Lord do? He hurls this huge storm over it. It was so bad the crew knew it was going to split the vessel apart. But through all the raging waves, through the thunder, the lightning, do you think Jonah noticed? No! He was down below—sound asleep."

The pastor steps down to the main floor. Ten rows away from me. His dark eyes roam over the crowd, but when they float over our direction, I'd swear they land right on me.

"Sometimes we are so used to the thunder and the noise and the rough turbulence of our crazy lives, we don't even think about it anymore. We just go on. We sleep through the storms. My brothers and sisters, is that you today? Those of you who've lost your jobs, are you just sleeping through your pain? Or are you giving it to God? Those of you who have lost a child to an addiction—are you ignoring the call of God while the wind rages? Are you running from your past? It's going to find you. Just like Jonah, you can't outrun God."

The pastor reads from the Bible, and I flip the tissue-thin page and follow along.

"When that big whale swallowed Jonah, that was God saying, 'Boy, you need some thinking time. You gotta quit running and get your head straight.' Because I'm here to tell you, God'll get your attention."

The pastor's next words have the hair on the back of my neck standing straight up.

"'The waters engulfed me up to the neck; the watery depths overcame me; seaweed was wrapped around my head.'"

Flashes of color shoot through my mind. Fragments of movement. Hands outreached. Water flooding my ears, burning my eyes. Weeds wrapping around my legs.

And then it's gone.

I press my hand to my pounding heart. Was that a memory? A piece of a dream? *God, help me remember that night my mother drowned. I want to see that moment again. I have to know.*

Pastor Thomas holds up his Bible, reciting the rest from memory. "I love the last of this passage. Jonah's drowning in the belly of that giant fish. He's all out of places to run. Death has come for him. And yet he says I called out to you one last time. And you heard me and saved me—despite all my running."

Feeling a sting in my palm, I look down and find my hands clenched, nail marks in my skin. I rest my hands on my skirt and take a breath.

"You can run, folks. But you can't hide." The pastor looks right at me. This time there's no mistake. His words sink into my heart like seeds in the ground. "Fear is the opposite of faith, and where does that get you? Swimming in the guts of a fish. You can't outrun God. But you know what the good news here is? You also can't out love him. So when you're up to your neck in water and all the other things you've let hold you down, you just call out to him." He smiles and scans the room. "You may have years of fish gunk in your life . . . but it only takes a second to be spit out into freedom. I'm asking you today—stop running from your past, your fears, and his call. Surrender right now."

The pianist plays a familiar hymn as we're led in a prayer of invitation.

All around me people move down front. The woman beside me

tips over her purse getting out. A man across the aisle brings his baby daughter and weeping wife.

And I just sit there.

My mouth silently shaping the words.

All to Jesus, I surrender;

All to Him I freely give;

I will ever love and trust Him,

In His presence daily live.

I surrender all . . . I surrender all . . .

Chapter Twenty-Five

"Quit looking at me like that." My dad jerks open the refrigerator door and pulls out a bottle of Coke.

"Like what?" I watch Riley play with the puppy in the backyard. She runs a few feet, then turns around and waits for Matilda to attack her ankles. The most heavenly sound of giggles follows. I can hear her all the way inside.

Dad pours the drink in a jelly glass. "Like you're waiting to see if I'm going to change my mind and take that dog away from Riley."

It had crossed my mind. "I just don't want her getting all attached and then you remember how much you dislike animals."

"She's past the point of being attached, and I'm glad Connor asked me about it. Riley would've been heartbroken if the dog had gone to another family."

I guess in his own way, Dad loves Riley. She's the closest thing he has to my sister. Speaking of that—"Have you heard from Allison?"

Dad takes a long drink from his glass. "I'm sure she's fine."

"How can she stand to be away from Riley? How can she just be content that Riley's being taken care of?"

"Drop it, Maggie."

"What if . . . what if we needed one of Allison's kidneys?"

"We don't."

"What if Riley had a rare blood type, and her mom was the only match?"

"She's not."

"What if—"

Dad's elongated sigh could blow over a tree. "There's no reason for Allison to not have peace of mind that her daughter's being well taken care of."

"Well, I couldn't leave my child."

He sits down in a chair at the table. "You never did understand your sister, so there's no reason why you'd start now."

"Don't you hold her responsible at all, Dad?"

Riley squeals outside, and he shifts his attention to the window. "She's not like you. Allison's always been fragile, like your mother."

This mention of Mom has me on alert. Dad never mentions my mother. Ever. It's like after the funeral, she was not only gone to him, but she was forgotten. It was the sprinkling of nuts on top of our dysfunctional family sundae. Sometimes I'd pull out old photo albums just to remind myself that indeed, at one point, I did have a mother.

"Mother was not fragile. Eccentric, maybe, but she wasn't weak."

He rubs a hand over his five o'clock shadow. "Forget what I said."

"No." Heat crawls up my neck as I hold my ground. "You can't just say something like that about Mom and let it go."

Dad looks at the clock hanging on the wall. "It's five-fifteen. Don't you have a date to get ready for?"

I study the man beside me. His dry, cracked hands, worn from years of work and his refusal to take anything but the occasional vacation day. The strong angle of his nose and chin, always tipped slightly down, whether from a sign of respect or just to make it easier to glare. And those eyes that would widen as he yelled when I was a child. I spent very little of my youth making any sort of eye contact with the man. But now I'm thirty. And I'm staring him in the face.

"Why'd you marry Mom?"

Dad looks at me like I just sprouted a top hat and belted out a show tune. "What kind of question is that?"

"An easy one, I would think."

His eyes follow Riley as she runs back and forth across the yard. "I was ten years older than your mother." He straightens a small stack of bills on the table. "Just got out of the service when I met her. Here I was, this small-town guy. An average Joe. I was in a bar with some navy buddies in San Diego, and I had a week until I went home to Ivy." His hands wrap around the glass in front of him. "Your mother was eighteen at the time. Too young to be in a place like that. I saw her as soon as she walked in."

I try to picture my mom as an eighteen-year-old. I can almost see her curly red hair. Wearing that favorite lipstick that made her look like she had been eating strawberries off the vine.

"She was beautiful. Had a laugh that could turn a man's head." Dad spares me a glance. "You've got that same laugh."

I want to embroider his words on my heart. That my dad noticed one single quality about me is a rare gift. But to have it be something I shared with my mother makes my head spin in childlike giddiness.

He takes a drink of Coke and continues, "Out of all those men in the place, she zeroed in on me. I didn't know why. Maybe I'll never know for sure. But she approached me, introduced herself." He chuckles. "Gave me some ridiculous made-up name. Called herself Gigi Fontaine. I didn't know her real name until the next week. When I was applying for a marriage license."

I blanch. "You asked Mom to marry you after a week?"

"Asked her on the second date. I stuck around in San Diego a little bit longer. After knowing each other for one month, we were married. I picked her up at her parents' house and moved Connie and her one orange suitcase back to Ivy."

"What did Grandma and Grandpa have to say about it?"

"They stuffed a fifty in my pocket and told me I had to keep her forever." Dad jingles the ice in his glass. "And I tried. I really tried."

I let his words soak in, glad to have a normal conversation with my father—to hear something, anything about my mom. "And then you got home and realized you were night and day?"

Dad slowly nods. "Your mom wanted adventure. She wanted dancing and parties. I wanted a pot roast on the table when I got home."

"I remember she would watch *Breakfast at Tiffany's* over and over," I say. "She would shut herself in her room all day and say she had the mean reds." The locked-away memory unfurls in my mind. "And then the next day she'd be waking Allison and me up with singing and take us to the park. She'd slide and swing like she was one of us. The other kids would gather around her as if she were Glinda the Good Witch." And I would stand back as she dazzled them all and think, *That's my mother*. That's the woman who would pick me up when my father would find a way to bring me down. She was my champion. My lifeline. My oasis from misery.

Dad stands up and carries his empty glass to the sink. "That's enough boring talk. Go get ready. I need to start supper for Riley."

I stay in my seat for a few more moments, not sure what my next line should be. How do you transition from that? I want to ask him if he ever really loved her. If he ever truly loved me. And why I was never good enough, but Allison could do no wrong. She was the golden child. And I was the kid left to find my acceptance from others. While Allison crashed and burned, I would fly ninety-to-nothing, looking for that next daredevil stunt that would win me the love and adoration of friends.

"You know I don't like someone in my kitchen when I cook." Dad settles a skillet on the stove, the metal clanking against the burners. "Go on, now. Connor'll be here soon."

There's a shift in the air. And though I can't define it, it's there all the same. I have no idea what good our little talk did, but it definitely did *something.*

"Thanks, Dad—for the story."

He harrumphs. "You're welcome. Now get out."

At six o'clock, the doorbell rings. As Connor chats with Riley and Dad, I come down the stairs, my nerves bundled like a wad of computer cables. Forgoing the flatiron, I let my hair cascade in loose waves. I wear a pair of Rock & Republic jeans topped off with a fitted Gap tank, and slip my arms into a lavender cardigan as I reach the bottom step.

And there stands the cutest veterinarian in all of Texas. Waiting in the doorway. For me.

"Hey." His smile is sexier than any leading man Hollywood's ever dished up, and I fight the flutter in my chest.

"Hey, yourself." I wonder if he notices the nervous tremor in my voice. I mean, we've been out, he and I. But this is a date. A real date. No caves. No bats. Just a man and a woman who know there's an undeniable attraction.

This pretty much scares the crap out of me.

"You look nice," he says.

Nice? I've given stronger compliments to a pint of ice cream. "Thanks."

He leans in and inhales. "You didn't wear the perfume."

"Must've forgotten." And it's too early in the game for Dr. Blake to think he can snap his fingers and I'll dab on cologne in all the right spots. I'm sure.

But the bra's new.

Not that he'll see it.

But I'll know.

I walk into the living room and kneel down beside Riley. As the dog gnaws on my purse, I pull my niece in for a quick hug. "Behave for Grandpa."

She rolls her eyes. "Save the squeezing for the date."

"Connor and I don't do that stuff." I stand up and dust the dog slobber off my jeans. "I save that for all my Chicago boyfriends. Now you call me if your grandfather makes you watch the fishing channel all night. I'll leave wherever I'm at and come and get you." I bend down and kiss the top of her head. "Children have rights too."

Connor bids everyone good night as he gently pushes me out the door. He interlaces his fingers with mine as we walk to the truck. And though there's not a shot in heck of this going anywhere, I let him hold it again when I'm all buckled in.

"Where are we going?" I ask as he pulls the vehicle onto the road.

"It's a surprise."

"It better not be the kind that ends up with me picking out a Happy Meal toy."

His lazy smile sends shivers up my arms. "Close your eyes."

"No."

He shakes his head. "You seriously have some trust issues."

"And you have overblown ego issues. I have enemies all over this town for things I can't even remember. So the odds of me closing my eyes and letting you lead me around blindly are about as good as your being drafted as a backup dancer for Britney Spears."

Connor whips the car over on the shoulder of the road. He reaches into the glove compartment, his hands brushing my knee. "Here. Tie this on." He tosses a black bandana in my lap. "And if you don't put it on, I'll do it for you."

"Is that supposed to intimidate me?"

"If I can wrestle a cow, I can sure handle you."

"Such pretty words. You turn my head, Dr. Blake. Surely you do."

"Do it."

"Can't we just do dinner and a movie like normal people?"

Connor rests his hand on my leg. "Maggie, we both know you're not normal. Now tie the thing on."

I hold the bandana in my hands as the nerves take over. "You know, McDonald's wouldn't be that bad. Let's head for the Golden Arches."

Connor reaches for my hand. "Trust me."

"Is this a test? Like you're trying to see if I have faith in you? That I can trust you no matter what, even though we both know I'm a neurotic mess and have intimacy issues?"

"No." He drops his head on the steering wheel. "This is me trying to take out Maggie Montgomery, the girl who gets her kicks from leaping out of airplanes and climbing mountains in the dark. Do you have any idea what kind of pressure it is to come up with a date for someone who has the attention span of a two-year-old and gets bored in five-minute intervals?"

I bite my lip and hold back the laugh. "Well, at least help me with the thing."

His strong hands make quick work of fastening the bandana around my head, and soon we're driving again. And I'm so nervous I want to chew the Sally Hansen right off my nails.

The minutes dredge on as my body tilts with the motion of the truck. I grip the armrest until my knuckles cramp. Maybe if I just sneak a little peek.

"Maggie, you lift that bandana, I'm gonna dump you right in the middle of Mr. Tucker's pig farm."

I let my arm fall back down. "Somebody needs to take some Midol."

When I think I can't stand it anymore, the truck slows and finally comes to a stop. "We're here. I'm going to come around and get you."

"I'll be waiting, big boy."

He laughs as he shuts the door. The evening wind blows on my skin as Connor appears at my side and reaches for my hands. "Easy does it. Step down."

I misjudge the depth of the ground and catapult toward the grass.

Muttering, Connor sweeps me up in time and gathers me into his arms.

"Get your hands off my butt."

He shifts his grip. "Get your foot out of my face."

I lean back and rest my cheek against his chest. The blindfold gives my words a boldness. "You smell good tonight, Dr. Blake."

"I just came from Mrs. Rigglebink's emu farm."

For a moment I let my mind wander and imagine that he's my man. And he's always doing crazy stuff like this for me. I feel safe in his arms. Protected. Even with the pervy blindfold.

I hear Connor's feet hit pavement, and he walks a little ways before coming to a stop. Keys jangle, then a door squeaks as it's opened.

"If they find my body in a meat cooler tomorrow morning, I'm really gonna be ticked. I have a pet rock in Chicago to take care of."

Another door is opened, and the temperature change lets me know we're inside. Flashing lights filter in through the blindfold, and the soft strains of an old ballad play overhead. "Connor?"

"Okay, I'm going to put you down. Nice and easy."

As I hang on to his arms, he slowly lowers me, and my feet finally touch the ground.

"You can take it off now."

"I thought you knew I wasn't that kind of girl."

With an exasperated sigh, Connor unties the bandana and peels it from my eyes.

I blink a few times and adjust to the lights. Turning a full circle, I can hardly take it all in. I stand in the Ivy High School gym. A strobe light flashes overhead along with streamers in blue and white. An ivory runner on the floor leads to the center of the court where a table for two sits. Sprays of flowers are everywhere, with balloons hanging at different levels like kites on strings.

"You did this?" My voice is airy as a cloud. "You did this for me?"

"Welcome to prom."

A giant cutout moon sits over to the far left, with a huge faux carriage. I read the banner above it out loud. "A Starlit Night."

"It was the theme our junior year."

I do another rotation, buying some time to clear the moisture from my eyes.

Connor shoves his hands in his pockets. "What do you think?"

I shake my head, words completely unavailable to me. No coherent thoughts.

"Maggie?"

I propel myself right into Connor's arms. I hug him tight like I just want to press the feelings right into him. Like I need my heart to send the message to his. "I love it," I finally manage. "I love it." And I seal my lips over his, reveling in the texture of his mouth, his face in my palms. He kisses me back with a searing, slow tenderness that clears my mind of all thoughts. All worries.

He gradually pulls back and smiles. "I think they're playing our song."

Mariah Carey sings an ode to her lover. "I was more of a headbanger girl myself."

"We have all night." Connor holds out his hand, and I curl into his arm. He swings me back out, and with a laugh, swoops me to him, moving us in time to the music.

"You're a pretty good dancer for a nerd." Once again, my head tucks into his chest, like it was made to fit in that spot.

"I watched a lot of *Fresh Prince*. You haven't seen anything yet."

"How did you do all this?"

We cut a path across the floor, dancing in perfect sync. "The coach is a good friend of mine. I saved his horse last spring and he owed me."

"You decorated all by yourself?"

"Of course not."

I smile against his shirt. "Beth."

"And Mark. And the girls."

"They're the best." And I don't ever want to lose track of them again.

"They like you too." He kisses my temple. "So do I."

"Even if I'm a mess?"

He doesn't answer, and I let it go.

"I can't believe you did this."

Connor smiles down at me. "Every girl needs her prom."

"I'm not making out with you in the backseat when this is over."

He sighs. "You're never going to get prom queen with that attitude."

Watching the strobe lights, contentment fills me up until I could burst like one of the helium balloons. "This is the most amazing date ever."

"And you haven't seen me do the moon walk yet." He tips up my chin and captures my lips with his. My body melts into him, and my fingers tunnel through his thick hair.

"Maggie?" Connor says against my mouth.

"Hmm?" He changes the angle of the kiss, and I follow.

"We need to"—his lips move toward my ear—"talk about us."

I sigh and close my eyes as heat dances across my skin. "E-mail me later."

He lifts his head, draws back. "Now."

I stare at a spot on his shirt, tempted to tell him the bitter truth. I can't commit to anyone. I get claustrophobic in relationships until I find myself saying, "It's not you. It's me," and then suddenly I can breathe again.

And yet.

I've never felt this strongly about someone—this quickening of the pulse just to see him at my door.

Never felt this safe. Or cherished.

Or scared.

"Spill it, Maggie. Whatever's going through that red head of yours."

But I can't say any of that. "You know I'll be leaving soon and—"

"We could work around that," he says reluctantly, like he's been thinking about it, and he's not really sold on his idea.

"I—" My tongue won't seem to cooperate. "Connor, I'm going to be here intermittently whether I'm with National Geographic or *Passport to the World*."

"Is that enough for Riley? Is that your idea of a commitment to her?"

"I'm trying. It will have to be enough. And we could see each other when I come to stay with her."

He shakes his head. "That's not going to work. I'm not doing long distance again."

I stick pride in my back pocket. "But we could still hang out until I leave. You know, until you find your Stepford Wife."

"That's not a good idea and you—" Connor's interrupted by the ringing of his phone. He ignores it and opens his mouth again.

"You should get that. Could be an animal emergency."

He stares me down like he's facing off an opponent on the ten-yard line. Or in his case, like someone threw out his Lord of the Rings DVDs.

"Could be a sick horse. A puking puppy. A guinea pig with seizures."

With a growl, he whips out the phone and checks the display. His forehead wrinkles in a frown. "Hello? Beth?"

My senses go on high alert.

Connor plugs his other ear. "Speak up. Yes. Okay." His blue eyes move to me. And I see trouble there. "We're on our way." With the punch of one finger, he ends the call.

"What is it?"

"I'm afraid prom is over for tonight."

"Is it Beth? Her girls?"

He shakes his head. "It's your dad."

Before he even says the words, I see the plane to Los Angeles leaving without me. Taking my chance at a new life with it.

"Maggie, your dad's at the hospital. He's had a heart attack."

Chapter Twenty-Six

I run into the emergency room and skid to a halt at the receptionist's counter. "My dad." Breathing hard. Must cut back on the SweeTarts and Twinkies. "Heart attack."

Connor steps in, his voice as calm as one of those NPR hosts. "Benjamin Montgomery. Possible heart attack. Would've been brought in by Beth Sterling."

The woman types on her computer. I see the screens flashing on her bifocals. "Yes, he's in surgery right now."

I clutch the counter. "What kind of surgery?"

"I don't have any details, ma'am. If you'll go to the cardiac wing, there's a nurse's station and waiting room. Third floor."

"Follow me." Connor throws an arm around me and leads me down a long hall, where we wait half an con for the elevator.

"I could write a book in the time it takes for this thing to get here," I say, watching the floor numbers tick off above us.

God, I'm sorry for every bad thing I've ever said about my father. Yes, he wasn't a great dad, but I don't want him to die. Riley needs him. And I didn't get the chance to tell him . . . okay, I don't know what I'd tell him, but maybe that he's a good grandpa? That I forgive him? If you give me another chance, I'll come up with something.

At least I don't have to worry about where Riley is. Beth had immediately called back to tell us Mark was home, and Riley would be safely tucked away at their house, having a slumber party with the girls.

The door pings open, and I dart inside. Connor pushes the button, and we're sealed inside.

His hand settles on my back. "How about I pray for your dad?"

I nod and step closer to him.

"Heavenly Father, we ask that you be with the doctors. Give them wisdom and healing hands during this surgery. We ask that you strengthen Ben and mend his body. Give Maggie and Riley peace." He squeezes my shoulder, and I lean into his side. "God, we know you are in control, and we take comfort in that. In Jesus' name, Amen."

"Amen," I whisper.

The doors whish open, and Connor guides me down the hall.

"Maggie!" Beth rushes out of a waiting area. She pulls me into a fierce hug with those strong arms that have rocked four babies.

"What happened?"

"Riley called me in a panic. She had walked into the kitchen and found your dad in the floor. Unconscious. That smart girl of yours had already called 9-1-1. She was a wreck, though. Crying. Scared."

I squeeze my eyes shut against the image.

"She tried to call you, but kept getting voice mail."

Guilt pushes on my chest like a hundred-pound weight. "I had my phone on vibrate." When I listened to the calls on the way to the hospital, it was everything I could do not to throw up on Connor's floorboards. Her frightened voice, choked with tears. A child so alone and desperate. Again.

"Have you seen the doctor?" Connor asks.

"No. Haven't seen anyone since they wheeled him in. The

doctor who took him in said it looked like a heart attack, but I don't know anything."

"Thank you." I wring my hands. "I . . . I don't know what I would've done without you." What Riley would've done. "Go home to your family now." I hug my friend again. "Thank you." I say it three more times before letting her go.

After checking in at the nurse's station, I return to the small waiting area. Connor hands me a cup of strong, black coffee.

"You don't have to stay." I take a drink, the warmth sliding down my throat. "I'll be fine."

Holding my hand, Connor guides me to a couch. "I'm staying." I settle in beside him and rest my head on his shoulder.

Two nurses walk by in candy-colored scrubs, their tennis shoes squeaking on the linoleum floor. "I can't even imagine what Riley—"

"Don't think about it, Maggie." He kisses the top of my head. "It's over. She's safe with Beth's family."

"All she's known is trauma. One scary experience after another. My dad is her only constant"—my shoulders quake in a shiver—"and tonight she watched him suffer. Probably thought he was dead." Tears make slow treks down my cheeks. "I'm a terrible aunt. A horrible daughter."

He pulls me closer. "No you're not. You couldn't help it you didn't hear the phone. You were too dazzled by all my romantic moves. It's the Connor Blake love trance. Gets the ladies every time."

I give a watery smile. "It really was a great night. Until this." And until you asked me where we were headed. "Thanks for being here."

"I guess you'll have to reschedule your interview."

"Yes." And reschedule my life again. It's like that story of Jonah and the whale. God keeps dragging me back to Ivy. "If they let me. There are people lined up for that job."

Connor's voice rumbles near my ear. "Maybe this is your chance to do something different. Send your documentary into the world."

I sigh. "You don't understand."

"Funny, I was going to tell you the same thing."

Before I can set Connor straight, a man pushes through the double doors at the end of the hall and walks our way. "Are you the family of Mr. Montgomery?"

"Yes." I stand up. "I'm his daughter. How is he?"

"He has suffered a heart attack. We did a cardiac catheterization and things didn't look good. Unfortunately, it can't be treated with angioplasty or a stent, so we're setting him up for bypass surgery Tuesday morning."

Two hours later, I stand over my father's hospital bed. He sleeps quietly against a backdrop of beeps and the random clicking of the equipment nearby.

"Come on," Connor says beside me. "You're beat. The doctor told you he'd be out until tomorrow. You need to get some rest."

I glance at the chair in the corner and think of staying.

"He won't even know you're here." Connor's hand curves at the base of my neck. "You have Riley to think about."

Connor drives me home, coming in long enough to make sure everything's okay in the house. "Are you sure you're going to be fine here? I could take you to Beth's."

"No, but thanks."

"Do you need me to stay? I'll sleep on the couch."

I give him a tired smile. "It's three a.m. and you're still trying to put the moves on me." I lean up and kiss his cheek. "You're amazing, Dr. Blake." Something settles around my heart. Something foreign. Strange. Probably just fatigue and too much waiting-room coffee. "Good night."

He wraps his strong arms around me for one last hug, then lets himself out the front door.

I brush my teeth, slip my weary body into a T-shirt. And collapse on the bed. Makeup still on.

I dream of my mother.

And the lake that took her life.

The lake that holds me prisoner still.

At seven a.m., I stand on Beth's doorstep in my baseball cap and Nike yoga wear, a box of donuts in one hand and a gallon of milk in the other.

"Good morning." Mark lets me into the living room where Dalton goes scurrying by naked as the day he was born, clutching a diaper. "How are you?"

"Fine." Exhausted. Feel like I ran a marathon on no sleep. "Is Riley up and around?" I hand him the food and peer around.

"She's in the backyard letting the puppy out."

"Thanks for taking her and Matilda last night, Mark."

He smiles, his white teeth a contrast to his dark skin. "Glad to. Maggie, I know things are crazy for you, but God's got it all under control. Your being back in Ivy, taking care of Riley, even your dad's heart attack none of this was a surprise to him."

I shift uncomfortably. "Yeah . . . thanks. Um, I'm sorry about your job. I've been praying for you. I know how nerve-racking that must be."

Mark tilts down that chin and looks at me like a stern parent. "Did you hear what I just said?"

"I haven't slept much."

"Dude, I don't spout off that stuff and then not believe it myself." He opens the box of donuts and takes one out. Biting into it, he points it at me with each word. "God is on the job. Even when I'm not. Between unemployment, my part-time work, and Beth's crazy pizza-delivery gig, things are fine. I've got my family and my faith. And that's what counts."

His brown eyes look so sincere. Like he means it. How do you just free-fall into faith like that? "I better get Riley. Thanks again."

From the back of the house, I hear the sound of Beth hollering at one of her daughters to stop throwing shoes at her sister. Slipping through the dining room, I open the back door and step into the yard. Riley sits at the edge of the privacy fence, her back to me, the curl of a puppy tail hanging over her leg.

My running shoes crunch in the grass. "Riley?"

She doesn't turn around.

"Riley? Sweetie?" I tap her on the shoulder as she cradles her dog. "Hey—"

She twists her body around, her eyes swollen and red. "Where were you?" she cries.

I drop to my knees beside her. "I'm sorry. Riley, I'm so, so sorry. I didn't hear my phone. But I came as soon as I could. I know it was awful to see Grandpa like that, but you were so brave and—"

"No!" She swipes at her nose, her gaze outraged. "I was alone. Like I always am. Doesn't anybody even care?"

Jesus, help me. "I'm here now. I love you, Riley. And between Grandpa and me, you're not going to be alone anymore."

She pulls away and picks up her puppy. "I'm going inside now."

I reach out my hand. "Wait—please." She stops. "We're going to make sure you're taken care of from now on."

Riley runs her hand over the dog's amber-colored head. "How?"

"What?" My head throbs with a dull ache.

She looks up from the dog and pins her stare on me. "I said *how* are you going to make sure I'm taken care of?"

I open my mouth. And snap it shut. I have no idea. "I—" I fumble for words. "I'm working on it. I—"

"Forget it." She pivots on her shoe. "I don't need you."

And she walks away.

Ready to face the world alone.

Again.

Chapter Twenty-Seven

I massage my back and consider rubbing my sore backside. Eight hours of surgery. Lots of time to consume massive amounts of second-rate coffee and stale vending machine delicacies. And I won't even mention what I've eaten since I've been sitting in my father's room.

The ICU room curtains block sight of the moon, stars, and city lights outside the window. Wish there was something to block out the noise. Dad's hooked up to so many things, it's like a symphony of medical equipment.

Beside me, Connor reads a *Sports Illustrated*.

Dad stirs in the bed. First his hand moves. Then his eyes.

Unfocused, he squints and slowly takes in his surroundings. I stand up and go to his side.

"Hey, Dad," I whisper.

He struggles to see me. "What . . . what day is it?"

"Tuesday. But don't you worry about work. They've got it covered just fine."

He licks his lips. "Allison?"

"No, I'm Maggie." The daughter who put on five pounds just today to sit through your surgery.

Dad closes his eyes, his face scrunched in pain. "Money in my wallet. Need you to . . ." He rests a moment, and for a second I think he's gone back to sleep. "Put it in the shed for your sister. Be by tomorrow."

"What?" My voice sounds loud in the hushed stillness of the room. "You've seen Allison?"

"Tomorrow."

I reach for his hand. "Dad?"

Then Connor's beside me, holding my shoulders. Pulling me back. "Maggie."

I turn around, sputtering. "But he said—"

"He's out of it. Let him sleep."

The nurse had given me his wallet Sunday night. His dulled gold wedding band. And I'd stuck it all in my purse. I bump out of Connor's path and grab my purse, sitting under a chair. Pulling out his leather wallet, I flip it open and peer inside.

"Oh my gosh." I hold up three crisp hundred-dollar bills. "He's been giving her money. All this time. Right under my nose." And I had no idea. Was I ever in the house when she stopped by? Was Allison ever tempted at all to come in, ask me how her daughter was?

"People say crazy things under anesthetic," Connor says, watching my face.

"Only one way to find out." I slip the wallet back in my bag. "Has she contacted you again?"

"Don't you think I'd tell you if she had?"

I don't come up with an answer in time.

He massages the back of his neck and shakes his head. "You're a piece of work, Maggie Montgomery." I steel myself for him to say more. But he only sighs. "You need to go home and get some rest. Just looking at you makes me tired."

"I guess I should go. Riley's at Beth's. Not that she'll want to go home with me." She's been doing an excellent job ignoring me. And today her teacher e-mailed and said she failed her spelling test and refused to go outside at recess. But on the positive side, I called the paper yesterday and my ad for a nanny will start running tomorrow. I feel better about it already . . . I think.

At Beth's, Mark leads me into the living room, where Beth sits at a small foldable table with a sewing machine zipping over some material. She's surrounded by piles of homemade costumes. Riley and the two oldest girls spin around in long, frilly dresses.

"Beth, those are amazing." I pick up a vest off the floor and inspect her handiwork. "You did this? On our budget?"

She straightens from the machine and checks her baby monitor. "Yeah. I found some really cheap scrap material in Grapevine the other day."

I watch my niece pull her dress over her head. "Where'd you get the patterns?"

"Who needs patterns?" She taps her head. "I got them all right here." Holding up a sketchpad, she smiles. "And here."

I take it from her and flip through the pages. "This is incredible. I can't even believe what I'm seeing. And to take it from here"—I point to the costumes—"to that. Unreal." I keep searching the pages. "What are all these?"

She licks some thread and sticks it in the needle. "Wedding dresses. I've made a few on the side. Some bridesmaid and flower girl dresses. Just a little hobby."

I stare at drawings that could come from a Vera Wang design studio. "It must take you hundreds of hours."

"It's like therapy. I love almost every minute of it." Beth snaps her fingers like a drill sergeant. "Josie, get your baby brother. He's trying to eat that dog's tail again."

An idea blooms in my head. "Could I borrow these drawings for tonight?"

Her hand stills on a piece of material. "Why?"

"I have a friend who's been looking for a wedding dress. She wants one-of-a-kind. Very picky lady. I'd love to fax these to her."

Beth waves her hand and snorts. "I'm so sure."

"I'm serious."

She pulls two-year-old Dalton into her lap. Kisses his dark curls. "I guess. But I'm no designer, Maggie. I just like to play around with fabric and stuff. It's nothing."

"Beth, this is definitely not nothing." I hug the book to my chest. "I can't wait to show her." I glance at my niece, who now sits on the couch, her stony gaze on the TV. "Riley, let's go home."

Stomping all the way to the car, Riley shuts herself in. She holds the squirming puppy in her lap in the car and stares out the window.

"Want to tell me about school today?" I ask.

"Nope." And so it goes. Single word answers all the way to the house. And we had been doing so well.

Later that night, I slip into Riley's room and check to see if she's sleeping. She lies on her pallet on the floor, Matilda curled in a ball beside her.

God, help me reach her again. I can't stand this. Is this how you see me? Hard-hearted, wounded, and too afraid to let anyone in? Just . . . heal us both. Show me what to do.

I feel like there's so much at stake. And so little time.

The next morning I call Carley. "Did you get my fax?"

"Yes. What are these dresses? They're beautiful."

"My friend Beth created them."

"Is she a designer?"

"A very gifted one." She also delivers pizzas in her minivan, but no need to share that detail right now.

"Has she done any other work?"

"Oh, lots." Like Riley's costume of a horse's butt. "Amazing craftsmanship."

"Does she have a Web site?"

"Um, not yet. Very exclusive still. She usually handpicks her clients, but I told her about you, and she said she'd consider creating a dress for your wedding."

Carley gushes about a few of the designs in detail. "I really want to talk to this girl. Give me her number."

I smile and take a bite of toast. "I'll have her call you when she can work you in. She's a little pricey, though." Nothing compared to what Carley's been looking at. "But still, cheaper than most in her caliber."

"Make this happen, Maggie. I want to be the first in town to wear one of her designs. My cousin Bitsy will have an envy-meltdown. It's perfect."

"I'll let you know what Beth says."

"Will I see you next month in Nepal for our first shooting of the season?"

Disappointment burns in my stomach. "Yes." Especially now that the National Geographic job is gone. "Where else would I be?"

Deciding I'll wait until I pick up Riley to visit Dad, I get settled in for the day. And by settled in, I mean stake out the shed in the backyard, then sit in the floor of the kitchen with my laptop, a glass of tea, and watch for my sister to show up.

At one-thirty, my butt's asleep, I'm sloshing with liquid, and I'm dying to stretch my legs.

And then I see her.

A flash of blue T-shirt. Red scraggly hair, a lopsided ponytail whipping in the wind. Worn-out jeans. She unlatches the shed door and, with a nervous glance over her shoulder, steps inside.

I shake out the stiffness and head to the backyard.

In the dim light of the shed, I find my sister tearing through shelves, cussing loud enough to scare the neighbors. "Where is it? Where did he put it?"

"Looking for this?"

As Allison whirls around, I hold up the stiff bills from my father's wallet.

"Give that to me. It's mine."

"Actually it's our dad's money. So he's funding your drug habit these days?"

Her eyes narrow like a cobra ready to strike. "No. It's for food."

"Is that what you tell him?"

"It's the truth." She swipes her limp bangs out of her face.

"Why don't you let me take you to the treatment facility in Dallas, and I'll give you the money."

"I'm not an idiot."

"Or maybe I'll just give the cash to Riley. You know, your daughter?"

"You leave her out of it."

"You certainly do." The toxic words roll off my tongue, words I know I'll later regret. "Your father's in the hospital, by the way. He had a heart attack." My sister gives no reaction. "Do you know what the only thing on his mind was? You. He wanted to make sure I took care of you."

Allison laughs, revealing a few lost teeth. "And that burns you up, doesn't it? That he loves *me* more than you. He always did."

"It doesn't bother me. Not anymore. What bothers me now is that your little girl is suffering every day. And you don't even care."

My sister's sneer wavers. "I want to see Riley. You're keeping her away from me. Brainwashing her. I know you are."

"It doesn't have to be this way. You need to get some help." I step closer and try to keep the judgment out of my tone. "Let us help you. I know we're a messed-up family, Allison, but we're all you've got. We care about you. And we care about Riley. If you would take the correct medication maybe it would make things a little clearer." I take a wild stab. "Make the pain not so bad. And that's it, isn't it? You like the escape of it all."

"You don't know me," she hisses. "Don't stand there and talk to me about help and caring about me. And this high-and-mighty routine? It's getting old, big sister. You're the one who treaded water and clung to the leg of the pier while my mother drowned. So I'm the crazy one? I don't think so."

"I never said you were crazy."

"But we're all a little insane. That's how Crazy Connie raised us."

"Don't say that," I whisper. "She loved you. *I* love you." At least I'm trying to. "And Riley needs you. She misses you."

"Dad's already made me sign my kid away. He won't even let me see her until I go to rehab."

"Just until you get your head straight."

"My head's never going to be straight!" Allison screams. "Don't you get it? I'm cursed. Just like Crazy Connie. And you"—her eyes travel down my form like I'm sewer sludge—"you're so perfect. You deserved this disease, not me!"

Pieces shift into place. "What are you saying? That Mom—"

"I have to go." She shoves past me, her frail arms surprisingly strong. I bounce into a wall of boxes. "You can't keep me from my kid forever."

"Wait!" Heaving myself upright, I run after my sister. "Allison! The money!" I call after her, but she sprints across the yard, straight for the street. I run after her, yelling her name. Following her past three houses, I stop when the yellow SUV roars toward us. The vehicle pulls over. A man throws open the passenger door, and Allison jumps in.

They speed by, leaving me with the money.

And a perfect view of the license plate

Chapter Twenty-Eight

A week and a half later, I stand at the stove and make my fourth attempt at steel-cut oats. I follow the directions on the bag, but these things are just tricky.

"Here you go." I set a bowl down beside Riley. "Eat up and I'll take you to school."

She stares at the bowl like I just scooped it up from the back end of a cow. "This is lumpy."

"You call them lumps. I call them clusters of whole-grain-oatey-wonders."

She rolls her eyes and sticks her spoon in her oatmeal. It stands straight up. On its own. "I'm sick of your cooking."

"Well, I'm sick of your griping." And I miss my giggling, sassy niece. The old, miserable Riley is back with a vengeance, and it's sucking the life out of me. "We have to eat healthy now that Grandpa is watching his diet."

Propping her chin on her fist, she sighs. "Can I have a Hot Pocket?"

She finishes her breakfast, draining her milk but leaving most of the oatmeal, then tromps upstairs to get dressed. I check on Dad, who's still sleeping, before I peek in Riley's room.

I take in her ratty old jeans and too-short T-shirt. The clothes she had when I first met her. "You're not wearing that. There are plenty of things in your closet."

My niece folds her arms over her chest. "This is what I want to wear."

"Too bad."

"I ate your stupid oatmeal, so I should get to wear anything I want."

"Riley, we're running late. Either you pick out something else or I will."

"Fine." She stomps to her closet and flings it open, the door crashing against the wall.

Anger flares like a geyser. "Do *not* do that again." I move into the closet and grab a shirt and some capris. "You can wear this."

"I hate that outfit. It makes me look stupid."

I think you're confusing the outfit with your attitude. "It makes you look cute. Put it on. And for your little temper tantrum, you can forget TV tonight."

"So?"

I take a deep breath and count backward from ten. In three languages. "Riley, I know you're mad at me—"

"I'm not mad. I don't care."

I start over with a gentler tone. "I know it's scary—everything that's going on in your life right now. And you're wondering what's going to happen to you. But I promised you I'd make sure you were taken care of. I'm not going to leave until Grandpa's on the mend. And I've got some nanny possibilities lined out."

"A nanny?" She snorts. "What am I, two?"

I bite my lip to keep the smart retort in check. How do parents do this stuff? "A nanny just to help. You know, someone to bake cookies and help you with your homework. And then I'll fly in once a month to stay a few days." I finally feel like I've landed on a logical solution that suits everyone.

"Don't bother." Riley storms out of the closet and picks up her backpack sitting by the unused bed. Her puppy nips at her heels. "I don't need you."

Bullet wounds probably hurt less than those words. "Well, you've got me, so too bad."

"My mom was right—you don't care anything about me."

With a Herculean effort, I lower my voice and speak calmly. "You know that isn't true. I love you. I know I'm messing this up, but I'm trying. And it's okay to be scared after Grandpa's heart attack. But the doctor says he's going to recover and be around to drive us nuts a long, long time."

She shoots me a well-practiced look of disgust, then marches downstairs.

As Riley rockets out the front door, Mrs. Bittle, the neighbor and now part-time caregiver, walks in. Luckily I was able to talk her into helping. She'll be coming over every day, especially when I'm not here. Or when I need a break from the crabby patient.

I greet the woman, then follow my niece. "Did you finish that English homework last night?" I ask as I start the car.

"No."

"When I left, you only had half of it to do."

"I got busy with something."

"Riley, I received an e-mail from Mrs. Ellis two days ago about your history grade sliding. This is not acceptable." I pull out of the subdivision. "You don't blow off your homework."

"I do."

I grip the steering wheel until my knuckles turn white. "Fine. No TV for the next week. That way you'll have plenty of time to do all the school work you've opted out of."

She gives me the silent treatment the rest of the way, and nothing I say gets a rise out of her. When I pull up to the school, she hops out, slams the door, and storms into the building like she's part of an elementary school S.W.A.T. team.

I dig into my purse and pull out an address I got from Beth. I drive out to the west side of town and turn into Harbor Meadows, a neighborhood built around a meadow of trees. Two-story brick homes line either side of the streets. I wave at a woman getting her morning paper. A man walks his dog. Normal everyday life. Doesn't resemble where I grew up at all.

I stop the Focus at the third house on Maple Leaf Drive. Neat shrubs line the front of the yard. The grass is green as Astroturf and has the diagonal pattern of a very attentive lawn mower.

Raising the brass knocker, I pound it twice. And wait.

Steps thud from the other side, then the door swings open. Mary Katherine Blake stands in the entry.

Her face shifts from confused to a look of hesitant pleasure. "Maggie! What a surprise to see you! Come in. I just took some blueberry muffins out of the oven."

Another woman who can cook. How do you get to be one of those?

"I, um"—I slip inside, uncertainty gnawing at my gut—"I just wanted to talk to you about something. I'm sorry to stop by uninvited."

Her glossy coral lips lift in a smile. "You're welcome here anytime." She gestures to the overstuffed couch in her living room. "Take a seat. I'll be in shortly."

I take my time traveling to the couch, stopping by the mantle to look at an eye-catching piece of art, surrounded by family pictures in coordinating black frames. Connor and his sister in elementary school. The entire Blake clan on a vacation at Yellowstone. Mary

Katherine and her toddler grandson. Connor coaching a little league team. He smiles in every shot and wears the expression of a man sure of himself, his God, and the love of his family.

"That one on your left is my favorite."

I jump at Mary Katherine's voice. She sets down a tray on the coffee table and floats to the fireplace. "That's Connor as a six-year-old. He's bottle-feeding a baby bird he found in the woods. Everyone told us not to let a rambunctious child near that bird, but Connor held it like it was as fragile as spun glass. He nursed that thing back to health. Didn't even cry when he had to set it free." She presses her lips together and smiles. "He just knew it was the right thing to do." She rests her hand on my shoulder. "He's always had good instincts like that." Her eyes rest on me, and I just stand there. Unsure of what it is I'm supposed to say.

"Um . . . so I wanted to speak with you about—"

"Let's have some tea." She claps her hands and takes a seat in a cranberry wingback, her posture straight as the chair's. "Sugar?"

"No, thank you."

She hands me a cup and saucer in a matching pink rose pattern. "Take a muffin. They're still warm. I hope you like butter. Are you one of those healthy eaters?"

"I had cake for dinner last night."

She laughs and pats my knee. "I knew I liked you." She takes a delicate bite from her blueberry muffin. "Have you seen Connor lately?"

"Yes. He's been great to come over and check on my dad every day. Even brought dinner a few times." Played with Riley. Helped her with housebreaking the dog. Even helped her with her science homework. And just stayed and talked with me on the front porch swing like we were two of the closest friends.

"Mrs. Blake, I—"

"Please, call me Mary Katherine."

I twist the napkin in my lap. "Mary Katherine, I've been thinking about all the times I went to the drug store with my mother." Do I even want to know this? My mother is dead. Why am I so compelled to tarnish the image I have of her? "I know there are rules about confidentiality, but"—I take a sip of tea for encouragement—"do you know why she was on medication?"

Mary Katherine's eyes widen slightly as she stirs in a teaspoon of sugar. "It really isn't my place to talk about this."

"I know." I lean forward, my eyes pleading. "But you're all I've got. My sister has a chemical imbalance. She's bipolar, schizophrenic. And those are on the good days. I think I've been in denial about the fact that my mother must have suffered in similar ways." I picture her laughing, swinging at the playground, serving us ice cream for dinner. "When my mother was in a good mood, it was magical. We were her favorite people. She'd devote her every minute to us, keep us entertained with crazy stories or some made-up game. But lately I've been remembering those other times—things I had blocked out. Like when she was down, she'd shut herself in her room and spend the whole day alone. In the dark with the covers over her head."

"Shouldn't you ask your father about this?"

"He doesn't talk about my mom. Ever. I . . . I just needed some confirmation."

For a moment I don't think she's going to answer. Her delicate fingers secure the back of a gold earring. Then she sweeps some crumbs off the table. Pours herself another cup of tea.

"I'm sorry." I set my flats on the floor. "I should go. I shouldn't have bothered you like this and—"

"She took medicine for her chemical imbalance," Mary Katherine says, reaching for my hand. "The doctor would often call and change her prescription. He couldn't seem to get it regulated. And then she'd go to another doctor, and he'd put her on something different. She'd complain to the pharmacist about horrible reactions, and eventually she'd find another doctor. Finally"—Mary Katherine covers my hand with hers—"she just stopped taking everything."

"Are you sure? Why would she do that?"

She shakes her head. "I think she just got tired. When she'd pick up her medicine, she'd say, 'One more try. These will be the pills that are going to change my life.' And then she just stopped coming in, except to occasionally bring you girls by for some ice cream."

The muffin is a growing bubble in my stomach. "So she just quit trying?" My adventurous, daredevil mom. Simply gave up.

"Maggie, she was in a lot of pain. She didn't know what she was going to wake up with from one day to the next. She was trapped in a body that didn't work. In a brain that often didn't belong to her. Neither one of us has any idea what it was like to be Connie Montgomery."

But my sister does.

A shiver dances across my skin, and I hug my arms. "Thank you. I appreciate the information. I'm sorry I asked you to break your confidence."

I walk toward the door, my heart as heavy as the purse I sling over my shoulder.

"Maggie?"

My hand stills on the knob.

"Your mother loved you girls. I think you were the only thing that *did* make sense in her life."

I nod, unable to look at Connor's mom, tears pooling in my eyes.

"She would be so proud of who you've become. To know that you're living your dreams and pursuing life just as hard as she did."

Is that what I'm doing? "Thanks." I race outside and start the car, my shaking hand grabbing for my phone. Connor picks it up on the second ring.

"Hey." I pull the car out of the driveway.

"Maggie, are you okay?"

I sniff again. "Yeah. I know it's your day off, but I was wondering . . ."

"If you could come over and help me clean a stable?"

My smile is wobbly as I turn onto Elm Street. "No."

"What do you need?"

"Skydiving."

Silence. "Can't you take up knitting or that scrapbook stuff?"

"Don't worry about it. I'll go by myself."

I hear his ragged sigh. "I'll be at your house in ten."

Chapter Twenty-Nine

I sit in the grass in a Dallas field and watch Connor and his tandem partner come in for landing. His smile is wide, his parachute red, and his dismount close to perfection.

Minutes later, he eases down beside me, his shoulder touching mine. "Almost as exciting as a Star Wars marathon?" I ask.

His blue eyes glance toward the sky. "Almost."

"I'm proud of you for not screaming like a girl. But you probably save that for contact sports."

Connor reclines on the ground, his muscular legs sprawled out to catch some sun. His hand makes a sweeping circle motion on my back. "You want to tell me what this was about?"

I frown and block the sun with my hand. "Something to do. Between the hospital and the house, I've been cooped up for nearly two weeks. I just needed to get out." Without invitation, I lie back, resting my head on his chest and feeling the steady heartbeat beneath his shirt. I don't even let myself think about how perfect my cheek fits in the spot under his chin.

"Talk to me, Maggie."

"I am."

His hand stills. "What happened today?"

Sometimes a girl just gets tired of holding it all in. Like a New Orleans levy, I guess I can only keep so much inside. The words just pour out. "And then your mom said she had the same mental issues that Allison has."

He's quiet for a long moment. Then finally, "I'm sorry. You should've called me. I would've gone over there with you."

"I needed to do it alone." I hear something like a growl rumble in his throat, but I wisely ignore it. "She said my mom stopped taking her meds."

"Just like Allison."

"Well, Allison takes drugs—just not the right ones."

"And now you're sitting here mulling over how you're going to fix this."

"She is my sister."

"But she's not your mother. Saving Allison won't bring your mother back."

I stiffen. "I know that." Sitting up, I draw my knees to my chest. "I need to tell my dad about seeing Allison. And the money."

"You need to talk to your dad about your mom. It's time to get that out in the open and have some closure."

I twirl a blade of grass in my hand and watch the sun cast shadows on Connor's face. "Maybe. But until I remember the night of my mom's death, there's never going to be closure."

An hour later, I pick up Riley at school and start an early dinner. My goal for tonight's meal is to get everything in the pot without burning the kitchen down. As the water and chicken broth heat to a boil, I sit down at the table with my laptop. Ten minutes later, I'm so engrossed in my work, I don't even hear my dad come in.

"What is that?"

I nearly jump out of my seat. "Dad! What are you doing up?"

His face pinches in a frown. "I haven't been up much yet. Doctor said I need to walk some every day. So I figured a walk to the john and the fridge would be my exercise." He peers over my shoulder. "Wedding dresses?"

"Yeah, it's a Web site I've designed for Beth. I found a cool template online. It's still a work in progress, but so far I think it's pretty chic. My friend Carley got Beth three more orders this week. She's going to be swamped in wedding dress demands." And she's loving every minute of it. She's calling her business Ivy Girl Designs.

"Why does she want to do that?" He pulls out a chair and eases into it.

"Because from the sale of one dress, she's made her house payment this month. And because it's been her dream forever."

He snorts. "Job's a job."

I open my mouth to set him straight. Then let the words die on my tongue. He'll never understand. Work's always just been what you did. Didn't have anything to do with passion.

Going to the fridge, I pour my dad a glass of water. "Here. Take your pills."

He swallows two. "What are you cooking?"

"Chicken soup."

His droll eyes sweep from the stove to me. "If the heart doesn't kill me . . ."

"Thanks a lot. My cooking's improved, right? I mean, we're getting healthy. Fruits, veggies—"

"Mrs. Bittle sneaks me in her leftovers."

"Oh." I pat his hand. "Don't worry. You didn't raise a quitter. I won't give up."

He rubs his upper chest. "That's what I'm afraid of."

The doorbell rings, and I jump up to get it. "That's our next nanny candidate." The first one I talked to this afternoon on my way back from Dallas didn't even make it past the phone interview.

I open the door to reveal a short woman, her hair in a severe bun, glasses pushed to the edge of her nose. "Mrs. Persimmon?"

She nods.

"Please come in." I step back and watch her assess the house, her brown eyes sweeping the living room and into the kitchen.

She spies my father sitting at the table. "I only watch children. I don't take care of the elderly."

I can hear his sputtering from here. I plaster on a smile. "Oh, don't worry. Give him a box of Depends and he's self-sufficient."

Dad shakes his head and grumbles all the way back to his bedroom. I know he'll be asleep in minutes.

I lead Mrs. Persimmon to the couch, and I sit across from her. We get the niceties out of the way, then I get down to business.

"Do you cook?"

"Who doesn't?"

Snippy. Strike one. "My niece can be quite the handful, but she's also led a very . . . difficult life and sometimes acts out. Tell me your philosophy on discipline."

The woman purses her pale lips. "I believe that discipline is discipline. It doesn't matter what the child's excuse is. Wrong is wrong, and I won't be indulgent."

"Uh-huh." I jot down some notes on a legal pad. "And if Riley did act up, what would a typical punishment be? For example, I grounded her from TV recently."

Mrs. Persimmon rests her hands in her lap. "I don't believe in television, so that would have to go right away anyway."

Strike two.

I remind myself to stay positive. "Would you have activities planned for my niece to take the place of TV?"

"Yes. I have many books that I'd love to share with her. Classics, of course. Charles Dickens, Shakespeare, Jules Verne, and—"

"Other dead white men?" I stand up and try for an encouraging smile. "I'm going to be honest with you. My niece dislikes me enough as it is. This would push her right over the edge." I lead Mrs. Persimmon to the door. "Thank you for coming by. Have a safe drive home." *And you are never getting within five feet of my niece.*

Riley appears at the top of the stairs, holding Matilda. "Was that my new governess?" she says in her best British accent.

"Avon lady." I lean against the door. "I told her you didn't want any Skin So Soft, and she left."

Riley's eyes do a full rotation before she returns to her room.

After sitting through an awkward dinner with Riley during which she alternates between sighs and throwing me the death stare, I wash the dishes, then take Dad a tray of soup and crackers.

"You awake?" I bump the door open with my hip as Dad raises himself to a seated position. His breath is ragged from the effort. So surreal to see this hard man brought down to quivering weakness.

He leans against his pillow and sniffs the air. "Is that the soup you were making?"

"No. The garbage disposal was asking for a sacrifice, so I had to give it up and pour it down the drain. But the good news is, I spared your granddaughter." I set the tray over his legs. "This is Campbell's chicken noodle. Just like Mom made it."

A hint of a smile appears. "Your mom never could cook. If it weren't for me, you'd have grown up on ice-cream sundaes and chicken nuggets."

"Yes." I tuck a napkin into his T-shirt collar. "Thank goodness you saved me from that."

I help him eat as much as he'll allow before shooing my hands away. Finally, I collapse in a nearby chair as he moves on to some Jell-O that I'm proud to say I didn't screw up.

"Do you remember what you said to me after first waking up from surgery?"

His spoon pauses near his lips. "No telling."

I pick at an imaginary piece of lint off my jeans. "You told me to get in your wallet and leave the money out back for Allison."

He slowly nods. "I've been wondering about her. She hasn't called me to harass me for any more cash, so I assumed she was okay."

"You can't keep feeding her habits, Dad."

"She's my daughter."

"She's my sister. And Riley's mother, and she's a mess." The stubborn lift of his chin tells me what he thinks of my opinion. "I saw her last week. I waited for her, actually." At this I have his attention. "She said something that I hadn't put together myself yet. Probably hadn't wanted to—that Mom was mentally ill like Allison."

He dips his spoon into the bowl. "Not that bad, but yeah."

"Why didn't you ever tell me? Why didn't we ever talk about this?"

"There wasn't anything I could do about it."

"We could've helped her."

"Don't you think I tried?"

I just stare at the man. Unable to agree. Unable to believe he did a single thing.

Dad focuses on the blanket covering his legs. "We didn't know what to do for her. She didn't know, and I sure didn't. The doctors weren't much help. Her condition was an even bigger mystery then than it is now. I—" He takes a sip of water and rests a moment. "I failed her. I know that. Your mother was this erratic, unreachable person. Every day she was different, and you couldn't reason with her."

"Did you ever love her?"

My father shoves his bowl to the other side of the tray. "I was a good provider for your mother and this family. If you want to stand there and tell me it wasn't enough, then you go ahead. But that's all I knew how to be."

"You worked so much because you didn't want to be home with her." My dad, the man of the house, didn't know how to take care of his own wife.

"Did you give Allison the money?"

I don't even bother getting into that story. "No, she didn't take it."

"Put it out there in the shed. She'll get it."

"Dad, she's really unbalanced right now. She was saying crazy things about you not letting her see Riley. I don't really think—"

"Put it out there, Maggie." He turns his head into the pillow and his eyes blink with heavy fatigue. "I couldn't help your mother, but I'm not going to lose your sister."

I pull his door shut, take the tray downstairs, and pad to the kitchen. Later, I sit in my room, my laptop on the bed beside me, and I stare at the faces of all the children who need me. But how can I help them when I can't even help my own sister?

The dream finds me again that night.

I wake up drenched in sweat, gasping for breath, and afraid to close my eyes. I reach for the phone beside me and hit redial.

"Hey," comes Connor's sleep-laced voice. "What's wrong?"

"Just felt like talking."

"Another nightmare?"

I close my eyes and see the water. "Yes."

A few seconds pass before I hear his voice again. "Want to hear about crazy Mr. Jasper's ferret collection?"

"Connor, I would love nothing more."

Chapter Thirty

The rest of the weekend was filled with more of the same—visits from Connor, angry comments from Riley, and waiting on my surly father hand and foot.

Monday morning I survive the car-rider line without hurting anyone or demonstrating that the crazy gene didn't exactly leave me alone either. After dropping Riley off, I head home, check on Dad, then open my Bible. I had to miss church yesterday, and surprisingly, it felt weird. Like I had missed an important meeting. That church has burrowed its way into my heart. I mentally add it to the growing list of things I'll miss when I leave Ivy.

I open my daily devotional and read the selection for the day. As my eyes pore over the words from 1 Thessalonians, six simple words reach out and tap me on the shoulder. *He who calls you is faithful . . .*

God, obviously you brought me back to Ivy to take care of some business. But why do I keep feeling like I'm not done? Coming back home every four to six weeks is the only possible solution. I have a home. Friends. I have a career that's taking off. Please help me stay on track, get things done, and get back to my life. I know it won't ever be quite the same. I've learned I need to try harder with my father. And I'm going to be a constant presence in my niece's life. And as for Connor . . . I'm so grateful for our time together. It was the last thing I ever expected—and like nothing I've ever experienced. But I'm not girlfriend material. And I know he deserves more. Oh, but please don't let it be Danielle Chapel. That would make me barf continuously every day of my life.

Jesus, you've called me here. I'm trusting your word—that you'll be faithful to help me see this through.

My cell phone rings, interrupting my quiet time. I check the screen and groan. "Hello?"

"I'm calling from Ivy Elementary. Your niece has been in some trouble, and you need to come down here right away."

I fall back against the pillows. "I'll be right there."

I repeat the Bible verse over in my head until it becomes my mantra for the morning. When I see Riley sitting in a corner seat in the school office, my mind empties of anything holy.

"What happened?"

Danielle Chapel sticks her head outside her door. "Please come into my office so we can talk."

"Let's go." I help Riley to her feet.

Danielle shakes her pretty brunette head. "Just the two of us."

I stare her down. "No, this concerns Riley. And she will be participating."

The principal hesitates for only a moment. We follow her inside, and she immediately opens that supersized file.

"Riley started a fight yet again." Danielle shoots my niece a look meant to reduce a rule breaker to tears. Riley shrugs and picks at the neon polish on her thumbnail.

"Your niece only shoved the girl this time. But same child as always, and it will not be tolerated. We have a strict policy on bullying and do not take it lightly." She reaches in her desk and pulls out a DVD. "This is a video on how to parent a child who harasses others. I really recommend you watch it."

I turn to Riley. "What happened?"

"I said she pushed a child and—"

I hold up a hand. "I'm talking to my niece. Riley, tell me in your own words what happened."

"Why?" She flicks away more polish. "No one believes me."

I unclench my jaw. "Try me."

Her cheeks billow with a sigh. "Megan was making fun of Sarah again. Sarah started crying, and I asked Megan to stop. Then she and her friend went to making fun of me. Calling me stupid." She turns her bitter face to the principal. "I don't really care if they say that because I have a higher grade in math than them now."

I nod in support. "Go on."

"Then they went back to saying mean things about Sarah. Said her house was so bad she lived with rats. And she was so poor she couldn't even get her clothes washed." Riley tells this in a monotone, like she's said it all before. And no one listened. "I asked them to back off. They were all in her face. I asked them. And they didn't. So I pushed Megan." She looks at me with unfiltered disgust. "I know you said to get a teacher if it happened again, but there wasn't any time. And I couldn't let them talk to Sarah that way. She can't help how she lives."

Said from a kid who knows. "And you asked them to stop?"

"Yes, Maggie."

I turn to Danielle. "Well then, I guess that's that."

"Yes, indeed it is. Megan and a few other girls absolutely deny this. And once again, little Sarah went along with them. I'll be suspending Riley today and she will not be allowed to participate in the class play."

"If my niece says that's how the story went, then that's how it went."

Riley and Danielle speak at the same time. "What?"

"She said the girls were harassing Sarah. I believe her. If there's anything I've learned from our reading lessons and nightly homework sessions, it's that Riley is a very smart girl. And she wouldn't be dumb enough to keep repeating the same story over and over if no one believed her the first time." I slide the DVD back to Mrs. Chapel. "Maybe you want to give this to Megan and the other girls' parents?"

"My punishment still stands."

I glance down at the girl who's looking at me like she's about to bet money on my odds. "Riley, go sit outside while Mrs. Chapel and I finish our conversation."

She scrambles out, grateful for the freedom.

I press my palms on the desk and lean down. "Danielle, I know you don't like me."

She smiles coolly. "On the contrary, when you drive off and leave Ivy, I'll like you more than you know."

"When I drive off and leave Connor, you mean." *Honey, you're not his type either.*

She lifts a shoulder beneath her tailored jacket. "I'm sure I don't know what you mean."

"My niece is telling the truth. She may be trouble, but she is not a liar. And somewhere in that cold heart of yours, you know I'm right. Now I want this ridiculous prison sentence reduced. And I want her back in the play. Because *no one* can play a horse's butt like my niece can."

She taps her red nails on her pen. "In school suspension for one day. And no deal on the play."

This is so ridiculous. "First of all, you'd just be hurting Mrs. Ellis, who's going to have to find a replacement on short notice. And second, consider it a parting gift to me by letting Riley remain in the production."

"One more misstep, Maggie Montgomery, and I call the state department and have them investigate your home."

I find my first genuine smile of the day. "Oh, you do that. I'd *love* to hear their assessment."

Later, I walk out into the main office. My niece sits in an ugly blue chair, her hands fisted in her lap. "The good news is you have the day off."

Her eyes drop to the floor. How many times can the world reject a kid before she just gives up? "What's the bad news?"

"There's not any." I wrap my arm around her narrow shoulders as we walk. "There's the even-better news. And that is that you still have your part in the play."

"I'm still a horse's butt?"

"You are indeed."

Her grin grows like a flower under the sun. She doesn't speak again until she's buckled into the Focus. "Thanks . . . and stuff."

I start the car and flip down the visor. "For what?" I shouldn't make her say it. But I am.

Riley takes a long study of the Ivy scenery before providing an answer. "For taking up for me." She rubs a pattern on the armrest. "No one's ever done that."

My heart nearly folds in on itself. "Well then, it was way past time!" My voice is as perky and pity-free as possible. "But we can't keep going on like this. Obviously your friend Sarah is afraid to take up for herself—or you. What we need is a plan."

Riley nods. "I've been thinking about making a stink bomb."

"Did you have a plan B?"

"Putting worms in their P.E. clothes."

"I do like your creativity. But maybe we should go with my idea." I drive toward Beth's neighborhood. "It involves a little acting. Are you up for that?"

Her chin lifts a notch. "Look, I got robbed in the class play. Because I can totally bring it."

"Well, good." I park the car behind Beth's pizza delivering minivan. "This part's got Oscar written all over it."

Riley and I just get seated in Beth's living room when my phone chimes with a text. Connor.

U+Me=Date 2nite.

I text back and remind him I'm currently Florence Nightingale.

I smile at his reply.

U underestimate me. Mom babysitting Riley and the grumpy patient.

"Girl, you have the biggest, dreamiest grin on your face." Beth ties off the hem of a small presidential costume.

I slide my phone back in my purse. "Just Connor."

Her brown eyes twinkle with laughter. "Mmm-hmm. So what are you going to do about him?"

I clutch a throw pillow and run my fingers through the fringe. Probably a pillow of Beth's making. "Nothing as long as I'm here. But when it's time to go back, we'll have to part as friends."

"Is that what you want?"

"It's the right thing to do for the man. He's not going to accept a part-time relationship."

Beth snips the thread with her orange-handled scissors. "I said, is that what *you* want?"

I become aware of my niece taking in our every word. "So how are the costumes coming along?" For a lot of them, Beth had cut out the patterns and sewed just enough for a thankful parent to take over and finish. With the help of some iron-on bonding stuff from the craft store, even I had been able to complete quite a few while staying home with Dad.

"Y'all are boring me." Riley stands up. "The swing set is calling my name, and I must answer." She lets herself outside, her shoulders a little straighter than yesterday.

"The costumes are basically done as of this jacket." Beth holds up a small blue blazer. "But what's got me on overdrive are the orders your friend is sending me for bridal dresses." Beth shakes her head. "I had to take off two nights from delivering pizzas just to get some sewing done. In fact, I've got Mark cutting out the material just so I can get ahead."

"Sounds like a great problem to have."

My old friend looks at me, her eyes glistening. "The Lord is working in a big way in our family, Maggie. And if you hadn't been faithful to come to Ivy, that wouldn't have happened. I can't thank you enough for hooking me up with your friend Carley."

Uncomfortable with the raw emotion—hers *and* mine—I wave it away. "It was nothing. You're an awesome designer, and they're getting their dream gowns for a fraction of what they'd pay in a boutique."

Beth whistles low. "Those prices you told her. I didn't think I'd be able to sleep at night getting *that* kind of money for my sewing." She tosses back her head and laughs. "But aside from two kids in the bed, I slept like a baby."

Beth and I talk about Web site updates, her ideas for a line of chic, unmotherly mother-of-the bride dresses, and how she's teaching her husband to sew. After some iced tea and Oreos, the conversation winds down. "Now you better tell me what you stopped by for before Dalton and Delilah wake up from their naps and my peaceful living room becomes a war zone."

I quickly fill her in on Riley's ongoing problem at school. "So I wondered if maybe Josie would like to get in on the preshow entertainment."

Beth drags in a breath as she considers them. "It's a little deceptive."

"Yeah, I know." Kind of the kink in it all.

"And it's a little risky."

"That too."

"And it's not the most honest way to handle this."

"I completely understand if you don't want Josie to be a part—"

"Are you kidding? I'm in." Beth holds up her hand, and I high-five it. "Megan Oberman's mom has been a thorn in my P.T.A. side for years. Her child can do no wrong, and it's time somebody gave her a little enlightenment."

That evening I stare at my face in the mirror and brush blush over my cheekbones. Just as I reach for the lip gloss, my phone rings.

"Hello?"

"Maggie Montgomery?"

"Yes . . ."

"This is Ted Phillips from National Geographic."

I sink onto the bed, my breath catching in my throat. "Hello, Mr. Phillips."

"We were really sorry you couldn't make it to the interview for the producer position, but we understand there was a serious family emergency."

"Yes. I hated it that I missed the interview." Why is he calling? It's definitely not to get an update on my dad.

"Maggie, we were very disappointed in the pool of applicants we had. None of them compared to your work or your résumé. None of them came with your stellar references."

"Wow . . . um, thanks."

"The committee met today, and if you're still available for the job, I'd like to have the privilege of interviewing you again."

My heart jolts in my chest. "Sure . . . when?"

"How about now?"

An hour later, Connor stands at my door holding not flowers, but a bag of convenience store candy. I ignore him and immediately stick my head in the bag. The bounty there I see has tears stinging my eyes.

"It's so . . . perfect." I hold up the chocolate minidonuts, the cheap kind—my favorite.

He kisses my cheek. "Nothing's too good for you, Maggie."

I hand the bag off to Riley and lean toward her ear. "If I come back and the SweeTarts are gone, I will make your life miserable."

She rolls her eyes. "What are you gonna do, make me eat your cooking?"

Mrs. Blake pops in behind her son, a giant beach bag on her arm. "Hello!" She hugs me, then her son, and finally Riley. "We're going to have so much fun. I have games and movies." She pats her bag. "And homemade cookies." She glances at my dad in his recliner. "And I hear you need to eat something healthy."

He nods and shoots me a look. "I just want to eat something I can recognize."

"Oh, you guys are too funny. I'm bowled over by your loving support." My brain spinning with anxiety and my heart completely weighed down, I pull Connor toward the door and lead him outside.

By the time Connor turns down Main Street, I can see a restaurant is not part of our destination. "Where are you taking me?"

He laces his fingers with mine, resting my hand on his knee. "My house."

I sit at the granite-topped island in the kitchen while Connor comes in and out checking on the steaks. The aroma that seeps in through the open door should make my mouth water. Instead, it has me wishing for a double shot of Pepto-Bismol.

Connor talks about the vet clinic as he gets me started making the salad. I vaguely remember eating salads before I came back to Ivy. At least this is something I can make without messing it up.

One and a half chopped tomatoes later, he's holding my hand under the faucet. "It will stop bleeding in a second."

"There's just nothing domestic about me," I sigh. "Why do I even bother?"

He turns his face to mine. "You've come a long way, Maggie. Give yourself some credit."

My eyes linger on his lips, and automatically I lean forward to kiss him. Then back away, vetoing the idea. "Thanks." I remove my hands from the water. From his grip.

Without a word, Connor disappears down the hall and returns with a Band-Aid. He brushes my fingers away, and with his deft hands, presses the bandage around my thumb. His eyes hold mine for a moment. He says nothing. And neither do I. Yet the room seems to be filled with millions of words anyway.

Connor lets my hand drop, then goes to the oven and removes the bread. "Why don't you get our drinks and bring them outside to the deck?"

Puzzled, I bring two lemonades to the one of the tables outside. Where we have a perfect view of the lake. "We're eating out here?"

He shoots back inside, only to return carrying the salad. "Nice night out."

I glance toward the water. It sits in the distance, but it's there all the same. Nothing nice about it.

"Do you need me to cut your meat?" Connor asks. "I don't want to interrupt dinner by having to sew a finger back on."

I pick up my fork and push some potatoes around. "I'm good."

He prays for our food, then hands me some French bread. "All right. Spill it. What's going on?"

"What do you mean?"

He doesn't speak until I meet his gaze. "Maggie, if you've got something to say, then just say it."

I bristle at his toneless voice. It does nothing for my frayed nerves. "I . . . I got a surprise call from National Geographic this afternoon. It's the funniest thing. They couldn't fill their producer job and gave me a phone interview."

A hawk circles overhead, its cry piercing the sky. Below us two squirrels scurry through some leaves and scamper up a mighty oak.

"When do you leave?" He moves the butter knife deftly over his bread.

"It's not a done deal yet." I swallow twice. "I go in and meet the team. Do another quick interview, and if I pass the test, I'm in."

"When do you leave?" he asks in that same neutral voice. Is this really all he has to say?

"I wanted to be here for Riley's class play, so I told them Wednesday." In less than a day and a half.

Connor leans back in his chair, his muscular arms crossing over his button-down shirt. "Are you seriously going to take this job?"

I blink at the force behind his words. "Yes."

"Why?"

I'd even take some of those Pepto tablets. The nasty ones that make you feel like you're crunching up chalk. "What do you mean, why?"

"Why are you taking the job, Maggie?"

"Because I want it."

"Do you?"

I think of Riley and know she would be rolling her eyes at this point. "I've worked long and hard for this. I came from nothing. I put myself through college and nobody cared if I made it or not. But—"

"And you *still* think no one cares." It's not a question. The muscles flex in his jaw as he studies my face. "And you're still working like a maniac to get someone's approval. To make Ivy sit up and take notice."

"That's not true."

Connor throws down his napkin and stands up. He walks to the edge of the deck and peers out at the water. "Your dad hurt you a long time ago. I guess he still does." He looks back over his shoulder. "But you can't fill that space with job accolades or by climbing any ladder. Seeing your name on the National Geographic credits isn't going to do a dang thing for you."

The chair slides across the floor as I shoot to my feet and face Connor. "*I* want this. For me. It's what I've wanted since the beginning."

"Dreams can change. I thought you wanted to make your documentaries."

"Nobody wants to see them. The economy is in the tank, the world is inundated with bad news, and the last thing people want to see right now is a movie about hurting children who get beaten or sold into prostitution."

"Excuses. You're just running scared. Why can't you go after what you really want?"

"I am."

"No, you're not." His voice raises, and he runs his hand over his face, his fingers scraping across the light stubble. "Everyone thinks you're this big daredevil. This legend of courage with a wild streak as big as this town. But you're not." Connor steps closer until our feet are touching. "I've never met anyone more ruled by fear in my life."

"I jump out of planes, for crying out loud. I travel all over the world in—"

"You're just running scared. That big job you're going after? It's safety. That's what it is. I've seen you huddled over that laptop when you were sitting in the hospital with your dad. I've seen you jotting down notes in the middle of our conversations because you couldn't let an idea go. I've seen the way you hold your video camera like it's some sort of extension of you. It *is* you. That's who you are."

"The documentary business is a tough market. Impossible."

Fire flashes in his eyes. "Then fight for it."

"I have to take this job, Connor."

He steps back, making no move to touch me. "Is God telling you to do your documentary?"

Yes. No. Maybe. "I . . . don't know."

"I think you do. You just need to get out of your own way. You have to let God have the driver's seat, Maggie."

Now I'm the one who's loud. "I *have* surrendered my life! I got saved last year and—"

"All of it?"

My chest rises and falls with each breath. "What?"

"Have you surrendered all of your life? Every decision?" He stabs his finger toward the lake. "Every horrible thing in your past? Every rotten thing that's ever been said or done to you?" Connor looks down that arrogant nose. "Because I think you're still on the bottom of that lake waiting for your mother to come back. Waiting for someone to pull you out and tell you everything's okay."

A slap could not hurt worse.

Connor's hands grip my shoulders. "You didn't kill her. It's never been your fault she died. Let it go. You don't owe anyone anything—not your father and certainly not your sister."

I cough at the tightness in my throat. "It's over."

He doesn't mistake my words. I watch his eyes narrow. Then he nods that dark head. "Okay."

I swipe away a tear. Just like that? Just okay and he's turning me loose? "I can't do this, Connor. It's too hard. You're . . . this huge force of life, and I'm"—I throw up my hands—"just me. You're strong and full of all this faith and confidence. I can't compete with that."

"It's not a competition."

"You want things from me I can't give you." I go on before he interrupts. "I feel it every time I stand next to you. I think I knew it from that first night at Beth's."

"You're right I want things. I want you to be yourself. I'm one of the rare few who get to see glimpses of the real Maggie Montgomery—the girl her daddy ignored and her sister can't stand."

I blink the moisture from my blurry view as the words twist into my soul.

Connor brushes a tear from my cheek. "And the girl Riley loves and has come to depend on. Who's helping Beth and her husband get back on their feet. Who's nursing her father back to health."

I search those sky blue eyes. *And the girl you might care for? Ask me to stay. Give me one reason, something that has nothing to do with work or family. Just you. Just me.*

Connor presses his lips to my forehead, and I close my eyes against the pain. The good-bye.

"You've got more than a lake holding you down, Maggie. I hope you find what you're after. And I hope it makes you happy."

I drag in a ragged, choking breath. "I care about you, Connor. I don't want to walk away from this"—*at all*—"don't want to walk away from this angry. I hope that when I come back into town we can still be . . . civil. Even friends."

Connor shakes his head and gazes out toward the lake. "That's not what I want from you. It's all or nothing."

All or nothing.

Isn't everything?

And funny . . . because nothing's all I have to give.

Chapter Thirty-One

"Mrs. Lewis, you were a teacher for thirty years?"

"Yes, dear. First grade." My sixth nanny candidate sits on the couch. She's not dressed prim and proper. She doesn't even have comfortable shoes on. She looks like she's probably been known to drive a convertible up and down the hills of Ivy Lake blasting Rolling Stones at noise-polluting decibels.

I like her instantly.

"And then you retired?"

"Yes." She plays with the diamond pendant resting on her sweater set. "My husband was diagnosed with terminal cancer, and I retired so I could take care of him. That was three years ago. I don't want to go back into the teaching profession, but I love children." She laughs, a melodic sound that fills the room. "And I'm bored. My kids are all grown and moved away, and I have no one to cook for, no one to take to soccer practice. Sometimes you just need someone to bake for, you know what I mean?"

"Actually my family calls the fire department every time I get near the oven." I smile and move on. "Your letters of recommendation are excellent. I called them all, and your old boss at Ivy Elementary wants you back. And the woman who now stays at home with her kids said you did a better job with her little Joshua than she did."

"I understand life hasn't been easy for your Riley."

"No." But she's improving by the day. Last night she let me tuck her in—into her own bed. And right now she's upstairs doing her homework before the play. "She's been tossed around a lot. Things still haven't settled down for her. Sometimes she acts out. Gets in trouble at school."

The fine lines around Mrs. Lewis's eyes turn into full-blown crinkles. "Then we'll just have to love her through it, won't we?"

I shut my folder and say a silent hallelujah. "Mrs. Lewis . . . when can you start?"

"Okay, Dad, I'm going to wheel you right here." I dig in my heels as I roll my father's wheelchair down the sloped floor of the Ivy Elementary auditorium.

"Don't get any ideas about letting go and sending me crashing into the stage."

"Never entered my mind." Okay. Maybe once.

"Don't need to be wheeled around like a darn invalid anyway."

I pat his hand. "Well, that's what you are, so suck it up." Sure, he could walk, but no sense in pushing it. He was up and around more than ever today, and I knew he was exhausted. But he refused to stay home and miss Riley's play.

Dad's face changes as he raises up and kisses her cheek. She and I share a look. I just shrug.

"You're gonna be great, kid." Dad busses her on the chin. "And later you can autograph my program."

"Thanks, Grandpa." Her sigh drags out. "I guess I better go put on my costume."

I pat her back. "You'll be the best horse's patoot ever." I give her a wink. "You ready for a little preshow excitement?"

Dad props his head in his hand. "I don't even want to know."

With a wave to Beth and Mark in the third row, I lead Riley

backstage. Mrs. Ellis claps her hands for attention and shouts some orders.

Riley sends an uncertain look over her shoulders. "This might get Sarah's feelings hurt again."

"I know." Another weakness in my evil scheme. "But then we'll end it for good. You can do it. You were born for the stage. Think Reese Witherspoon. Julia Roberts."

"Those are all old ladies. How about that dark-headed girl from the Disney Channel?"

"Even better." I hug her to me. "You're so brave, Riley. You're my hero." I hold out my fist and she bumps it. "Go get 'em."

As Riley casually strolls toward this Megan girl and her pack of mean girls, I greet Mrs. Ellis and draw her as far away as possible from my niece.

Ten long minutes later, when I've fixed Abe Lincoln's tie, powdered Martha Washington's hair, and located Teddy Roosevelt's cowboy hat, Riley gives me the look.

The voices of twenty-five children with stage fright make for a loud backstage area, and I have to do very little to muffle the sound of my approach. I stand a few feet away near a loaded coat rack. Far enough to not be noticed. But close enough to hear.

". . . So that's why I think you should leave Sarah alone from now on."

Megan curls her lip and laughs with her friends. "We'll do anything we want. Sarah's not going to tell. She's too stupid to say a word. And Mrs. Chapel believes me. She's always going to believe me. She and my mom are best friends."

Well, the final puzzle piece clicks in place.

"Leave her alone, Megan," Riley says. "I mean it. Don't touch her again. And unless you're telling her to have a nice day, don't even speak a word to her."

"What are you? Her mommy?" The girls dissolve into giggles. "It's not like you can do anything about it."

"No." I step forward. "But I can." I rest my hand on my niece's shoulder. "I'm Riley's aunt. And I'm going to need you ladies to have a nice long talk with Mrs. Ellis and Mrs. Chapel tomorrow morning at school. I believe it's time you came clean about your little bullying game. Sarah's suffered enough. And so has Riley."

I wait for them to break down into tears, to pour out the remorse, and beg me not to tell.

"Whatever, lady." Megan twists a curl around her finger. "I'm, like, Ivy Elementary royalty."

"So you don't want to come clean? Mend your ways? Go the straight and narrow?"

The girl looks at me like I'm generic tennis shoes. "I'm *not* ratting myself out and telling Mrs. Chapel."

"Yeah." I share a smile with Riley. "I think you will."

Megan laughs. "What do you want to bet I don't?"

"One video?" I turn behind me. "Oh, Josie, dear. Do step out here for a moment." From the coat rack comes Josie Sterling. "Did you get it all?"

She hands me my camcorder. "Every snotty word."

Josie, Riley, and I stand together, united in bringing down a brat mafia. "Excellent work, girls. It's going to make a lovely movie for Mrs. Chapel."

Riley smiles. "I'll bring popcorn."

Megan turns on her heel, her posse right behind her. "Mom!" she wails. I think the little princess knows her days as Ivy Elementary royalty are numbered.

I wish Riley good luck one more time and follow Josie toward the exit.

"Maggie, wait!"

I turn around at the curtains as Josie goes on ahead. Riley runs to me, her red curls bouncing. She stops. Then promptly stares at the floor.

"Did you need something?"

She shakes her head.

"Okay, then. Um . . . I'll just go get my seat. I'll be on the—*oomph*!"

Riley throws herself at me, her arms wrapping around my waist. "I love you."

Speechless, my brain numb, I slowly pull her close, my hands on her back. "I love you too." And the stupid water works start again. Like I haven't been crying nonstop since last night. Like I didn't just pour an entire bottle of Visine in each eye. "I love you too, Riley. I mean it."

She pulls away, still focused on the tile beneath her. "Okay then." And then she races back to her class.

I stand there just watching. Replaying it in my head. Marveling in the shock . . .

. . . the peace.

Thank you, God. Thank you.

I walk back to Dad. But find he's not alone.

"Hello, Maggie. Riley asked us to come." Mary Katherine Blake stands visiting with my dad, along with her husband. And her son.

Mr. Blake continues telling my father a story, with Mary Katherine chiming in.

I feel Connor's eyes on me and force myself to meet his gaze. "How are you?"

He nods, then gives me the once-over, taking in my flirty skirt and funky hat. "You look nice tonight."

"Thank you. So do you." His pink button-down could make

some men look feminine. But not Connor. He could wear a tutu and still be the most masculine guy in the room.

"Good luck on your interview tomorrow. I think I might've forgotten to say that last night."

Oh, when I left my heart bleeding on your back deck? "Thank you."

"Connor!"

I twist my head around just in time to see Danielle Chapel flouncing down the aisle.

"There you are! I have our seats on the front row." She greets his parents and paints on a smile for me. "Hello, Maggie. Are you looking forward to the play?"

"Yes. But the preshow entertainment was not to be missed." I hand her my camcorder. "I'm going to let you borrow this. It's a taped confession of your future *Gossip Girls*, admitting to harassing Sarah and my niece. Maybe you can watch it during intermission. You can give the camera back to Riley tomorrow." Now I'm smiling. "When you call her to your office for an apology."

When Connor and his parents escort Danielle back to her seat, she's still stammering.

"I guess someone finally took up for our girl," Dad says watching them walk away.

"Yes."

He nods. "About time." His pale hand slides over the armrest of his wheelchair and rests lightly on mine. "You never needed me, Maggie. And I didn't know what to do with you."

I startle at the topic change. At his hand holding mine.

"You were always so independent. So normal. You were this whimsical sprite like your mother, something that couldn't be tamed or understood. While your sister was the needy one. Always upset. Unhappy. In pain."

"I needed you too," I whisper. "When Mom died, I had no one.

You didn't talk to me unless you were yelling. My sister hated me. And most of my friends just hung around me because I was the life of the party. I had to be." Because I was afraid when the fun stopped, everyone would walk away. Kept me in detention a lot. Riley and I have that in common.

"I'm sorry." His voice is low. Reluctant. "I did everything wrong, and you still turned out fine. I gave any time I had to your sister, and she's completely messed up. Maybe I did you a favor. Because you sure have it together."

My eyes travel the room and land on the first row. Connor laughs at something Danielle says. She gazes into those familiar eyes.

"Yes, my life turned out perfect."

Chapter Thirty-Two

"The sample of your work is amazing. Your eye for the landscape, your subjects—just second to none."

I sit at a conference table in Los Angeles and let the compliments soak in. I should be eating this up. Heck, I should be writing this down. The vice president of the National Geographic Channel just said I'm amazing.

"You would be in charge of all aspects of production, Ms. Montgomery. From idea development, some writing, shoot supervision, even managing your crew. We have every reason to believe you're prepared for that."

"I am." I sit up straight, the waistband of my pencil skirt cutting into my circulation. Stress-eating may be good for the taste buds, but it's wreaking havoc with my ability to breathe. "As you'll see from my résumé, I was the assistant producer on many of our shows this past year. I worked very closely with Carley Fontaine. She taught me a lot."

Mr. Torkelson, the gray-haired gentleman beside me, smiles. "Life is different when you're not behind the camera."

"It certainly is."

"Will you be able to relocate? You'll be traveling a good part of the year, but we like most of our staff to live close to the studios."

"Yes." I think of Riley. Of Ivy. I see Beth surrounded by white taffeta, her sewing machine flying. Her smile beaming. And Connor. His healing hands, and those eyes that seem to read my every thought. The night he took me to the prom. "Relocating won't be a problem. I never really put down roots in Chicago."

The VP fills me in on the team I'll be supervising, the plans for the upcoming season, and, finally, my salary. It's enough to buy Riley all the Disney movies she wants. My mind reels at this incredible opportunity. Girls who graduated with a 4.0 in trouble do not turn this kind of chance down.

"We also viewed the documentary you sent in with your résumé. Very impressive as well."

My pulse quickens. "Really? You like it? Because I have so many more ideas and—"

"But it's not what we're looking for."

I close my mouth. "Of course not. I understand."

"But we like your creativity. And your vision. We like how you're obviously a global-minded thinker." A man in a golf polo nods his head. "Exactly what we're looking for."

"I think that about covers it," Mr. Torkelson says. "The show will be much like the one you're leaving. Same focus—but now you'll be in charge. The job starts next week. What do you think?"

I think about how soon I can change into sweats. "It will be an honor to work for you." I reach out my hand and shake his. "I can't wait to get started."

"Flight 1085 to Dallas–Ft. Worth has been cancelled. If you would like to make your way to the ticket desk, we will be glad to assist you with getting a later flight."

"Great." I sling my backpack over my shoulder and get in line.

At least I have a romance novel, a movie on my iPod, my Bible, and a *People* magazine. And an outside zipper pocket of enough Jolly Ranchers to do some serious harm to my blood sugar.

Three hours, two Starbucks, and one Happy Meal later, I buckle myself into seat 16A. I take out my *People* and slip on my headphones.

I barely glance up as the woman sits down beside me. She stands on tiptoes to shove her carry-on into the overhead compartment. Casting furtive glances all around, her lips moving as if talking to herself. Oh, fabulous. It's like I couldn't escape crazy if I tried.

I slide my legs over to the side so she can move to her seat.

She taps me on the shoulder. "Excuse me."

I pop out one earbud. "Yes?"

She points to the window. "Would you mind—that is, would you consider trading me seats?" She fumbles with the chain around her neck.

"Sure." *Just leave me alone.* I scooch down, taking my backpack with me. Man, I cannot wait to get back home. I miss Riley. Round trip to California in one day is exhausting.

Connor's words come back to replay in my mind. Surrender, he said. I surrender plenty. I've stayed in Ivy far longer than I intended. I got to know my niece and have provided a caregiver for her. I've got someone coming in for my dad for the next few weeks. And I reconnected with Beth.

God, everything's perfectly lined up. The new job. The nanny. Even got some closure from my dad. I can leave Riley with all my loose ends tied neatly in a bow. Then why do I feel like I ate a bad cheeseburger?

"I'm afraid to fly," the woman says beside me.

I give her a thin-lipped smile. "You'll be fine." *As long as you leave me to my magazine and don't expect me to hold your hand.*

"I'm Jane, by the way."

"Nice to meet you." I don't even bother giving her my name. You know, it's like the elevator. Just because you're shoulder-to-shoulder doesn't mean you strike up a conversation. It's one thing to say, "Can you let me out to pee?" It's quite another to give some-one your life story.

"I know you think I'm silly."

The captain's voice booms over the intercom and is so garbled it's barely audible.

"If he just said something important, I sure didn't catch it." She wipes at her forehead with a tissue. "They need some better speakers on here, don't you think? Maybe some surround sound? I don't know whether he said the weather in Dallas is a nice seventy-eight or we'll be flying with one engine."

I find myself smiling. Jane's not crazy. She's just panicked. "I fly all the time. I'll let you know when you need to use your seat as a flotation device."

She snorts. "Skip that. I'll grab the nearest man instead." Jane reaches down and pulls a Bible out of her purse. "I see a Christian counselor for this little issue, and he gave me some scripture to pray over. Calm the nerves. Allay the fears." She fluffs her salt-and-pepper hair. "What do you do that you fly so much?"

"I work for a travel channel. And as of today I work for National Geographic."

Her eyes widen. "Wow. That is something. Just got the job today, huh? You must be ready to burst with excitement."

I flip a page of the magazine, my eyes glazing over an article on secret celebrity boob jobs. "I'm excited."

Jane does a double take. "Now that didn't sound very convincing."

I shut the *People* and dig out some Jolly Ranchers. Passing one to her, I sigh. "Have you ever had a plan, and you followed that plan, and then things happened and you didn't know if you wanted that plan anymore?"

Jane clutches the armrests as we hit the air, the plane bobbing as it struggles for balance. "Is that supposed to happen? I haven't flown since I was twelve. That's been forty years ago, and it was not a good experience. Somehow I've managed to avoid it ever since. Lots of car trips. Drives my husband nuts." She pauses for a breath. "Now what were we talking about? Oh yes. Plans. This National Geographic job. Is this the good part of the plan or the part you don't want?"

"It's my dream job." I pop a candy in my mouth. "Or it used to be. No, it is. It definitely is." I can't just quit my job and do independent documentaries, I can't. I could fail. And then what would people say? What would I have? I have a pet rock to support.

Jane leans in. "If you knew this plane was going down—and if it does I will scream all the way to my Maker—but if you had minutes to live, what would you regret?"

"Not trying." The words tumble from my lips, without thought. Defying logic.

Jane's brows lift to her forehead. "Very good." She swats my hand. "I'm channeling my therapist here, in case you didn't know. Okay, so not try *what*?"

"It's nothing. Forget I said it. Just a knee-jerk reaction."

"Oh, honey. Those are the best kind. Keep talking—you're minutes away from kissing the ground. Who would you think about? What would you want to say? And you can't say 'oh crap' because I've already got dibs on that."

"I'd . . ."

"Yes?"

"I'd want to live more fearlessly."

Her mouth forms an *O*. "That is good. I like that. Me too."

"I'd want to stick my toes in the ocean. And . . ." So many thoughts pound my brain. Memories whiz by like a movie on fast-forward. Voices overlap, faces fade in and out. "I'd want to redo it all. Start over and"—I inhale the stale cabin air—"be bold."

"It's hard, isn't it?"

I nod my head toward her Bible. "I get that God says to be fearless, but how? Knowing and doing are two separate things, you know? I tell myself not to be afraid, but what good does that do?"

Jane pulls the ribbon marker on her Bible and opens it up. "You know what my pastor says?"

I shake my head.

"He says that it's okay to be fearful. That some of God's strongest warriors were frightened. The difference between a believer and the rest of the world is that we press on. We can be shaking in our boots, but we don't turn back. The hopeless—that's what they do. They give up on their mortgage. They give up on the unemployment line. They don't get on this plane. But I can sit here and know that my God saves. And no matter what I go through, if I keep pushing through, he's there in the end. So, honey, having fear doesn't mean you're on the wrong path. It just means you put on your helmet and your jersey and you plow right on through."

My skin tingles as the thoughts take root in my brain.

"My pastor also said, 'Jane, you get your butt on that plane.'"

This drags my attention back to the conversation. "Interesting pastor."

She pats her hair again. "He's also my husband. Good thing he's hot. With a bossy attitude like that, a man wouldn't get very many home-cooked meals." She flips another page in her Bible. "I'll let you get back to your iPod. I'm going to sit here and pray and panic. Then pray some more."

"I think you're very brave for being on this plane."

She gives me a shaky smile. "First air pocket we hit, I'll probably pee my pants. But thank you. It will be worth it in the end. I'm going to visit my son and his wife. My first grandchild is due any day. I'm already feeling a little liberated." She opens her candy. "And a bit queasy."

A few minutes later, I return to my iPod and *People*. But my eyes wander over to Jane's Bible. Her lips are moving again, and she fingers the cross dangling from the chain around her neck. She runs her hand over words line by line. The highlighted portion calls my attention, and I read it.

Isaiah Forty-three.

It's the same passage from the sermon I heard that first Sunday in Beth's church. I can hear the choir in my head, singing the verse aloud.

Do not fear, for I have redeemed you.

I have called you by your name; you are Mine.

I will be with you when you pass through the waters,

and when you pass through the rivers, they will not overwhelm you.

You will not be scorched when you walk through the fire,

and the flame will not burn you.

My heart stops when I come to the middle of verse four.

I love you.

The words loop in my mind. Repeat like they're straight from heaven.

God, you love me? I don't know how. Or why. But I want to love you back with all I've got. Connor's so right. I haven't surrendered it all. I sit there in church on Sundays and just go through the motions. I take up a seat. And give nothing back. You gave up everything. And I come to you with empty hands. No part of me. I'm tired of being in charge. I totally stink at it. Take my life. All of it. Redeem me. Claim me. Again.

"Honey?"

A hand closes over mine.

"Honey, are you okay?"

I hear Jane's voice and realize I'm crying. Tears streaming down my face. "I want to create documentaries." I rub my hand over my dripping nose. "I see children everywhere I go. And they have stories to tell. No voice of their own." I grip her hand. "I want to tell those stories. I think God is *telling* me to do that. It's not a hobby. And it is a risk, but I have to do this."

"Well, praise the Lord you work for National Geographic now!" she beams.

"No. They think the idea sucks."

"Oh."

"But that doesn't matter. There has to be someone out there who will want to see my documentary."

"You mean you already have it made?"

"And I want to stay with my niece. She needs me. She told me she loved me yesterday. And I can't just weave in and out of her life when I can squeeze her in."

Jane can only nod. Because now *she's* sitting next to the crazy person.

"And then there's Connor. I've never loved a man in my life."

She shrugs. "Sometimes I doubt the sense of it myself."

"But I walked out on him. Just threw it away. He just happened so fast, and it scared me. But I think it's the real deal. *He's* the real deal."

"Is he cute?"

"Oh yes."

"Even better." She twists in her seat until she's facing me. "Do you want me to pray for you?"

I can only nod, as I snot-cry right in front of a total stranger.

"God, we thank you for saving us. We thank you for your love that heals. And for being with us when we pass through those troubled waters . . ."

At Jane's amen, we lift our heads. I laugh and search in my bag for a Kleenex. "I'm sorry. I'm a mess."

"Here you go." She hands me a tissue. "And this."

I hold her card in my hand.

"I want you to e-mail me and let me know how it all turns out."

With my eyes, I plead with her to understand. To see the sanity beneath all the blubbering. "I know I sound insane."

She grips my hand again. "Insane? Honey, this was better than *Desperate Housewives* and I'll be dying to know how it ends."

Peace whishes into my spirit as light as the clouds outside my window. "Thank you."

"No, thank *you*. We just killed thirty minutes in the air"—her smile is radiant—"and I've yet to tinkle in my pants."

Chapter Thirty-Three

It's ten-thirty when I pull into the house on Mockingbird Lane.

"I'm home," I say as I turn off the car.

Stepping onto the porch, I run my hand over the railing, so in need of a paint job. Where my sister and I would run and jump off, pretending we were fairies. The step where I tripped as a four-year-old and knocked out my front tooth.

I find the front door unlocked and step inside, my heels clicking on the floor. "I'm home!"

The house is dark, except for a light at the top of the stairs. I'm sure Dad's fast asleep. I make my way up the steps, my head spinning with all I have to tell Riley. And I have to call *Passport to the World* and tell them I'm quitting. Then explain to National Geographic why I won't be taking the producer position. I have a decent nest egg. I can survive here in Ivy while I pursue my dreams. Like the documentary. And Connor Blake. And detoxing from all the candy.

I knock on Riley's door and let myself in. "Riley? I have big news!" I flick on the lights.

But the room is empty. Except for the clothes strewn on the floor and Matilda, who runs to me and rests a mangled chew toy at my feet. I reach down and scratch her head.

I check the rest of the upstairs rooms, then holding the puppy, go back down. When I don't find Riley in the kitchen or the backyard, worry sets in.

"Dad?" I tap on his door. "Dad, wake up."

I flick on the lamp as he sits up. "What? What is it?" He shields his eyes from the light.

"Where's Riley?"

He blinks and rubs his neck. "Upstairs. She sat in here and watched Nick at Night with me until nine. Then she went to bed."

"Did you check on her? You know she went to bed?"

"Yes, yes. What's wrong? What's going on?" He throws off the covers, alarm sharpening his features.

"She's not in the house." I step back outside and call her name. Three times. Four. No answer.

"Maggie!" Dad yells, shuffling into the living room. "It's Allison." He holds up a piece of paper. "There was a note on the kitchen table."

I wrench it from his hands.

You can't keep me from Riley forever.
She's my child. She belongs to me.
—Allison

"Allison must've used her key," Dad says.

I grab a chair to keep from doubling over. "That day in the shed—Allison said you weren't letting her see Riley."

"I wasn't. Allison was getting too unpredictable. Dangerous."

"She told me she wanted to see Riley. That she *would* see her."

Dad sinks into the couch, resting his elbows on his knees. His head falls into his hands. "I didn't hear a thing."

I set the puppy down. "What time did you go to bed?"

"Ten."

"Did you go right to sleep?"

"I was out cold. I haven't felt good all day. Mrs. Bittle left a little after nine."

And this is the last thing he needs. I throw my bag on the ground and rip out my phone. I punch in the dreaded three numbers, 9-1-1.

"I need to report a missing child . . ."

My next call is not any easier. "Connor?"

His voice is clipped. "What do you need, Maggie?"

I take a deep, steadying breath. "Riley's missing."

"I'll be at your dad's in five minutes."

I hang up and call Beth. Then Mrs. Bittle, and a few neighbors. Anyone I know who might've seen or heard anything.

But no one has.

"Maggie?"

I pace back and forth in the living room. "What?"

Dad rolls the tie of his robe in a ball. "Why don't you, um . . . pray for Riley."

Resting my hand over my galloping heart, I nod. "Okay, Dad." We sit on the couch together, and I hold his hand, and I give it all up to God. Because if there was ever a fire to walk through, this is it.

I run upstairs to change quickly into jeans and a T-shirt, and when I return two policemen sit in the living room talking to my dad. I watch the strain build in his shoulders and say another prayer for his heart. I give another officer all the information I have about my meeting that day with Allison.

Connor walks into the house without knocking. I run straight into his arms.

"What happened?" He smoothes my hair, my back. "What in the world is going on?"

I dash away tears and step back. "Riley's missing. Allison has her." I recite the note. "I don't think Riley left voluntarily. She wouldn't have gone off without Matilda." I point to the dog curled up at Dad's feet. "She takes that dog with her everywhere."

"Okay." His hands run up and down my arms. "We'll get her back. We'll find her."

And I was doing so good with this fear thing. *God, help me to not fall apart. I can't stand this. Please bring Riley back. I want to spend the rest of my life taking care of that little girl.*

"Wait." I rummage in my bag again. "I have the license plate number of Allison's friend—or boyfriend." Or dealer or whatever. "Here!" I hold it up like a gold medal.

Connor takes it and hands it to Officer Peyton. The policeman calls Connor by name, and somehow this makes me feel better. As the two talk quietly, I consider telling Connor about all of my revelations. That I want to be Riley's guardian. That in all my awkwardness, I'm falling in love with him. And that he was right—I was running scared.

But now isn't the time. He wouldn't believe me. And I don't have the energy to do anything else but focus on getting my niece back.

Ten minutes later, Officer Peyton hangs up his phone and gives Connor the latest update. Connor nods and joins my dad and me on the couch.

"I have a name and address. Bobby Driscoll."

Dad nods. "She ran around with him a lot last year. Got into some trouble."

"He's got a rap sheet a mile long. Minor offenses."

I close my eyes. I could've done without that piece of information. "Let's go talk to him."

Though it takes some arm-twisting, I convince my father to remain at the house while Connor and I follow the police to Bobby Driscoll's. My unease grows as we drive at least ten miles out of town. The three squad cars ahead pull into a rural trailer park neighborhood. They turn in a driveway marked with a broken mailbox and overgrown weeds. I take in every detail of the single-wide trailer. The peeling roof. The dog on the front stoop. The seven cars in the yard.

"Stay here." Connor gets out with the police. I sit in his truck, my body racked with tremors, my mouth moving silently in prayer like Jane's on the plane. *Please help us. Please help us.* I recite what I can remember of her Bible verses over and over. *Bring us through, Lord.*

Five minutes later, I'm still sitting in the truck shivering, my hands pressed to the windows to see. Obviously my niece isn't here.

When Connor walks out, I open the door and go to him. "What did you find?"

He shakes his head. "Nothing."

I close my eyes against a wave of nausea.

"We'll find her." He pulls me to him, whispering prayers over Riley. Pleas to God for us.

"Why are there so many cars here?"

Connor drops his arms. "Officer Peyton says Mark Driscoll is known for his parties on the lake. Judging from the beer cans in the yard and the bonfire ashes, I'd say they got started early, then maybe moved it to the water this evening. Peyton's calling the marina right now to see if anyone's rented a pontoon."

"The lake?" *God, is the very same body of water that killed my mother going to take my niece as well? Why would my sister even want Riley with her at a party?*

I call my dad and update him. Then I phone Beth and give her the same information.

"We dropped the kids off at Mark's mother's," she says. "We're driving around town looking for her. Or Bobby's yellow truck. Or that crazy fool sister of yours."

"Thanks."

"I'm praying, Maggie. Mark and I are nothing but hopeful. We're gonna find Riley."

I should be bolstered by her never-ending optimism. But I'm not. I'm too bone-deep numb.

"Maggie?" Connor stands with Officer Peyton.

I walk to them, my head aching with guilt and fear.

"Bobby rented a party barge at about eight this evening," the police officer says. "They're out on the lake somewhere. We don't know for sure that he has your niece, but it's a lead we're going to pursue. We're heading out to comb Ivy Lake right now. County's on their way too, as is the Corp of Engineers."

We get back in our vehicles and caravan the direction we came.

"I'll drop you off at your house." Connor turns on some heat, even though his truck reads sixty-eight outside. "I'll get my boat and search the lake too."

"It's so dark." And the lake's so big.

Connor makes a few phone calls as he drives to my dad's. I hear him asking friends to pray, others to join the search.

He stops his truck outside my house, puts it in park, but leaves it running. "I'll keep you posted."

I absently nod and shut the door. As he pulls away, I'm bowled over by grief. The fear gnaws at me like a parasite. And the worst of it all, I simply feel helpless. Powerless.

And that just ticks me off.

"Stop! Stop!" I take off running after his truck, my hands waving over my head. "Connor, stop!" I scream with every bit of air I've got.

And his brake lights appear.

Then he backs up the truck. And I jump in.

"I'm going with you."

"Maggie, we don't have time for you to—"

"Freak out. Yes, I know. I won't." At least I'll try not to. "I have to go, Connor. If we find Riley, she'll need me." And this gives me some hope. This child loves me. I may never have been grounded to this earth by the stable love of my father, and my mother is long gone. But my ten-year-old niece is the reason I'm here. And I'm not going to sit in that house and let a moment pass by that I could be searching.

Connor nods in approval as he drives. "Next you'll want to declare victory over cooking."

"Let's not get crazy. I think I'm retiring my skillet for life." Sometimes you just have to know when to hang your impossible hopes on the Lord . . . and when to cut your losses.

We get to the center of town and I see a familiar minivan.

"Is that Beth?" Connor asks.

"Yep." I smile as my best friend and her husband zoom by us, the Peppy's Pizza sign lighting up the top of her van. *Fast Delivery Guaranteed.*

Two minutes later, we see more familiar cars. "There's Michael and Jermaine." Connor points out even more.

Tears spring to my eyes. But not of fear—of hope. Twelve years ago I left Ivy as fast as I could. I had to get away, make something of myself, and remove all traces of the girl I was and the town I loathed. But now this is home. Where people get out in the dark of night to help you. Even if you stood them up at the spring dance or depantsed them in P.E. This is home.

As the seconds turn to eons, we finally reach the Ivy Lake Marina. We jump out, and I follow behind Connor inside. Without speaking, he takes my hand and guides me over the wobbling dock. *Don't look down. Do not look down.*

We walk by six boats before coming to Connor's.

In my delirious state, I read the side of his boat and laugh out loud. "*Jedi Lovin'*?"

He pats the white-and-navy Bayliner. "May the force be with us."

My laughter fades as he helps me onto the boat and fits me with a life jacket. He moves my fumbling hands out of the way and snaps me in.

"Take a seat and hold on."

He fires up the boat, turns on all the lights, unties us from the dock, and out we go. The night air is slightly chilly on my skin, and I adjust my eyes to the dark of the sky above the lake. *Let us find her, God. Show us where to go.*

Connor builds up some speed, and the wind whips my hair in my face. I want to hold it back, but I need both hands to keep my iron grip on the rail. My stomach churns like I've just eaten my weight in hotdogs and gotten on Space Mountain.

"What if we're wrong?" I yell over the motor. "What if we're wasting time on a false lead?"

"It's the best tip we've got." His focus remains on the water. "There are tons of people out searching. Within the hour, the county will be covered."

Connor keeps the phone close and pulls it out every few minutes to check in. And each time he looks at me and shakes his head. He stands at the helm like the captain of a pirate ship. Wind-blown hair, confident in his abilities, and intent on his prey.

We weave through islands and coves. We cross to the other side and check the docks on the border of the next town. Connor stops and questions the occasional late-night fisherman. But there's no sign of Bobby Driscoll and my sister. No trace of Riley.

He checks his texts again, then nods. The boat slices the water in a quick turn, and he aims *Jedi Lovin'* down an alley of water I think we passed awhile back.

I slide myself across the seat cushions, take a few steps on legs of jelly, and sit right behind Connor.

He turns around. "An old fisherman and his son were listening to the scanner. They called in and said they saw a pontoon down at Maple Cove. It's about ten minutes this way. There's a narrow channel that I didn't try, but I guess it's wide enough to get through. Police are on their way, but we're closer." Connor's eyes lock with mine. "We've been told to wait."

"No." I shake my head, the blood rushing in my head. "We have to go. Now."

He nods once. "That's all I needed to hear."

The boat's roar builds, and I squeeze my eyes shut as the water sprays my face. I focus on breathing in and out. Because it would be really cool if I didn't puke right now. I hang on to the armrests like the seat could self-eject at any second.

Just when I think I can't take any more, Connor jostles my arm. "There it is."

I peel open my eyelids as he points to a pontoon fifty yards away.

The boat noise plummets to a whine as Connor brings down the speed. The pontoon gets a little closer, and I can make out some people dancing on board. They're packed on there like a swarm of ants. Drinking. Laughing.

Let my niece be here. Please, Jesus. Let her be safe.

A few minutes pass as the boat idles. The current pulls us closer to the larger craft.

"We can't ride right up to it," I say. "We have to be as subtle as possible. My sister has to be out of her head tonight. I don't want to scare her into doing something crazy." If she's there. And if she has Riley.

Connor lowers the anchor. "You stay here while I swim over to them. But do not so much as move a muscle on this boat. Do you hear me, Maggie?"

"I'm going." I stand up and grab on to the seat back for support.

"I'm going with you." I nod, whether to assure myself or Connor, I don't know.

Connor hesitates. Shakes his head.

"Yes." I jerk my hand toward the boat. "If my niece is there, I'm taking her back with me. You can beat up any goons that get in my way."

His left cheek dimples. "This isn't a movie. I don't expect a showdown."

I pat his hand. "Then just stand there and look pretty."

When I stand on the seats and look down into the lake I must jump into, my bravado sinks like a fish carcass.

"You ready?" Connor whispers.

"Uh-huh." The water dances below me, lapping at the boat. If it had a voice, I know it would be mocking me. Taunting my cowardice.

With a battle cry, I fling myself off the slick boat and flail feet first into the lake. I hold my nose. I squish my eyes shut. I scream out a prayer to the Father, Son, and Holy Ghost.

And on Jane's behalf, I'm pretty sure I pee my pants.

The water explodes by my shoulder as Connor cannonballs next to me. My arms and legs are a spasm of movement as I pull my chin up, squirt out water like a fountain, and wonder at the sheer stupidity of my action.

"I can't swim." I pant and paddle. "I can't swim."

Connor's hand reaches for my vest and pulls it up. "Breathe. Maggie, look at me." His voice is sharp as steel. "Stop moving!"

I cease my floundering. My legs go limp. My arms latch on to his. "Okay, okay, okay. I've got it."

"You should get back in the boat."

"No." I clamp my teeth together. *What* was I thinking? My dad's critical voice pierces my memory. *What kind of idiot can't swim? You are such a baby.*

"Let the life vest do the work." Connor's words are softer, a contrast to the loud party noises coming from the pontoon. "You don't have to know how to swim. Just tread. Push the water away with your hands." He demonstrates. "You got it?"

I nod like an idiot. Of course I don't have it.

Resembling a dog in its first bath, I become a catastrophe of movement, my clothes clinging and weighing me down. But somehow I keep up with Connor, as he deftly glides across the lake. I hear a few voices calling attention to our presence, but mostly the party seems to continue without pause.

Connor jerks his head toward the back of the boat. "Around here." He pulls me to him, and I make a pathetic *eek* in the back of my throat.

We swim around to the other side. A ladder hangs over the edge, and he helps me up. My feet slip off the first rung, but with a push to my backside, I move up to the top. Glancing back, I see Connor's right behind. And with the hope that Riley is on board, I keep going.

And fall right over the edge and into the boat.

I land in a heap, bringing down a girl in a bikini top.

"Hey!" she yells.

"Sorry." I want to inform her that I just swam all by myself, but I don't think she'd care. And I don't have the time.

Connor's hand beneath my armpit hoists me up. "Stay with me." And I don't know whether he means stick by his side or just do a better job of staying upright.

We weave through the crush of people, and my senses are overwhelmed by the odd smells, the sight of drugs, and the fact that it is a huge injustice that any dope-head should have the gift of looking amazingly toned in a two-piece.

Connor and I make a full circle around the boat. And finally I spot my sister. She dances to a rap song, a drink in one hand, a cigarette in the other. Three people crowd around her like she's the center of her own party.

"Allison!" I toss out any ideas of being calm and subtle. "Where is she?"

My sister continues her dance, her eyes hazy and slow in finding me. "Hey, Maggie." She spies Connor and a little frown puckers her brow. "What's the deal?"

I move a couple out of my way and step closer. "Where's Riley?"

She tilts her head. "I don't know what you mean. But she's my kid, so it's none of your concern."

Sloshing in my life jacket, I charge Allison. I reach for the neck of her T-shirt and drag her to me. "Tell me where my niece is!"

Strong arms pull me back. Connor tucks me to his side. "Allison, Riley is missing, and we're really worried. The whole town is looking for her."

Allison takes a drink and giggles like a junior-high deviant. "You're not invited, so get off the boat. I'm the mother, and I'll take care of my own kid. You think you know what's best for me, but you don't." She staggers and waves the bottle in my face. "We were fine until Dad started interfering. Then you."

"Please." My voice is hollow with desperation. "Please tell me. She has a puppy now. I just want to give her the dog." The lie sounds ridiculous even to me.

"What's going on?" A pot-bellied man with a sleeveless shirt that reads *Tanksley's Body Shop* stumbles to us. His eyes glow pink, and he reeks of sweat and something I can't even begin to guess at. "These people bugging you, Allison?"

"Yes," she pouts. "Get them out of here, Bobby."

He rounds on us, and I instinctively shrink back. Connor does not. "You have a child somewhere." Connor's face could scare the fun out of any party. "Hand her over and we'll leave you and your friends."

"You think you're so much better than me." Allison steps around Bobby. She shoves at me with her unsteady hand. "You have to ruin everything. My kid, my party, and don't forget—my mother. *You* should be the one who's screwed up, not me. *You're* the one who watched our mother die. You just stood there." She pushes me again. I edge toward the side of the boat and ground my feet. "You can't have my daughter back!"

"Noooo!"

I turn at a sound equivalent to angel's singing. My niece digs herself out from beneath a row of seating. Shoving upholstery pillows off, she flies straight to her mom

"Stop it!" She pushes her whole body into Allison.

"Allison." I steady my voice. "You know this isn't right. Just let her come home with me. For tonight. You can pick her up tomorrow." *When the police are waiting for you*. I turn to Connor for help, but he's got Bobby pinned in a headlock, shoving another guy off with his elbow.

Allison grabs Riley by the hair and pulls her to her side. My niece gasps, her mouth open in pain.

"No way, sister. I'm not as dumb as you and Dad think I am."

Riley's eyes beg for me to intercede. "You're hurting your daughter. This isn't you." I advance a step.

Allison takes two back. She inches away from me, dragging Riley with her. She takes a drag of her beer. "You can't have her. You will never have her. She is all I have left."

I make a dive for it, and in the seconds that pass, I watch in horror as Allison flings out a hand to hold me off. Riley's head connects with Allison's glass bottle. Pain makes her eyes go wide. Then they close.

A cry rips from the depths of my soul as Riley tips backward. Her small, limp body hits the water.

And sinks.

Chapter Thirty-Four

I fling off the life vest, shove my sister out of the way, and stand at the edge of the boat. My breath catches in my throat.

Somewhere behind me I hear Connor call my name.

Right before I dive in.

The water stings my eyes, and I fight to gain balance. My body plunges down. *God, help me. I learned how to swim. Show me what to do. Remind me. Move my arms. My legs.*

Above me the water splashes as someone else joins me in the lake. Connor. But I have no time to wait. Must find Riley.

I kick out, reach for anything. But there's nothing to hold. Where is Riley? Pressure builds in my chest, and my head throbs.

I close my eyes against the dirt. The darkness.

And I see my mother. A glimmer of a memory flits through my mind. On the pier. She twirled and twirled, moving closer and closer to the edge. I had followed her. Watched from a distance.

And then she jumped off.

I screamed for her. I sobbed out her name. My mother couldn't swim.

And neither could I.

But I plunged into watery depths. My hands lashed out in every direction. Nothing.

I swam lower. Deeper.

Finally, I touched something.

My mother's arm.

I clutched on to it. I jerked her toward me. Spots swam before my eyes. The pain in my chest was unbearable. My air was gone.

Her hand flitted across my cheek.

My mother shook her head, her red hair spilling around her.

Then she pushed away.

And let go.

I swam as hard as I could toward her.

But she only moved away. Until I couldn't see her anymore.

When I crashed to the surface, the air stung my lungs. I breathed it in great heaving gasps. Swimming to the legs of the pier, I held on.

Threw up.

Let some stranger pull me to safety.

And promptly blacked out.

The missing piece. All this time. It was hidden in my head, locked away like a coded secret. My mother took her own life. And I had watched it all. She made me a victim, a prisoner of my own guilt.

God, not again. Help me find Riley. It's so dark. But I'm not coming up alone this time.

My chest aching, I stroke through the water, my legs and arms finding some synchronicity. I have to get to her. Time is running out. I can't see a thing.

The waters engulfed me up to the neck; the watery depths overcame me;

Seaweed was wrapped around my head . . . but You raised my life from the Pit.

. . . As my life was fading away . . .

I remembered the Lord.

I push through the lake, reaching out, grabbing. I'm a windmill of movement.

And finally I make contact. My hands feel in front of me. Rush over the shape.

It's Riley. I clutch her limp body to me. And paddle toward the top.

My legs weaken. My arms can't carry the load. Not much farther. I have to keep going. *God, give me strength. Where is my help?*

I press on for what seems like an hour. My head grows light. My limbs soften and grow weightless. I tighten my grasp on my niece.

And accept the fact that we're going to die together.

I give in. Use the dregs of my strength to keep her at my side. And just float.

I didn't get to clean up all I wanted to in this life. But I was on the way. I would've told Connor how I felt about him. I would've kept Riley with me forever. I would've moved to Ivy. Occasionally I would even invite my dad over for pot roast. From the deli.

I would have told Beth she was the best friend I ever had. I would've stopped blaming myself for the way my sister's life turned out. And my mother's death. I would have told the world about those children who lived on the other side of my camera lens.

And I guess that's enough. Just that I knew. And I finally dove in. I finally got it.

When the light flashes in my eyes, I don't even have the energy to blink. Is this Jesus? Coming to pluck me from the depths? To take Riley and me home?

Hands reach for me, and I lean into them. *Yes, get us out of here. I'm ready. I don't have one single thing left to surrender, Lord.*

My body bends as I'm pulled up. Riley's taken from my arms, and I let her go. My fingers can't hold her any longer.

I feel the water sluice off my skin. I'm raised up. Stretched out.

Lips press against mine. Air blows into the back of my throat, straight to my lungs. My chest rises. Expands. Hands press at my stomach.

I cough. Water trickles out of my mouth.

My eyes lift the barest of centimeters. Just one.

And I see Connor's face over mine. His mouth wide open. Aiming toward me.

"No." It comes out as a croak. A grunt. I flop my hand toward him. "No more."

"Maggie, thank God." And I'm in his arms. Gathered to him.

My throat hurts with the force of pushing out one single word. "Riley."

He nods against me. "She's okay. She's gonna be okay."

I give a weak laugh against his bare chest. "You would do anything to make out with me."

The hospital room is filled with flowers, balloons, and more importantly, boxes of candy.

I lean my head against the pillow, Riley spooned against me. I brush my hand over her hair again, needing to remind myself once more than she's alive. And she's here. Where she belongs. And I never have to relive last night again.

"I'm sick of watching *The Price Is Right*. I want to turn it back to Nickelodeon." She pops another SweeTart in her mouth and wrangles for the remote.

"Give me five more minutes," I say. "I want to see if the short guy wins the final round."

The model steps back to reveal the prize he could win. A shiny new bass boat.

"You're right. I've been selfish." I take the remote myself. "Let's turn it."

As SpongeBob SquarePants squeals on the television, Connor sticks his head in the doorway. "Anybody home?"

"I am!" Riley jumps from the bed and runs to hug him.

"I brought a friend who really wanted to see you." He sticks his hand from beneath his unseasonable jacket and pulls out Riley's wiggling puppy.

"Matilda!" She grabs her puppy and lets Matilda lick her face. "You missed me, didn't you?" Riley giggles and plops on the floor to play with her dog.

With his hands in his pockets, Connor walks to my bedside. I resist the urge to explain my disheveled appearance. My lack of makeup. The pudding on my shirt. Riley and I were too busy lounging around to shower. Or do much of anything hygienic.

"How are you?" His voice is too polite, too formal.

"Good." A million things scramble through my head. I have so much I want to tell him. "You saved our lives." I look over to my niece, who is completely absorbed in Matilda. "Thank you doesn't even begin to cover it." I reach out my hand, but he steps away.

"Beth said you and Riley are going home today."

"Yes. Connor, I have to talk to you. I know you're busy with all the reunion preparations, but maybe this evening we could—"

"I don't think so, Maggie. We need to just let this go and move on."

"But—"

"I should go." He steps toward Riley and rubs the top of her head. "I'm afraid Matilda has to leave with me. She'll be waiting for you when you get home."

"Awww." Riley gives the dog a small squeeze, then hands him over. "You're so awesome for bringing her. Isn't Connor the best, Maggie?"

I swallow past the lump in my throat. "Yes . . . the best."

I watch Connor walk out the door. And out of my life.

After the doctor gives us the final all clear, Beth drives us home in the pizza mobile, with Dad strapped in the passenger seat. He listens to Riley chatter all the way to the house.

With the resiliency only found in a child, Riley bounds up the steps with Josie and the two play video games while the puppy nips at their toes. My dad shuts himself in his room to take a nap.

I pick up my phone and call Connor, but it goes straight to voice mail. All seventeen times.

When Mrs. Bittle comes to check on us, I convince her to stay for a bit while I get out of the house.

The cemetery looks mournful today as the sun remains hidden behind the clouds. The grass reaches out to tickle my ankles as I kneel down in front of my mother's grave.

Constance Marie Montgomery
Beloved Daughter, Wife, and Mother.
Fearlessly She Lived. Joyfully She Loved.

I trace my hands over the script. "Fearlessness means never giving up. And you did. But I can forgive you. I can't imagine what it was like to live in your head." I swipe at some dust on the top of the stone. "You have an amazing granddaughter. She's a little like you. And scarily enough—a lot like me. And I'm going to take care of her, Mom. And she's never going to have to run from anything in her life." I wipe a tear with the back of my hand. "Well, unless I try using the stove again."

Chapter Thirty-Five

"Are you sure about this?"

I run a swath of hair between the paddles of the flatiron. "Yes. Don't talk me out of it."

Riley sits on the bathroom counter, her legs kicking a staccato beat on the cabinet. "I'm just saying, if you're going to go after Connor, you should stuff your bra. Cody told Zach who told Hannah who told Josie that guys like big boobs."

Ten. She's ten! "Brains. I'm sure he meant to say boys like girls with large intellects."

"Oh. Can you get those at Victoria's Secret?"

"Wish me luck?" I lean down and give her my cheek. She kisses it and squirts me with some perfume.

"You look great. Especially for a lady who was fish bait only two days ago."

"Thanks." I walk into my bedroom and grab my new handbag. Its black patent leather matches my sleek new dress and my sassy hot-pink heels.

"Be home by midnight," Riley says, picking up her squirming puppy. "It's important you set a good example for me."

I pause with my hand on the door. "I love you, kid. I really do."

She rolls her eyes. "You too." She rubs her dog's silky ear. "Aunts are so gushy sometimes, Matilda."

I blow her a kiss, then make my way downstairs. My father is waiting at the bottom.

"What's this?" I frown at the box behind his back.

"It's nothing." He can't even look at me as he rests the box on the banister and removes a corsage. "Just a flower for your dress. Silly thing. Mrs. Bittle told me to get it for you."

I take the rose from him and pin it on myself. "It's perfect."

We stare at one another for a moment. Finally he clears his throat, leans in, and pecks me on the cheek. He steps back, his face as pink as my shoes. "Well, have a good time. Go get 'im, and all that stuff."

"Thanks, Dad."

"I really messed up with you, Maggie."

I nod once. "I know."

"I'm gonna have a lot of time on my hands now that I'm retiring—again—from the factory. I just . . . I just thought maybe when you buy your new house you and Riley could still come over some."

"Of course we will."

"For the food?"

"It's a big draw." I laugh and squeeze his hand. "We'll find our way."

"I'm glad you're back home. For good."

"Me too."

I race out of there before I have to reapply mascara. There's something about coming home that can make a girl cry more in one month than in her entire life. Maybe I'm just getting it all out of my system. Clearing the way and making room for the happy memories.

My stomach is tied up like a sailor's knot as I enter the Ivy gym. My date stands in the lobby and waits for me.

"Hey, Jermaine." I loop my arm in his.

"Some fellow already get you a corsage?"

"Yep." I smile. "He's an okay guy. But he's not you."

Jermaine booms with laughter. "This better not ruin my chances for picking up some chicks. My mama wants to see me married."

"If you want, I'll tell all the ladies here that you were the best kisser who ever walked the halls of Ivy High."

"I like the way you think."

"I'll also give you all the shrimp puffs off my plate tonight."

"Let's go get your man back."

We mix and mingle for a while. I apologize to the few remaining people I hadn't run into or offended again since being in town. Then my date and I head for the dance floor.

"There they are." His whisper is a buzz in my ear. "I'll take her, you take him."

I bite my lip on a smile. "Good plan."

Jermaine drags me by the hand toward Danielle and Connor, who sway to a slow ballad. Danielle's glowing smile fades as she sees us.

"May I cut in?" Jermaine doesn't wait for her agreement. He pulls Danielle's body to his, presses her head to his chest, and gives me the okay sign as he leads her away.

Connor turns to me, his expression completely neutral.

I clear my throat and square my shoulders. "You look amazing." His tux makes him look like he's leaving any minute to walk the red carpet. But the glower is not going to win him any Mr. Congeniality awards.

"I think we've said all we need to say."

"I haven't. There are more words." My brain starts and stops. Freezes and shifts. "More words to say that weren't said before that would be good words right now. Here. For this moment. In time. And space." Omigosh. I must still have water floating between my ears.

"Maggie, I don't need—"

"I'm falling in love with you," I blurt out.

Beside us two couples slam into one another.

"I am." I nod like a bobblehead. "And not because you saved my life—though that was really cool. And I'm grateful. Because I didn't want to die. I really didn't. And it was dark down there and quiet and creepy." It's like I left all my good lines at home—where I practiced! "I know I'm not the safe, sweet flower of a girl you think you're looking for, but you shouldn't look for her. Because she's probably in a watercolor class somewhere or taking care of her plants or making a casserole, and I don't know how to do any of those things." *Lord, a quick, painless death right now, if you please. One of those disappear-in-a-cloud numbers.*

"Why are you back, Maggie?"

"Because I'm moving to Ivy. I quit my job. Well, both my jobs. I got the National Geographic job, but I'm not taking it. I can't. You were right—it's not what I want. I'm bored with my work, and I know I'm supposed to do something else. But that's really scary, and I don't really want to think about that right now because I left my Pepto-Bismol at home." I hold up my bag. "It wouldn't fit in here. I totally tried to stuff it in."

Connor moves as if to leave. "I need to see if Beth needs some help."

"No!" I grab his sleeve. More reuniongoers stop what they're doing and watch the attraction in the center of the court. But I don't care. For the first time in my life, I don't care what people think of me. "I'm staying in Ivy. I'm keeping Riley. She's mine, Connor. My sister is probably going to be gone for a long time, and I'm raising my niece. And she's going to be loved and encouraged. And she's going to be brave. Braver than I ever was."

He runs a finger under his collar and looks at me like he's

seconds away from physically removing me. But I can't turn back now.

"The water was rushing to my ears. All this time. But then I called out to God, and I just let it go. I surrendered everything. I had been holding back. I was just going to church and not really living for God. Or myself. And Connor"—I take a bold step forward as he glares down—"if I had died in that water, I had already decided all these things. And I was at peace with it all. Except for the fact that I didn't tell you how important you were to me."

Something flickers in Connor's gaze. His jaw unclenches. He starts to speak and I hold up a hand to stop him. He has to hear all of it.

"You're right, you know. I am afraid of everything. I'm afraid of spiders with weird spots. And tornadoes. And airplane chicken. And rusty nails. And deleting e-mail forwards without sending them to twenty friends. And being like my mother. And *not* being like my mother. And my job." I step closer. "I'm afraid to not matter. To not leave my mark on this world. To die and be so insignificant, no one would know."

His voice is ragged, hoarse. "I would know."

Hope flares like a bottle rocket, but I press on. "I'm afraid of the directions on pasta. I don't even know what al dente means. And I'm afraid of loving someone . . . and him not loving me back. Because that's all I've known." I grip the arms that once held me tight with a promise I couldn't handle. "And I'm quite scared of you, Dr. Blake. You make me all weird and tingly inside. And sometimes you'll look at me a certain way, and I'll get to feeling panicked. But then you just reach out your hand, like you understand, and my heart stops racing. And I stop looking for the nearest plane to jump out of. It's quite possible I love you, Connor. And I don't know what to do with that yet. And no amount of hand-holding can calm that huge, ginormous, monstrous anxiety right now. And I don't know if I can make you happy or if I'm going to botch this up royally. But I want to try. God sent someone to tell me that it's okay to be afraid. But until I push through and keep going, then I've lost . . ." I take a deep, cleansing breath. "And I don't want to lose you."

The room around us explodes into applause. I ignore them all. I just focus on the man in front of me.

"Please," I whisper. "Tell me you'll stop looking for Miss Boring and Perfect."

A smile spreads on Connor's face. Then he crushes me to him in a kiss. His warm lips press on mine, and I wrap my arms around him, smooshing my corsage. And the padding in my bra.

Connor dips me back and kisses me until I don't have a thought in my head. "You don't ever have to fix pasta for me," he says against my lips.

"I'm not ready to give up on that either. I'm going to keep trying."

He laughs and drags me to his chest. "Maggie Montgomery, I don't know if this world is ready for the bolder, braver you."

"You know what this makes me in the mood for?"

He groans. "Skydiving? Bats and caves?"

I smooth the front of his shirt. "Chess." I brush my lips over his. "A big old sexy game of chess."

Epilogue

ONE YEAR LATER

"I knew I should've gone with the tuck pleats." Beth runs her hands down my ivory gown and clucks her tongue. "Riley, please get off the floor and leave that dog alone before she drools on your dress again."

"Beth, relax." I pin my veil in place and check myself in the mirror. I see hints of my mother's face. Her eyes. Her smile. But not her fear.

I mean, sure, I have enough butterflies in my stomach to cover a botanical garden. But today I marry Connor Blake. Doctor, best friend, hero, and studliest thing to ever drive a pickup in Texas.

Carley was upset when I quit *Passport to the World*, but not so mad she didn't fly in for my wedding. National Geographic upped their offer on my contract, but I had to tell them no once again.

Because my home is here.

Jane from the airplane? I e-mailed her back and gave her that update. And what a story I had to tell. I went down to the pit like Jonah. I felt the water close over my head. And I cried out to my God. But I rose from the waters with a firm resolve to live my life like it mattered.

I also rose from those waters with a few ticks and a minnow in my pants.

Turns out Jane was the mother of a Discovery Channel executive.

And although they too passed on my documentary, Discovery introduced my work to three other companies. And one of them even bought it. They call themselves HBO. I'm working on my third project right now, and we'll be traveling to Cambodia for part of our honeymoon.

Today my dad won't walk me down the aisle. He asked me if he could, but I kissed his cheek and kindly told him no. I wanted him to have a front row seat to the new me. And besides, Riley's the girl for the job. We'll walk down that aisle together, hand in hand. The new regime of Montgomery girls. Ready to take on the world. For real, this time.

So here I go. "Let's do this thing, girls!" I gather my bouquet, sweep my veil over my face, and fling open the door.

I am Maggie the Fearless.

Maggie the Brave.

"Maggie, your skirt's tucked up in your hose."

Maggie the Exhibitionist. I close us back in and brush my dress in place. Riley giggles beside me.

Beyond this door, Connor waits for me.

The man who was strong enough to tell me no and point me to Jesus.

My future husband. My future.

The doors swing open again, and the wedding march plays. Carley and Beth give me a hug, then walk out in time to the music.

Riley and I stand in the entry as a church full of guests rise. All eyes on the two of us.

"Are you scared?" Riley whispers.

"Terrified." I give her hand a squeeze.

"I'm a little nervous too."

"I think we're supposed to be. The important thing is we charge on. Face our fears. Meet that giant on the battlefield and—"

"Is there cake when this is done?" Her earnest eyes blink back at me.

I nod.

"Then let's go. There's a corner piece calling my name."

Together we march down the aisle, me in my Ivy Girl designer gown, and Riley in a confection of satin that makes her look like an angel. Minus the Converse Chucks.

I stop before Connor and give him my hand. And my heart.

I will be ninety-eight and remember his smile in this moment. The way he's looking at me right now.

Riley steps to the place in front of Beth. My niece holds her bouquet like it's as important as the Olympic torch.

The dimple deepens in Connor's cheek. "Did I ever tell you I'm glad you stopped in Ivy?"

I squeeze his hand. "To think I traveled the world looking for something. And everything I needed was here all along."

"Admit it, you've been in love with me since high school. You took one look at my math club jacket, and you were gone."

I shake my head. "Our children are going to be nerds, aren't they?"

Pastor Thomas clears his throat and begins. "Today we welcome you to the joining of two lovely people—"

"Wait."

My eyes widen as Connor turns to me. "What are you doing?"

"Maggie, this isn't just between you and me."

I release the breath suspended in my chest and let the peace settle in. "No. It's not."

Connor holds out his other hand. And my niece runs to his side.

He winks at Riley. "Now you may begin."

"Dearly beloved, we are gathered here today . . ."

Life is full of uncertainties. I don't know if I'll ever be an award-winning documentarian. I have no idea if my sister will ever be able to live with her daughter again. And heaven knows I have yet to figure out that Betty Crocker cookbook I got at my last shower. But we press on. Because once you walk through that fire, it's so much better on the other side. And I could've missed it all.

". . . And Maggie, do you take Connor to be your husband? To love him, honor him, comfort him, and keep him in sickness and in health, forsaking all others, for as long as you both shall live?"

I lean down to my niece. "What's our answer?"

Riley giggles. "I think you should say yes. Don't you?"

I smile behind my veil. "I do."

Reading Group Guide

1. The insightful Eleanor Roosevelt once said, "What you don't do can be a destructive force." How was this true in Maggie Montgomery's life? Do you have any examples of your own to share?
2. *What would you attempt to do if you knew you could not fail? —Robert Schuller*

   What things got in the way of Maggie's dream to become a documentarian? Brainstorm a list of five things that you would do if you KNEW you could not fail. Be as impractical as you want. Now, beside each one, write what stops you from going after (not realizing, but pursuing) that dream. Consider giving each of those excuses or roadblocks up to God in prayer.
3. Connor tells Maggie to get out of the driver's seat and let God take control. In what areas did she need to apply this advice? What about in your own life? Can you think of any areas where you tend to take the reins and push God aside? Think about children, family, work, personal fears.
4. Fear abounds in our society right now—from the economy, the housing market, to a decline in family values. Why is it so hard to trust God for all our needs, even in the scary, uncertain times?
5. What fears did Maggie have? What about Connor?
6. Imagine you are Maggie. What advice would you have given Riley to allay her fears? When things occur that are so unfair, how do you explain to a nonbeliever that an invisible God is in control?

7. Not only does Maggie learn a lot from her old friend Beth Sterling, but she also comes to trust and rely on her as well. What are some ways Beth is there for Maggie? Describe a time when a friend came through for you in a dark time with help or just the right words. Have you ever been able to pass that favor on?
8. Maggie struggles with her past holding her back. In what ways can our families and past events become like shackles and prevent us from truly living a full life?
9. *Do not fear, for I have redeemed you; I have called you by your name; you are mine. I will be with you when you pass through the waters, and when you pass through the rivers, they will not overwhelm you. You will be scorched when you walk through the fire, and the flame will not burn you. For I am the Lord your God.*—Isaiah 43:1–3

   What did this verse mean to Maggie's life? What does it mean to yours?
10. We all know Satan loves to get a good foothold. What better opportunity than when things are going wrong, and we're weakened with doubt. What things did Maggie doubt? What about Riley? Describe a difficult time when you struggled with doubt? What did you do to overcome it? Can you think of any times when fear got the best of you?
11. In the Bible, David went up against the giant Goliath, despite the warnings and discouragement of others. In this novel, Maggie decides to pursue her dream of producing documentaries, even though it's a pursuit where few succeed. Why is it our nature to play it safe? Is this good common sense—or lack of faith?
12. Do we pass fears and phobias on to our children? How can we break that generational habit?
13. Describe how Maggie's phobia of water got in the way of her life. Do you have a phobia? Could it be preventing you from fulfilling your life purpose?

Acknowledgments

I would like to thank my readers for opening these pages. I have never prayed over a book or relied on Scripture as much as I have for *Just Between You and Me*. It's funny—whatever theme I'm developing for a novel always seems to be the exact one God wants me to get through my own head. I hope at least one of us gets it. I'm usually on the remedial plan, so keeping my fingers crossed for you. ;)

I am also enormously, monstrously grateful to my amazing editors Natalie Hanemann and Jamie Chavez. We all went on a trip writing this book, with lots of rushed, stressful stops along the way. But I wouldn't have wanted to created this book with anyone else. Thanks for sticking with me and for all the support, input, encouragement, and hand holding. You guys are the best. You should totally get a raise.

I'm so grateful to all the fiction staff at Thomas Nelson. I am humbly in awe of all you do. You are simply awesome, and I'm one lucky girl to be on the team. Thanks for investing in me and this book.

Thank you to Kim Traylor and members of the fabulous ACFW for giving me information on horses, which I knew nothing about. I'm a cat girl. So my litter box expertise was absolutely useless. I have the same problem at dinner parties . . .

To my family for putting up with me during one hard deadline.

Please let me rejoin the Jones clan once again. You do remember me, right? Short girl? Tan-resistant skin? Frequently in sweats?

Muchas gracias to Chip MacGregor for your advice, which is always so spot-on. And usually funny. I'll agree with anything that includes one liners. Thank you for the laughs, assistance, and support.

Finally, and most importantly, thank you, God, my father and redeemer. I so want to be the girl who surrenders her fears and lives life to its fullest. Thanks for putting up with me, even though I'm afraid of planes. And wasps. And circus clowns. And green peas. And standing before a crowd with my pants unzipped. And that one infomercial guy in the ugly sweaters.

When the storms hit, may we be the ones who press on, stand apart, and just keep going.